Torn Apart

Dedicated to

Daryl, who's taught me more than anyone about unselfish love;
my children, for never complaining about pancakes for dinner—again;
my mom, who never stopped believing;
Shawna, who had faith when mine faltered;
Rick, for sitting by me in a crowded room;
and most of all, my Heavenly Father for giving me the words.

Foreword

Torn Apart is not an isolated series of events in a fictional person's life. It is a compelling, true story about a woman who is no different than you, your friend, your sister, or your daughter.

What happened to her could happen to anyone.

She hardly noticed the cracks at first. Then, like a stone hitting a window, her life shattered when she discovered a secret her husband tried desperately to hide. The pain and heartache his choices brought her and her children were horrible. However, she eventually came to understand that he, too, was a victim.

Her story is a powerful wake-up call to what's increasingly becoming accepted in society today—the expanding, predatory pornography industry.

Pornography is a trap that is distorting truth, clouding minds, and damaging whomever it touches. It is savaging marriages, tearing apart families, and destroying our children's innocence. The devastating effects of pornography won't disappear by pretending it's harmless or insignificant—and no one is completely safe from its influence.

Pornography is a five billion dollar a year industry, and there are more than four million pornographic websites on the Internet, including 100,000 offering illegal child pornography. More than a third of all internet users are exposed to unwanted sexual material. The average age of first internet exposure to pornography is just eleven years old; 89 percent of all sexual solicitations of youth take place on the Internet.[1]

This is a story from which anyone can learn; the fear, the hope, the tears, the joy, the compassion, the forgiveness and, ultimately, the message of faith. Alyson's trust in God sustained her. His love changed the darkness in her life to light and her sorrow, so overwhelmingly painful, to new joy.

—Richard Paul Evans
#1 NY Times bestselling author

Prologue

April 1998

The snow had almost melted on the Chugach Mountains east of the city of Anchorage, Alaska, and the mud was finally drying out. The plentiful paper birch trees, willows, and alder shrubs had sprouted new buds, preparing to burst with color. Spring was definitely in the air, but it was a Friday, and Alyson Clarke was too tired to care.

It had been a long week, and she was glad for the weekend. Her eight-month-old baby, Alex, had been cutting a new tooth for three days, Jayden, her two-and-a-half year-old had spent the last twenty-four hours throwing up, and a mountain of dirty laundry was growing because the dryer had broken down on Monday. Nine-year-old Cade told her just last night that he needed four dozen cookies for a bake sale, and she had spent the last two afternoons driving Ryker, almost thirteen, around town for science project supplies. To top it all off, she had received a phone call this morning and found out the music for the women's class at church had been changed for Sunday. Alyson was the pianist. The practicing she had done all week had been for nothing.

Her husband, Jared, was working late again, so it was just Alyson and the boys for dinner. She had made biscuits and chicken noodle soup from scratch, hoping it would help Jayden's stomach improve. She was keeping her fingers crossed the rest of the family wouldn't get sick.

Once dinner was over and Ryker and Cade finished washing the dishes, they stretched out on the living room floor to play a game of checkers. Ryker had just made the first move of the game when Jared came home from work.

"Hi, guys, who's winning?" he asked when he entered.

"Hi, Dad," Ryker answered. "We barely started playing, but I'm going to win," he said confidently.

"Yeah, whatever, just wait," Cade replied.

"Boys, where's your mom at? I hope you two chow hounds left me some dinner. I'm starving," he added.

Alyson had come down the stairs with Alex in her arms during their conversation. As soon as the baby saw his daddy, he reached his arms toward him. Jared took him and gave his wife a quick kiss.

"What did you guys have for dinner?"

"Something good, of course," she said teasingly. "I didn't know when you'd be home, so I put it in the refrigerator. It won't take long to reheat. Would you like me to get you some?"

He nodded. "Thanks. That would be great." He walked to the couch where Jayden was laying down, halfheartedly watching his brothers play, and sat down on the other end, shifting Alex from his arms to his lap.

"How ya' doing, buddy?" he asked Jayden, rubbing his foot. Jayden moaned and rolled over, now facing the back of the couch. Alex started to squirm, so Jared repositioned him and began bouncing him on his right knee. He and Alex were soon giggling.

"Your dinner's ready, Jared," Alyson said five minutes later.

He stood up and went to the kitchen. He handed Alex back to her, glancing at the table before sitting down. "Thanks, babe, it looks wonderful."

Alyson got Alex a few toys out of a nearby basket and joined Jared at the table. She put the toys down and got the baby situated comfortably on her lap. He immediately reached for the closest one he could pick up and put it in his mouth.

Alyson and Jared discussed their day while he ate. During the conversation they could hear competitive comments between Ryker and Cade in the background. When Jared finished eating, he walked to the sink and rinsed his dishes before putting them in the half-full dishwasher, and then cleared the rest of the table. Turning back to his wife, his mouth opened in a big yawn.

"I'm so tired," he commented. "I think I'm going to go to bed early. I could use a good night's sleep after this week's hectic schedule."

Alyson could relate but knew she wouldn't get to bed herself anytime soon. "Okay, I hope you feel better tomorrow. Do you want to have family prayer before you go upstairs?"

Jared looked around the living room. The older boys were still involved in their game, and Jayden was asleep.

"I guess I'll let you cover that tonight," he decided.

"All right, sleep well," she replied, giving him a hug. "Good night." She tried to sound cheerful despite the fact that after taking care of the kids and house all day, overwhelmed and tired herself, he was the one who got to go to bed early. She also was disappointed that his early departure meant there would be no time to play a game or watch a video as they usually did on Friday night.

She shifted her focus to nursing Alex and getting him ready for bed. By the time she finished, Ryker and Cade had finished their game of checkers and were watching TV. When the next commercial came on, she asked Cade if he would quietly run upstairs to get pajamas and a new diaper for his baby brother. When he came back, he had the pajamas but no diaper.

"Mom, there weren't any left in the bag. I looked under the crib for another package, but there wasn't one."

"Oh, great," Alyson muttered. Had she forgotten to buy diapers? She couldn't believe she had forgotten something that important, but with the way things had been going, she wasn't surprised. Before she gave in to her growing frustration, she remembered there was an extra diaper in the bag she took to church on Sunday. She used it to change Alex. After checking the time on her watch, she told Ryker she needed him to keep an eye on his brothers while she went to the store to buy some more.

Alyson went upstairs with Alex and put him in his crib, glad he didn't protest when she covered him up. She switched on the small night light on the opposite wall, turned on the baby monitor, and glanced at him one more time. His eyes were already closed. She quietly left his room.

She walked to the master bedroom across the hall to get her purse. The door was shut so she turned the doorknob, opening it slowly so it wouldn't squeak. She didn't want to wake up Jared. She sighed with relief when she could hear his even breathing.

She went to the closet to get her purse and grabbed a light sweater as well. She slipped it on as she left the room. In the hallway she carefully closed the door and unzipped the top of her purse to get her car keys out. She fumbled around the bottom of the middle pocket without any luck and flipped up the light switch on the wall to see more clearly. She finally found them in the corner, wedged behind her checkbook. She took them out and closed her purse. When she turned the light off, they slipped from her hand, striking the baseboard of the wall as they fell, then bouncing off and landing on the carpet. She picked them up in frustration and headed for the stairs, barely making it down two when Jared called her name.

Shoot! So much for good intentions.

When she went back and reopened the bedroom door, she only went in far enough to see Jared. "Sorry I woke you. I have to run to the store to buy diapers, and I needed the keys and my purse."

"Hmm, okay," he said, the tiredness evident in his voice.

She began shutting the door for the second time.

"Alyson!" he called again, his tone frantic.

She looked back in the room and saw he was now sitting up, the bed covers down around his waist. There was a little light coming through the shaded window, enough for her to see his eyes wide with concern.

"What?" she asked, anxious to be on her way. She was hoping to have some time that night to relax, pop some microwave popcorn, and read a few chapters of a mystery novel she recently checked out from the library. That possibility was rapidly diminishing.

Jared lay back down, readjusting the pillow beneath his head before speaking again. This time the tone of his voice had changed considerably, as if the former outburst had been misstated and he wanted to downplay the concern he had expressed.

"Uh . . . there's a large envelope on the front seat. Don't touch it."

Alyson looked at him strangely.

He hesitated. "I mean . . . one of the secretaries at work asked me to mail it for her when I ran errands earlier this afternoon. I forgot. I'm going to do it tomorrow. Make sure it doesn't get bent or anything."

"Okay. I'll be home soon," she said, puzzled over the drama.

When she made it to the car at last, she noticed the envelope right away, exactly where Jared said it would be. On the way to the store she tried to understand why it had elicited such a strange reaction from him.

Ten minutes later, she turned into the parking lot, finding the first open space she could. After shifting the transmission to park and shutting off the engine, she looked again at the envelope. Her curiosity mounted as she stared at it, contemplating what to do.

Jared's story about forgetting to mail it for the secretary sounded fishy. He had acted too weird. She didn't want to be nosy—how embarrassing it would be if it really was boring paperwork from his office—but it was bugging her. If she could somehow open the envelope carefully enough, she might be able to reseal it without anyone having to know. She could buy a glue stick when she bought the diapers.

She reached across the seat and picked up the envelope, trying to ignore her rapidly increasing heart rate. The very instant the paper made contact with her skin, a horrible, sick feeling charged through her body, followed immediately by a clear and precise thought.

You can choose to open this envelope, which will start a chain of events that will change your life irreversibly, or you can set it back on the seat and continue with how things are.

What could possibly be inside? Whatever it was, she now knew for certain it was going to affect her more than she had imagined. Hesitations assaulted her brain as she tried to weigh both choices, and her body literally began to shake as old memories and experiences rewound at top speed. Did she have enough courage to logically face the facts about her life with her husband?

In recent months she had experienced nagging doubts and fleeting impressions; Jared was distancing himself emotionally from her. It was bringing up old fears. The past held something she couldn't bear to think about, something she kept securely locked, bolted, and sealed, with a red flashing light, behind a door in her mind.

Years before, Jared had wounded her deeply and their marriage barely survived. He had promised her nothing like it would ever happen again. He had also told her repeatedly how sorry he was and that he'd made a huge mistake. If he dared to reopen that door and force her to walk through it and feel that kind of pain again, she thought she would die.

No, that's ridiculous . . . it has to be something else. Remember what we've shared since then? Renewed love, a lot more laughter, and happy times with our boys—that was real. You know Jared loves you. No. It can't be that. It just can't.

So why did the horrible, sick feeling charging through her body feel so familiar?

Chapter One

"I am not afraid of storms, for I am learning how to sail my ship."[2]

June 1983

It was Monday morning and the air around Alyson was filled with the smell of freshly baked French bread. She was standing behind the counter of the bakery in the grocery store where she worked, waiting on a customer. As she placed a selection of fresh donuts and pastries in a bag, two young men approached the counter. She felt their eyes rest on her but didn't look up.

After the customer left, she flicked a stray section of her auburn bangs off to one side with her hand and shifted her blue eyes to them. The one on her right was Brent, a coworker several years older than she. He smiled warmly and she blushed.

"How's it going, Alyson?" he asked. He turned slightly and gestured to the guy standing next to him. "I want you to meet Jared. He's a good friend of mine."

Her gaze moved to his friend—dark hair, golden brown eyes, about six feet tall. He looked especially tall standing next to Brent who was shorter than average. She was pretty sure she had seen him somewhere before.

"Hi, Jared. It's nice to meet you. For some reason you look familiar." She watched as his face broke into a big grin.

"Guess I'm just a familiar-looking guy," he blurted out.

Alyson thought that was a dumb response. Before she could say anything else, another customer came to the counter—a woman with a tow-headed toddler sitting in the cart, loudly demanding a cookie.

"May I help you?" Alyson inquired of the woman, smiling. She reached for the open container of cookies behind the counter. "Is it okay to give your little boy one?" she asked.

"Yes, please," she nodded, looking relieved. "That's all I've heard from him since we came in the store."

Alyson laughed, "Him and every other child that loves cookies. No problem." She took a square tissue paper from the box and picked up a sugar cookie with it. She handed it across the counter to his outstretched hand. Instantly he was all smiles.

"Now, what can I get for you?" Alyson asked his mom.

Jared and Brent left before Alyson finished helping her.

Two days later Alyson got a phone call at work. "Hello, this is Alyson," she said when she picked it up.

"Alyson? Hi!" an exuberant male voice said on the other end.

She tried to place it, but couldn't. She hesitated, and he spoke again.

"This is Jared. We met the other day when you were working. Brent introduced us."

"Oh. Hi, Jared," she said, wondering why he was calling her.

"I wanted to see if you would like to go out on a date Saturday night?"

His invitation surprised and flattered her. "Thanks for asking, but . . ." her voice trailed off—he was basically a stranger. "I'm not sure if I'm working that night."

Jared's next question seemed out of place. "By the way, how old are you?"

She thought Brent would have already told him, but maybe he didn't know. "I'll be seventeen at the end of next month. How old are you?"

"I'm twenty-two."

Twenty-two!

She breathed in and out slowly, calculating the difference between their ages in her mind. "I'm not sure if my parents would approve of me dating someone so much older," she told him honestly.

"What if they knew I just returned from a mission last year?"

So that's where I have seen him before. At church. He's not a stranger after all.

Regardless of her parents' feelings, his comment made her feel better, and the thought of dating someone his age was becoming more intriguing by the minute.

"I'm sure that would make a difference," she told him. "Can you hang on while I go check my schedule for Saturday?"

"Sure."

"Just give me a minute." Alyson pushed the hold button on the phone, making it flash, and walked to the "employees only" room in the back. The posted schedule for the week was pinned to a bulletin board on the wall. She traced her finger across the page to Saturday and paused. The sides of her mouth turned up a little when she realized she wasn't scheduled to work the night shift. She got back on the telephone.

"Jared? I get off work at seven on Saturday. I would want to go home and change but I could be ready to go by, say seven-thirty?"

"Great! That works for me. I'll take you out to dinner."

"That sounds perfect. I'm always starving when I get off work."

He chuckled. "Since I have you on the phone, do you want to give me directions to your house?"

"Sure, I can do that. Are you ready?"

"Hang on. Let me find something to write it down on. Okay, now I'm ready." He listened without interrupting.

When she finished, she asked him, "Do you have any questions?"

"No. I think I got it. Thanks, Alyson. I'm looking forward to seeing you Saturday night."

"Uh . . . me, too." She was starting to feel a little unsure.

Should I have said yes?

"I'll see you then, Jared."

"Sounds great. Good-bye, Alyson." The phone clicked in her ear. She hung it back up and glanced at her watch—the conversation had lasted ten minutes. She was glad her boss hadn't been hovering nearby.

Saturday was only four days away, and they passed quickly. By the time Alyson's shift ended at seven, she was excited and nervous. Her stepdad, Nate, had let her borrow his truck for work and the drive home took less than fifteen minutes. She parked it in the usual spot and went inside the house, kicking her shoes off by the door on the way.

Her mom, Elizabeth, was in the kitchen emptying the dishwasher, and Alyson's nose caught the light scent of lemon in the air. "Hi, Mom," Alyson said as she hung the keys on the appropriate hook on the wall.

"Hi, sweetheart, how was work?" She put down the light blue glass she held in her hand and turned toward her daughter.

"It was good—busy—typical for Saturday. I have to hurry now, though. Did you remember I told you I was going out tonight with Jared Clarke?"

A fleeting look of worry crossed her mother's face and she looked more intently at Alyson. "That's tonight? Maybe I shouldn't have said . . ." her voice trailed off. "Never mind, I guess once won't hurt." She forced a smile and turned back to the dishes.

It was obvious her mom was worrying, but Alyson had no time for a discussion. "I'm going to run and change." She left the kitchen and went upstairs to her room.

When the doorbell rang she was still getting ready. Her mom let Jared in and she could hear bits and pieces of their conversation while she finished brushing her teeth in the bathroom.

Alyson came downstairs wearing a light gray corduroy jumpsuit with a fitted bodice that buttoned down the front, tied in the back, and flattered her slim frame. Her long auburn hair, released from the confining ponytail she wore for work, had been brushed and fell in soft curls on her shoulders. Her face was flushed from nervousness, something her fair skin made impossible to hide.

"Hi, Jared," she said smiling shyly as she walked in the kitchen. "Did you have any problem finding my house?"

"Hey, Alyson. Nope. Your directions were great." He noticed her outfit. "You look really nice."

"Thanks." Her eyes shifted to her mom, and Alyson walked closer to give her a hug. Alyson noticed right away she was more relaxed. "Bye. I promise I'll be home by eleven."

"All right, have a good time . . . and be careful."

"I will, Mom." She gave her a reassuring smile.

"It was nice to meet you, Jared," Elizabeth added.

"Thanks. It was nice to meet you too. Have a good night."

Parked outside was an immaculate Audi 4000. Alyson was impressed. Jared opened the passenger door, and she thanked him as she got in. While he walked around to the driver's side, she checked out the interior of the car, noticing the open sunroof. It gave her a perfect view of the beautiful evening sky. Even though is was 8 PM, the sky was still blue and filled with brilliant sunshine. It would be that way until sometime after eleven. The long hours of daylight during the summer in Alaska helped to make up for the short days during the winter.

Jared got in the car, secured his seat belt and turned the key in the ignition. As soon as it engaged, the sound of the pop group, Supertramp, filled the car. Music was their first topic of conversation.

They drove to a popular restaurant Alyson had never been to before, and Jared parked the car. Jumping out immediately, he opened her door before she could.

"Thanks," she told him, flashing a smile.

"You're very welcome," he said in a deep voice that made her laugh. Inside, Jared approached the hostess to get his name on the waiting list for a table.

Alyson sat down in a comfortable overstuffed chair, her eyes traveling around the interior of the restaurant, noticing the dark jewel-toned walls. One sported a stuffed boar's head, and another held a rich tapestry woven in intricate designs.

An old, weathered chest, dark with age, filled one corner and scattered rag rugs covered the floor. With the flickering candles and decorative pieces of pewter, it would be easy to believe she was sitting inside a tavern in a quaint English village.

Alyson enjoyed her dinner, especially the French onion soup served in small individual-sized ceramic crocks. Jared had encouraged her to try it instead of the salad with her entrée. She had discovered a new favorite.

While they ate, Jared did most of the talking and had her laughing several times throughout the meal. Her earlier nervousness completely disappeared.

After leaving the restaurant, they took a scenic route ending up at a neighborhood park near Westchester Lagoon. Jared parked the car and he and Alyson walked over to the nearby playground to sit on two of the empty swings. They talked while their feet lazily kicked at the rocks on the ground below. It couldn't have been more than five minutes when several annoying mosquitoes discovered their presence. Alyson swatted a few. It didn't seem to make a difference.

"Do you want to go?" she asked him. "The mosquitoes are really bad."

"No kidding," Jared agreed, flattening another one on his neck. "Let's get out of here." They made a beeline to the car, swinging their arms in annoyance at the insects that followed. By the time they were inside, they each had several fresh bites already beginning to swell and itch. Jared hurriedly closed the sunroof and smashed any unlucky prisoners he found buzzing inside.

"That was fun," he said to Alyson, enunciating every word with sarcasm.

"I can't believe how thick they were. It was like they appeared out of nowhere. I hate mosquitoes," she said as she began to scratch a new spot on her ankle.

"I think some ice cream would be good right now, what about you?" he asked.

The thought of eating more almost caused Alyson to groan out loud. She politely restrained herself, still so full from dinner.

"Thanks for asking, but I don't have any room. I'm fine with going though, if you want to."

"Oh, come on, there is always room for ice cream," he teased. "Promise me you'll at least try a bite. The place we're going makes some of the best."

"Fine, but just a bite," she smirked.

The cozy, family-owned café Jared referred to was downtown. The menu offered sandwiches, salads, and several flavors of homemade ice cream, including some made with local berries. Jared ordered two scoops of raspberry cheesecake ice cream in a dish.

While he ate, they sat at a table in front of a large picture window with a perfect view of Cook Inlet and Mt. Susitna. The deep, blue-gray water looked as smooth as glass. Alyson watched a trio of Bonaparte gulls forage for small fish and insects along the surface near the shore. Looking out in the distance, she hoped for a glimpse of a beluga whale with no luck.

Jared stopped eating. "Do you know the legend behind the 'Sleeping Lady,' the other name for Mt. Susitna?"

"A little, but I can't remember all the details," she told him.

"Want me to refresh your memory?"

"Sure."

"About a thousand years ago, they say giants inhabited the great land of Alaska, among them was a beautiful maiden who was in love with a handsome young warrior. They were planning to be married, but before they had the chance, their village received news that a tribe from the north was planning to attack. A council was held immediately to decide what to do.

"The young man was chosen to go to the tribe with gifts to show that their village was peaceful and friendly. While he was away, the beautiful maiden kept very busy. Eventually she became tired waiting for his return and laid down to rest.

"Soon after, the village received word that the offer of gifts had been rejected and a battle began. During the fighting, the young man was killed. The villagers didn't have the heart to awaken the sleeping maiden and tell her the sad news so they let her sleep on. She's still resting today, waiting for the safe return of her love . . ."

"That's right, I remember it now. It is such a cool story—but sad." Her gaze returned to the mountain across the Inlet. "It really does look like a woman sleeping."

Jared glanced at his watch. "Are you ready to leave?" he asked.

She nodded.

"Let me throw this away and we can go." He carried his empty dish and spoon to the garbage can and added it to the contents.

When they returned to Alyson's house it was ten-thirty. Her curfew wasn't for another half hour so she invited Jared in. They went in the family room.

"Have a seat, Jared," Alyson offered, pointing to the plaid couch under the window.

"Thanks," he said and sat down in the middle.

Alyson sat in a matching chair nearby.

She watched as Jared noticed that one wall of the room was stacked from floor to ceiling with a large variety of books. Although the shelves weren't crammed to overflowing, there wasn't a lot of extra space.

"Your family must really like to read," he commented.

"We all do, but most of the books are my dad's. He loves to read about the Civil War."

"Really?" Jared asked, sounding interested. He stood up and walked closer to the bookshelf, scanning a few of the titles. He picked one up about Abraham Lincoln and started to thumb through the pages.

They talked a little longer until Alyson started to yawn. Jared took that as his cue to leave. "I better go, so you can crash."

She made a move to stand up.

Jared stopped her. "Don't get up. I can find my way out."

She was feeling tired. "Thanks, Jared. I had a lot of fun tonight."

He smiled. "I did too. Catch you later, Alyson."

She didn't get up right away after he left. Being with him that night had been unexpectedly easy. She wondered why he didn't say he would call. Had he decided she was too young?

The gravel in the driveway crunched loudly as Jared backed out in his car. The sound brought Alyson back to the present, and she yawned again. She stretched and stood up. After locking the front door, she went upstairs to bed.

When Brent first told him about the cute girl at the bakery, Jared hadn't realized she was so young. Once he asked her out, he couldn't very well say "never mind." He probably should have found out before.

He made friends easily, regardless of the situation, and Alyson was no different, but there was something about her—more going on behind her eyes than she let on.

The next day at church, Jared talked to Trey Williams, a close friend. He was like his second dad, and they both loved motorcycles.

"How's it going, Jared?" Trey asked, patting him firmly on the back then shaking his hand. "How is that bike of yours running? Man, we need to plan another trip."

Jared grinned. "I'm in. Hey, Trey, I had an interesting date last night."

Trey laughed, elbowing him in the ribs. "You big stud, anyone I know?"

"Maybe," Jared told him. "Do you know Elizabeth Stewart?"

"Oh, yes. She's a neat lady, a really good person." His voice became subdued. "She lost her first husband, Jim, several years ago in a flying accident. He and two friends were returning from a hunting trip through

Telequana Pass. The weather turned nasty on the flight home. Bruce was in his own airplane and went on ahead. He made it out in time, but Jim got caught in the clouds, visibility was horrible. He ended up crashing into the side of a mountain. Both Jim and his friend, Larry, were killed on impact. It took almost a week to discover the bodies, waiting for the weather to clear."

He shook his head side to side. "It was a terrible tragedy. Each of them left behind wonderful wives and young children . . . yeah . . . I remember that."

Jared looked at him more intently.

"I know Bruce," Jared said. "I'm good friends with his oldest son." He shook his head. "That's really tough."

They stopped talking, their eyes reflective.

"So, Trey, I took Elizabeth's daughter out last night. Her name is Alyson. I didn't know how young she was."

"Yeah, how old is she?"

"She'll be seventeen in July," he said sheepishly.

Trey whistled loudly. Luckily they were outside the building. "You know what they say . . . train 'em young." He laughed, and then his face grew serious. "Jared, if she's anything like her mother, you better hang on to her."

Jared smiled widely. "Really?"

"Definitely. The only real problem I see is getting her to like a guy like you."

Jared laughed. "Thanks, Trey."

"I have a presidency meeting in about five minutes. I need to run. Take it easy, Jared . . . let me know how it goes with Alyson."

"I will. Catch you later, big guy." Jared headed to his car, anxious to get home and change out of his suit and tie.

Alyson didn't have to wonder very long if she would hear from Jared. He called her three days later. She was even more excited when he told her what a great time he had Saturday night, and she had been on his mind ever since. He asked her out for the following weekend. She said yes.

Reid, Alyson's older brother, had been eating a sandwich at the kitchen table while she had been talking to Jared on the telephone.

"Who was that, Alyson?" he asked her after she hung up.

"It was a guy named Jared Clarke. Why?" She was surprised he had been listening to her conversation.

"Jared Clarke? Mom and Dad are letting you go out with him?" Reid sounded astonished.

"Yes," she said, shrugging off his apparent concern. "Why? Do you know him? We went out last Saturday night. Mom knew about it."

Reid hesitated, a guarded look on his face. "I don't know him personally, but I've heard about him."

"Okay," she said, still taken aback he knew anything about Jared at all. "What have you heard about him?"

"That he has a reputation around church for being wild."

"Wild? Why do people say he's wild?" she asked, pressing for more information.

Sighing, Reid went on, "Okay . . . I don't know for sure, but I've heard rumors and I know when he went out with Samantha something happened. She wouldn't go out with him again."

Alyson rolled her eyes at the mention of Samantha. "She acts like she's better than everyone anyway. What supposedly happened?"

He hesitated again. "I . . . just don't think you should be dating him."

Alyson was tired of the conversation. "Thanks for your concern, I guess, but all you've given me are rumors. Jared was a perfect gentleman when we went out," she reassured him. "I'm not worried."

"Alyson, please be careful," he said, looking defeated.

"I will," she replied, annoyed.

When she and Jared went out again, she brought up her conversation with her brother.

Jared's reaction was unconcerned laughter. "That rumor started when I bought my motorcycle. People assume because I ride one, I fit that profile." His words held exasperation. "I hear it all the time and as far as Samantha goes, she loved riding on the back of my bike—until her dad found out."

"Oh, really?" Alyson knew there was another side to the story.

"Yep. After that, it was all over. We only went out twice." He changed the subject, acting bored. "Do you know Trey Williams?"

Alyson's eyes looked past him before focusing again on his face. "My mom definitely does. Isn't he involved with the Boy Scout program at church?"

"That's him. If your brother has any more concerns, Trey can vouch for my character. He and I are good friends. We have gone on a few trips together on our motorcycles, one to California after my mission." Jared smiled. "My bike is bigger than his."

Alyson tried to hold back her laughter. His statement was so . . . male.

To her that summer seemed magical. She enjoyed being with Jared and they spent most of their free time together. He sent her romantic notes and cards, showed up on her doorstep with flowers, and frequently told her how pretty she was. He always found fun things to do like the time he picked her up early in the morning to go trout fishing at a lake near Palmer. He even brought lunch. His maturity level didn't compare to any of the guys her age she dated.

On her birthday, Jared told her to dress-up because he was taking her to a five-star restaurant for dinner. When he picked her up that night, she met him at the door. He was holding an angel food cake—her favorite—decorated with flowers and her name.

Dinner was amazing. After they finished eating, he drove back to her house for dessert. Before they cut the cake, he handed her a pretty, wrapped box.

"Jared, I wasn't expecting anything else," she said, a little embarrassed. "You've already spoiled me way too much today, but thank you." She gave him a hug and took the box from his outstretched hands, curious about what it could be. The package looked too nice to rip apart. She removed the paper carefully.

Inside was an ordinary cardboard box, originally used for something else. The top flaps overlapped and folded underneath. Alyson looked at Jared.

"Well, go ahead and open it." He seemed excited.

She pulled apart the center and the flaps popped up. Inside were several small toys. She looked at his face, questioningly.

He was smiling. "Everyone needs toys for their birthday, right?"

"Sure, of course," she said, sounding as enthusiastic as she could at the moment.

He didn't seem to notice. "Come on, Alyson, see what you got."

"Okay." She picked up a plastic slinky that was on top, then a wooden paddle with a rubber ball attached to the center by a piece of stretchy elastic. "Wow, I haven't played with one of these for awhile." She laughed, moving the paddle back and forth a few times trying to hit the ball. She set it aside and took out a red Porsche matchbox car. "Sweet, how did you know Porsches are my favorite car? Wait till Reid comes home, and I can tell him what I got. He'll be way jealous." She was getting into it now.

Next she found a large bottle of bubbles. "I love bubbles." She unscrewed the lid, pulled out the wand and blew. Several iridescent bubbles rose in the air.

"Not bad," Jared said. "You have quite the talent."

"If you're really nice to me, I might share them with you," she said in mock seriousness, tilting her head slightly to one side.

"Isn't there anything else in the box?" he asked.

"I think that was all," she said, looking one more time. There was something in the corner she had missed. "There is! You're right."

Before she could take it out, Jared took the box from her. "Let me show you how it works." He put his hand inside and pulled out a small, orange-striped cat, made of plastic. It fit in his palm and had a curved tail with two small wheels underneath its body.

"That's cute," Alyson said. "You know I like cats."

He nodded. "If you wind the tail, it spins around. Try it." He handed it to her.

She moved her thumb and pointer finger to grab the tail and noticed something was around it, halfway down. Her eyes grew bigger and she broke in to a huge smile.

"Thank you, Jared. I love it." She slipped off the small gold ring and put it on the ring finger of her right hand. It fit perfectly. It had five red rubies—her birthstone—clustered around a small diamond creating a flower. It was feminine and dainty.

"I couldn't only give you toys . . ." He reached over and gave her a hug. "It reminded me of you as soon as I saw it."

"It's really pretty. Thanks so much. You had me wondering there for a minute with all those toys . . ."

His laughter broke in before she could finish. "You should have seen your face the first time you looked inside the box! It was great. He glanced at the ring on her hand. I'm glad it fits. I wasn't sure what size to get you."

"You got the right one." She gave him a sweet smile.

His face tinged with embarrassment and he looked away. "Hey, you still need to see how the cat works," he said in a childish voice, purposely creating a distraction.

Alyson picked up the plastic cat, wound the tail, and watched as it spun circles in her hand. "It works. And I know right where I'm going to keep it. Thanks, Jared."

He nodded. "Let's eat cake," and jumped up from the couch, still acting a little embarrassed. She stood up more slowly.

In the kitchen, Alyson got four dessert plates out of the cupboard and the same amount of forks from the silverware drawer. She handed Jared a serrated-edge knife. Her mom and younger brother, Michael, were home, so Jared cut a piece for them, too.

In late August, Alyson began her senior year of high school, continuing to work at the bakery. Jared left on his motorcycle to attend college at Weber State University in Utah.

The second day of Jared's trip down the Alaska-Canada Highway found him on the road at 7 AM, hoping to make some serious headway on the long trip. As the miles disappeared behind him, he enjoyed the changing scenery, the wind, and the feel of the powerful machine beneath him. The bike was running tight and smooth.

A lunch stop, a couple of bathroom breaks, and a fifteen minute downpour of rain were all that slowed him down. Other than that, the afternoon passed uneventfully. As dusk began to arrive, he kept going, wanting to make it to the next town thirty miles ahead before calling it a day.

With his headphones on under his helmet, Jared was rocking out to Journey when he came to a bridge. Although he was slowing down, halfway across the bridge the bike hit a slippery patch of pavement, beginning to fishtail.

Every cell in his body jarred to attention as the sliding motorcycle fell sideways, making contact with the hard, wet surface of the bridge. At the speed he had been traveling and the angle of the fall, the momentum caused the bike to roll several times—with Jared still on it.

The following Sunday, Alyson was sitting on a bench in the chapel with her family, waiting for the church meeting to start. She was flipping through the hymn book for the page of the opening song when someone sat down beside her. She didn't look, assuming it was one of her brothers. When she found the right hymn, she set the book on her lap and glanced to her left.

It was Jared.

He gave her a big smile. "Hi, Alyson. Is it okay if I sit with you?"

She blinked a few times, startled and confused. He should have been in Utah. She had been coping with "Jared-withdrawals" all week and wondering why she hadn't heard one word from him. She finally resigned herself to the fact that her life would go on just fine without him. The summer was great while it lasted, but there were lots of fish in the sea and she was planning to buy a new fishing pole to catch some.

Now, here he was sitting next to her, smiling as if they had been on a romantic date only yesterday. She tried to lower her pulse by taking a few deep breaths, tempted to wipe the grin off his face. Had he even gone? Was he playing some kind of a joke? She wasn't laughing and, good grief, they were at church! It wasn't fair. She couldn't blurt out what she wanted to.

Jared stared at her, watching the emotions he had unknowingly caused cross her face.

"Alyson?" he whispered. "Aren't you glad to see me?"

"Jared? What are you doing here? You're supposed to be in Utah." She tried to say it kindly and failed. It sounded more like a hiss.

"Alyson . . ." Jared looked confused by what he saw in her eyes. "I was in an accident last Tuesday and totaled my bike. I wanted to surprise you that I was back."

Her face paled. She felt like a real jerk. He had surprised her all right. Her pulse increased again, this time from fear and embarrassment.

"Are you okay?"

"Alyson, shh . . ." her mom whispered from further down the bench, pointing her index finger up, over pursed lips.

"Sorry," she mouthed back to her.

The opening prayer began. Alyson quickly bowed her head and squeezed her eyes shut. The next thing she knew, she felt Jared's hand slide into hers. It was extremely hard to focus on the reverent words of the prayer with her thoughts and emotions in a jumbled mess. She and Jared gave up talking until after the meeting ended, and they were heading to his car.

Jared filled her in on the details of the accident. "It all happened so fast. One minute I was cruising down the road, thinking about what I wanted to get for dinner and the next minute, I was doing uncontrollable somersaults with my bike. It was freaky. It took me a good five minutes after I stopped rolling to figure out what happened and where I was. Then it took a while to get out from underneath my bike—that thing is heavy. I was amazed nothing was broken, but I hurt everywhere. I couldn't stand up, though, until my equilibrium returned."

"I'm so sorry, Jared, I had no idea. What did you do? Was anyone around?"

"No cars passed from either direction for maybe twenty minutes and I was shaking. The first one that came did stop. It was two guys in a truck, and they helped me get my bike off the road. When they saw it, they had a hard time believing I was up walking around.

"They waited while I got my gear out of my saddlebags, threw it in the back of their truck and gave me a ride into town. Once I found the closest airport, I caught a flight out as soon as I could. My mom was able to get me on a pass with her airline connections. She picked me up at the airport in Anchorage. Trey said he'd drive out with me sometime next week to pick up my bike." Shaking his head he added, "I still can't believe it. I loved that bike. Hopefully I'll be able to part it out and get some cash at least."

Alyson reached over and gave him a hug. "How scary, Jared. I'm so glad you're okay. I know you were being watched over." She felt concerned about what he had gone through and was thankful he was okay but wondered what his unexpected return would mean. Thoughts of a serious relationship developing between them suddenly made her apprehensive and worried. She wasn't ready for that. But now that Jared was back, so were her feelings for him.

The accident changed Jared's plans for school. He hadn't registered yet at Weber so he wasn't out any fees, but no longer having his bike for transportation was an issue. He had to figure out something else.

At sixteen he had started flying lessons and absolutely loved it, planning to make commercial aviation a full-time career. The majority of the large airlines hiring nationally required their pilots to have a college degree. The FAA also required specific ratings to fly commercially and a certain amount of hours had to be flown under different conditions before an applicant would even be considered.

Jared had been steadily building hours but hadn't gotten his commercial or instrument rating. He was going to refocus on it part-time with the money he had saved for school. He returned to drafting at the architect firm where he had previously worked full-time.

The summer with Alyson had been great, but she still had some growing up to do. When he left for school, he figured things would change in both of their lives. He hadn't planned on missing her so much. Crashing his bike had been a major set-back for him, but once he returned to Anchorage, all he wanted to do was see her. Ever since then his feelings for her kept growing stronger.

She had an innocence about her that made him feel good. She never looked at him as if he was anything other than what he wanted her to see. She was young and trusting, untouched by the kind of things he had been involved with in his life. He liked that purity.

When he was with her, he felt like a better person and noticed others looked at him differently. And she made him smile. Maybe she could help him forget the others, especially Mandy and Tara. They both left scars on his heart for different reasons.

He had been hiding something from his family and friends for years and was tired of feeling guilty about it. He kept telling himself it wasn't a big deal. Porn. Everybody did it. It wasn't hurting anyone just to look. But what would it be like to have all his needs fulfilled by a real woman who truly loved him, rather than being turned on by a picture in a magazine or a hot babe in a movie?

Chapter Two

"And the heart that is soonest awake to the flowers is always the first to be touched by the thorns."[3]

February 1984

Alyson looked at her watch—six-thirty. She would be off work in half an hour. Jared was picking her up to take her out for a romantic Valentine's dinner. She was glad the stream of customers at the bakery had slowed down considerably since six. They had sold several dozen heart-shaped sugar cookies and single layer cakes decorated with red, pink, and white frosting.

She had finished some of the cleaning in the back early and things were looking pretty ship-shape. The last batch of freshly baked bread was sliced, bagged, and on the shelves. A few large, yellow trays needed to be washed and part of the floor swept. Once the trays were clean, she rinsed out the large aluminum sinks, wiping the few splashes of water that remained around the edges. It took less than five minutes to sweep.

Alyson looked at her watch again. Six forty-two.

"Sue?" she called to the woman by the cash register.

Sue turned to Alyson, looking expectantly.

"I'm pretty much finished. The shelves are stocked and everything is washed. Do you need me to do anything else?" she asked.

Sue was the manager and closing that night. She didn't mind. Her boyfriend was working all week so they had planned to celebrate their own Valentine's Day on the weekend. She walked to the back where Alyson was and looked around.

"Everything looks good." She glanced at her watch. "Can you double-check the employee bathroom first? Make sure the garbage is emptied and the toilet paper holder and hand soap dispenser are full. Then go ahead and punch out."

Alyson nodded. "Okay." She smiled. "Thanks."

"Do you have a hot date tonight?" Sue asked.

Alyson's smile grew bigger, and she glanced at the sparkling diamond solitaire on her left hand. Jared had proposed to her the week before. She said yes. Ever since she was a little girl, she dreamed about her wedding day. Now it was a little less than six months away. She never imagined it would happen so soon in her life, yet it felt right. They had set the date for early August.

"Yes, Jared's taking me out," Alyson answered.

Sue smiled back. "Have fun. You can tell me all about it tomorrow."

"I will. Thanks, Sue. I'll go catch the bathroom."

It took Alyson two minutes at the most to grab some more rolls of toilet paper from the supply shelf. She put one in the dispenser and one on top. She checked the soap and the garbage, which were fine, and then she punched out, put on her warm jacket and gloves, and grabbed her purse. On the way to the car, she dug out her keys.

The cold air made her shiver as soon as she walked outside. It was completely dark. The sky was clear, and she could see the stars. She let her '78 Monte Carlo run for a few minutes to warm up. She didn't need to scrape the windows. The clock on the dash said six-fifty when she left the parking lot.

The roads weren't too bad if she kept her speed down. Even though it had snowed heavily the day before, most of them were plowed and sanded. She was glad for the extra ten minutes. She wanted to be home before Jared came.

Traffic was light, and she made better time than usual. Making a left hand turn at the intersection of the Old Seward Highway and Klatt Road, she was less than three miles away from her house. The radio was on loud, and she was singing.

She had driven about a mile when in the opposite lane ahead she saw another pair of headlights rapidly approaching. She was shocked when suddenly they started to swerve into her lane. In a matter of seconds, the oncoming car was heading straight for her. Hitting the brakes, she turned the steering wheel as far to the right as she could. The compacted snow from the plows on the side of the road was piled too high and she had nowhere to go.

I can't believe it. That car is going to hit me.

A loud grinding assaulted her ears as metal impacted metal. Her car rocked hard as it was abruptly forced to a standstill. Alyson's body lunged forward and back, and forward and back again. When it stopped her mind tried to catch up. She felt no pain but was stunned. She had always heard how serious head-on collisions could be—often fatal—and she was still fully conscious.

Someone rattled the door handle and banged on the window to get her attention. She mechanically unlocked it and the face of a panicked stranger met hers.

"Are you okay?" he asked, eyes wide with concern. "I'm a doctor." Before she could answer, a woman joined him, and then another man. All three crowded in on her.

"I think she's in shock," one of them commented.

"Give her some space. Has anyone called 911?" the doctor asked.

Someone else was checking on the driver of the other vehicle, also a woman, who had gotten out of her car and was standing beside it. Two children remained in the back seat, moving and peering out the windows. None of the three seemed hurt.

Alyson heard more commotion outside her car door.

"Excuse me, I'm her fiancé, excuse me, please." She recognized Jared's voice immediately.

"It's her fiancé," the woman closest to the doctor said, getting his attention. She and the doctor stepped back and Jared was able to get to Alyson.

Jared leaned in as far as he could without actually getting inside the car.

"Alyson?" His eyes were full of worry.

She started to cry and talk at the same time. "The other car, it just came in my lane. I tried to steer out of the way, but I couldn't—oh, my car." The tears ran harder. She had paid cash for it less than three months earlier and earned every dime herself. She was furious with herself.

Why did I leave work early? If I hadn't, my car wouldn't have gotten hit . . . someone else would have.

That thought made her feel guilty. She glanced in her rearview mirror to see who was behind her.

"Alyson, look at me," Jared told her. "Don't worry about your car right now. How do you feel? Are you hurt?" he wanted to know.

The police and paramedics arrived, and one of the officers approached Alyson's car. Another officer went to the other vehicle.

"Is she okay? What happened?" the officer asked Jared.

"Apparently the other driver was going too fast, swerved, then crossed the center line and hit her head on. I was several cars back when it happened." Jared moved aside to let the officer talk to Alyson.

"Are you okay?" he asked her. "Do you think you can stand up?"

"I think so," she nodded. Her fingers fumbled with the seat belt until she got it unlatched.

He helped her out of the car. She was shaky and unsteady on her feet, but she stayed upright.

"I want you to go over there and get in the ambulance so they can check you. Can you do that?" he asked her.

Jared interceded. "I can help her."

"Who are you?" the policeman asked.

"I'm her fiancé."

"Oh, okay. Just take her arm and walk her over to the ambulance."

Jared linked her arm through his, and Alyson leaned into him as they walked across the street. She saw several cars backed up behind hers and was glad it was dark. She hated being the center of attention. She could hear the driver of the other car arguing loudly with the police officer.

Two male paramedics helped Alyson step up into the ambulance and sit down on the portable bed. "We'll take it from here," one of them said to Jared.

He nodded, "Thanks. Alyson—," he looked at her. "I'll be back in a few minutes. Everything's going to be fine."

She smiled weakly.

One of the men helped Alyson take off her coat, replacing it with a blanket he draped around her shoulders. He started asking her questions. The other man unbuttoned the cuff of her white blouse and pushed her right sleeve up, wrapping a blood pressure cuff around her arm above the elbow. It tightened rapidly. Once the needle gauge pointed steadily to a number, the pressure instantly stopped. The paramedic made some notes on a chart.

"Looks good," he said.

Jared found the insurance papers and the vehicle registration in the glove box of Alyson's car and was exchanging the information with the police officer. He was given the other driver's name, phone number, and insurance company. Two tow trucks arrived on the scene to remove the damaged vehicles. Once they left, traffic returned to normal.

When Jared finished dealing with the details, he walked back to the ambulance.

Alyson was much calmer and, according to the paramedics, doing quite well. They couldn't find anything needing immediate medical attention, but they did encourage Jared to take her to the hospital for x-rays.

Jared could tell Alyson was relieved to get out of the ambulance. He knew she wanted to go home and lay down somewhere dark and quiet. She said she still had a splitting headache, and her neck and upper back ached.

Jared put his arm around her and drew her close on the way to his car. He spoke his thoughts aloud. "Man, that was scary. It's one thing to have a car accident happen in front of you, but when you find out someone you love is in the car, it's a lot more traumatic."

"I'm sorry, Jared. I'm so glad you were here."

"I am, too," he said. "It could have been much worse."

Alyson began to feel dizzy. Thank goodness the car was close by. When Jared opened the passenger door she saw a dozen long-stemmed red roses taking up much of the seat. She gasped and found the energy to smile.

"Oops, I forgot about the flowers. Let me move them so you can get in." He picked up the bottom of the sturdy vase, anchored temporarily with his coat and a wrapped package. After Alyson was seated with her seat belt on, he handed her the roses.

"Can you hold them on your lap until we get to your house?" he asked her.

"Sure, Jared. They're beautiful. Are they for me?" She had gotten flowers before but never a whole dozen.

"Well, actually, they're for your mom. She's been so nice to me, and I knew you would understand." The sound of his words and the look on his face were serious until he broke into a grin.

"Of course, they're for you! Happy Valentine's Day. I debated whether or not to spend the money. Roses aren't cheap, but now with the accident, I'm glad I got them."

Alyson smiled even more widely. "You're the first guy to ever give me a dozen red roses. Wow. Thank you so much."

"And, hopefully, I'll be the last," he added, smiling back at her. He made one more turn, then pulled into Alyson's driveway and promptly turned off the ignition switch. "Hang on a second, Alyson . . ." He got out of the car and walked around to her side, opening her door and offering his arm. He helped her while she held on to the roses, inhaling their sweet fragrance on the way into the house.

Alyson put the roses on the kitchen counter and went in the living room. She removed the warm throw off the back of the couch and wrapped it around her, relieved to finally lie down. She fell asleep quickly.

Later that night, Jared took her to the emergency room at Providence Hospital for x-rays. Her parents were out of town. Her mom visiting a sister in Las Vegas who had just had a baby, and her dad flying the Anchorage to Seattle route. Nothing was cracked or broken; however, the soft tissue in Alyson's upper neck was strained from whiplash. She was given a prescription to use for the pain, which didn't hit her completely until the next day. She stayed home from work and school the rest of the week to recover.

After Jared got off work, he came over each night for a few hours until her parents returned. He dealt with the insurance company, and she received a check in the mail the following week, covering what she paid for the car and then some.

Alyson was grateful Jared had been there to lean on. The experience brought them closer. She was glad when she felt good enough to go back to work and school, plus several visits with a chiropractor eventually strengthened her neck and back.

A little over three months later in May, she graduated, receiving her diploma, and at the end of July, she turned eighteen.

Before Alyson knew it, August had arrived. They flew to Utah to be married in the magnificent, historic Salt Lake Temple on a brilliantly sunny day with blue skies and temperatures over a hundred degrees. Both believed they were beginning a marriage that would continue beyond their lives on this earth—one that would last forever.

When Alyson was in the bride's room with her mom, stepping into her white dress, it seemed like a dream. After she finished getting ready, she hugged her mom and walked out in the hallway to look for Jared. When she saw him, smiling and dressed in white, her heart took a picture she knew she would always remember.

They waited in one of the most beautiful rooms in the temple, side by side, until it was time for the ceremony. Light shades of green covered most of the walls, some with full-length mirrors. The carved moldings, intricate trim and detailed bordered ceiling were exquisite. Elegant, plush sofas and chairs were enhanced by gorgeous crystal chandeliers hanging from the ceiling, radiating thousands of tiny, sparkling points of light.

Alyson was in awe. The whole atmosphere was overwhelmingly peaceful. Jared was quiet and seemed to be taking it all in, too.

Alyson turned to him and whispered, "Can you believe we're here?"

He wrinkled his brow and said in a frustrated voice, "Shh! Don't talk!" as if she was a naughty child needing correction. The completely unexpected rebuke stung as though someone had suddenly thrown ice cold water in her face as she sat in front of a lit fireplace, relaxed and perfectly warm. The peace she felt so strongly vanished.

Jared's confusing words put a black mark on her wedding day that, along with the mental picture she had just taken, she would never forget. When their names were called, the irritation in Jared's face was completely gone. He gave her a warm smile as he stood up and reached for her hand. She shook off the hurt, reminding herself it was a joyous occasion. She was beginning a happy, married life with the man she loved.

Jared's thoughts paralleled hers, except the solid foundation he portrayed to Alyson was not solid, but cracked. He had been telling himself for weeks that once he spent a few minutes inside the temple, he would be at peace with his past and could begin the kind of life he wanted—as if the cracks weren't there. Alyson would never have to know.

The quiet words she had spoken had frustrated him, interrupting what he was trying to feel and erase from his soul. He planned to start over, draw the line. He promised himself. He would put it all behind him and not look back. Having someone like Alyson as his wife would make that craving for porn go away, help him become a man of integrity, honor, and someone God could love. He wanted to be a different person.

Their wedding reception was that night at Alyson's grandmother's church in the Sugarhouse area of the city. Alyson's mom was originally from Utah and many of her friends and family members still lived there. Utah was also where Jared had served his mission and he knew a lot of people, too. They would have another reception when they returned to Anchorage after the honeymoon with their friends and family in Alaska.

It had been a long and intense day, and Alyson wasn't used to the heat. Tired and headachy, she wanted to get out of her uncomfortable wedding dress. She was glad to leave the reception at about nine even though people were still eating and talking, grateful that her mom and aunts were taking care of the gifts and cleaning up.

It was a relief to return to their hotel in downtown Salt Lake. They parked and got out of the car. Jared had booked a very nice suite, and the air conditioning felt wonderful when they entered the room. She could finally relax. After a shower and two pain relievers, she felt even better.

While Jared showered, she looked through her suitcase for a letter. She had attended a youth conference at Brigham Young University when she was fourteen and one of the classes she went to was on dating. At the end of it, the teacher challenged each youth to write a letter to their future spouse, to make that person more real. The premise was that over the dating years, the letter could help guide their choices. When they found the person they would marry, nothing in their past would cast a shadow over the relationship. He told them to keep the letter somewhere safe and on their wedding night, present it to their spouse before going to bed.

Jared knew about the letter and had mentioned to Alyson earlier in the day he was looking forward to reading it that night. After he came out of the bathroom, they sat next to each other on the bed and she handed it to him. He opened it excitedly and started to read.

Alyson watched his face as his eyes moved back and forth over the handwritten page. Before he got to the end, it was apparent something upset him. When he finished, he said very little before setting it down on the bed. That was it. He didn't even look at her.

The feeling in the room had changed.

Alyson stared at him. *What could be wrong?* "What did you think?" she asked.

"Uh . . . yeah, it was nice," he responded, looking at her face while avoiding her eyes. Questions filled her mind, yet something warned her to drop it. She didn't understand but told herself it didn't matter. It was just an old letter. She leaned over and gave Jared a hug.

"I love you." She smiled, snuggling her face in his neck. She dropped the volume of her voice. "So, what do you want to do now?"

He turned toward her and smiled. "Hmm, I don't know, what do you want to do?"

Jared and Alyson's flight to Las Vegas left late the next morning so they slept in. When they got up, they ordered breakfast from room service and repacked. Las Vegas wouldn't have been their first choice for a honeymoon, especially in August, except they were given a free week at the Circus Circus hotel on the strip and budget-wise, it was too good to pass up.

It was a fun trip, only not quite what Alyson had expected. Even though they were now giving themselves to each other in every way, Jared seemed distant.

Six weeks later Alyson was cleaning the spare room in their apartment. When they had first moved in, they began using that room as a catchall for storage: items they used occasionally, and boxes they needed to go through. It was a Saturday afternoon and Jared had gone flying.

Alyson had baked cookies, done some laundry, and then decided to begin tackling the room.

She sorted things in piles, threw away junk, and did general reorganizing. There was an old dresser on one wall that was overflowing with miscellaneous items, and she spent time going through that. She started with the top drawer, mostly full of papers, assorted slides and snapshots as well as miscellaneous office-type items like ball point pens, paper clips and staples. She went through the papers first.

Among them was a wedding announcement addressed to Jared from someone named Mandy—the bride. The date caught Alyson's eye because it was a little over a week after she and Jared were married. She looked at the picture of Mandy and her fiancé and felt uncomfortably uneasy—weird. Jared never mentioned Mandy to her. If she had been important, he probably would have. They both had talked about other people they dated.

Alyson cleaned for another hour until Jared came home. He was a little surprised where he found her. "Hey Alyson, I'm home," he said, walking in to the room.

She immediately stood up and stretched, not realizing until then how stiff she was. She gave him a kiss and a hug.

Jared's eyes moved around the room looking impressed. "Looks like you've been busy today. It looks great—did I smell chocolate chip cookies when I walked in?'

She smiled. "What do I get if I say yes?"

"Oh, I get it." He pulled her closer for another kiss.

"Yes," she said as soon as he let her go.

"Yippee!" he shouted.

His silly exuberance made her laugh.

"Hang on and I'll get you some." She went to the kitchen, put three large cookies on a napkin, and poured a glass of cold milk. She carried it back to the room. Jared was crouched down halfway, balancing on his toes and picking through a stack of record albums.

"Here you go," she said, holding out the cookies and milk.

"Thanks." He was excited. He ate half of one in the first bite.

Alyson glanced around the room to see if she was at a good place to quit for the day. She noticed the wedding invitation again and picked it up.

"Jared, who is Mandy? She got married almost the same time as we did. We missed her reception."

He looked at her. Something she didn't recognize passed over his face.

"Mandy? Let me see it." He took it from her hand, glanced through it, and tossed it back in the pile.

"You've never mentioned her," she commented.

He studied her face before responding. "Let's go in the other room," he said. "Come on." He went and sat on the couch in the living room, Alyson sat next to him.

She could feel an underlying tension.

"Mandy is someone I met on my mission. I was attracted to her but I was a missionary. It wasn't the time for romance. We were just friends. My mission companion made a big deal about it. Even though nothing inappropriate happened between us, he went to the mission president and told him we had a 'relationship.' The mission president called me in. I told him the whole story, stressing we hadn't broken any mission rules. He didn't believe me and within the week transferred me to another mission. I didn't think it was fair and after a few days, I left and came home. In a few months the feelings I had for Mandy waned. We wrote for awhile and talked on the phone, but she was far away and I was dating other girls."

Alyson eyes had filled with tears as he talked. "Why didn't you tell me, Jared? I deserved to know. Leaving your mission early, that's a big deal."

The story had put doubts in her mind about him. She wondered what else he hadn't told her. She felt a headache starting.

"I know, Alyson. I'm sorry. I shouldn't have kept it from you. It wasn't right. The whole experience ended up in such a mess that it's hard for me talk about." He put his arms around her and held her close. "I'll make sure from now on that we talk about everything, okay? Do you need a Kleenex?"

She nodded.

He brought one from the bathroom and gave her another hug.

Four months later Alyson found out she was pregnant. She was ecstatic until morning sickness hit full force. She spent weeks feeling dizzy and tired, throwing up over and over every day. It was rough. There were moments when she questioned how she could have wanted this. She was miserable. When almost five months into the pregnancy the morning sickness passed, she was glad beyond words.

Jared was great. He frequently came home during his lunch hour to check on her and make her something to eat. Many times late at night he went out to get the specific thing she was craving from the grocery store or a restaurant. He told everyone he knew they were expecting a baby and, when Alyson was feeling huge due to her expanding belly, he reassured her that she was beautiful.

In the middle of October 1985, the first snowfall of the season lightly covered the frozen ground. It was a chilly Saturday morning and Alyson was two weeks past her due date. To her great relief, her doctor had decided to induce labor that day. She had been feeling as if she would be pregnant forever.

It was 6:00 AM when they left for the hospital. Jared had warmed up the car so Alyson wouldn't be cold.

"Can you believe the next time we come home, we'll have the baby with us, Jared?" Alyson asked in between yawns. The doctor was going to break her water first to see if labor would begin. If not, he would start her on an IV of pitocin, a synthetic hormone used to help induce contractions. Either way, their baby was finally coming,

Jared reached across the seat and put his arm on Alyson's shoulder. "I know. I can hardly wait to see what he or she looks like." He sounded happy and filled with anticipation.

She wasn't sure which of them was more excited, or which grandparent for that matter—all four told her they would be sticking close to the telephone all day.

At the hospital, Alyson got settled in her room. She changed in to a hospital gown and put her robe on over the top. Her feet were cold so she left her socks on.

The doctor arrived shortly and came to her room. He chatted with her and Jared for a few minutes and then had her lay down. A nurse assisted him as he ruptured the amniotic sac surrounding the baby. Alyson was nervous, expecting to feel some pain, but relieved when there wasn't any, only a minimal amount of pressure.

Her doctor encouraged her to take a long walk with Jared to see if the contractions would start. They walked around the hospital corridors off and on for the next two hours—she didn't feel a single labor pain.

Discouraged, she returned to her room. When the doctor checked her again and found no progress, the nurse started her on an IV and hooked her up to a monitor to watch the baby's heart rate. Within thirty minutes, her labor began.

From then on, the day seemed endless as painful contractions washed over Alyson, hour after hour, her body slowly making the progress required to give birth. Jared stayed by her side, encouraging her, feeding her ice chips, and reminding her it would be worth it when she said she wanted to go home and come back a different day. Jared and the nurse had laughed at her comment, but Alyson was dead serious.

She was starving, tired, and had been dealing with intense contractions for several hours. Jared helped her practice her breathing techniques. She was determined to have the baby without drugs but toward the end of the day, she wondered why she had ever felt that way. She couldn't have made it without Jared's support.

She was glad when she made it to transition, the shortest and most intense part of labor. When it ended she could finally do something, but after thirty minutes of pushing, she became discouraged. The doctor discovered the baby was in the wrong position. He talked about needing to use forceps, which stressed Alyson out even more. She didn't want her baby to enter the world that way. Fortunately, within fifteen minutes the baby had turned and, with great relief, she finished delivering him. A little boy.

It was just past nine on that cold night when their first son entered the world with a cry, his tiny face scrunched and red, but beautiful. She was exhausted but the tiredness receded as amazement, wonder, and happiness filled her heart to overflowing when she saw him for the first time.

"Alyson, look. He's here. We have a son," Jared said emotionally. "You did it," he said, smiling, "and now it's all over." He hugged her.

She felt immense relief that the pain had finally stopped.

Jared cut the umbilical cord and carried their son over to the nurses to be measured, weighed, and apgar scored, a test to evaluate his physical condition after delivery. Once he was done, Jared brought him back, wrapped securely in a blanket, and handed him to Alyson, smiling. Ryker was the name they had chosen. When she held him in her arms for the first time, she was entranced, and tenderly brushed his cheek with her lips, cherishing the first moments they met face to face. At that moment she felt her life was perfect.

Chapter Three

"A marriage that is filled with love, trust, faithfulness, and fidelity is a marriage that glows. . . . There is no love in pornography, only lust."[i]

Alyson loved being a mother and a wife, but by the time Ryker was about sixteen months old, some of the shine had worn off. She adored her son but there were times that his endless energy overwhelmed her, and it seemed all she did was clean up one mess after the other. She loved Jared but they had their differences—he didn't always know the right thing to say, and she didn't always know when to not say anything

Occasionally she caught a glimpse of something unsettling in their marriage. On the surface, her view of their relationship looked fairly calm. But something dark was lurking underneath the facade of their "happy" marriage. Its subtlety remained beyond her grasp. Alyson sensed it. She just didn't know what it was.

However, something tangible did concern her.

Jared's desire for sex had changed, and she didn't know why. She wanted to be close to him in the intimate physical way that bound them together like nothing else could. Increasingly he told her he was too tired and stressed out, dealing with other things or not in the mood. He acted as if her desires were wrong.

Out of self-preservation, Alyson learned to push those natural and important feelings for him away, ignoring them unless he wanted her.

"Jared, are you going to stay up for awhile?" Alyson asked about nine-thirty one night. He was stretched out on the couch, watching an episode of Star Trek, while she halfheartedly thumbed through a magazine. It was the first night in several that Ryker was in bed, sleeping contentedly by eight. He had been cutting a new tooth and today it finally broke through the surface of his gum.

During the next commercial, Jared answered, "No . . . I'm pretty tired. I have to open in the morning at eight. I'm going to bed as soon as this ends."

Alyson went in the kitchen and added two dirty cups and a bowl to the dishwasher, filled the dispenser with detergent, and started it. She checked to see that the dead-bolt on the front door was in place.

"I'm going to go brush my teeth and take out my contacts," she told him and gave him a kiss. I'll see you upstairs."

He came in the bedroom about ten after ten. She was reading in bed. He climbed in next to her, and she closed her book and switched off the lamp. He lay facing the wall. She moved next to him, snuggling close and kissed the back of his neck.

"Stop it, Alyson, you're crowding me," he told her, sounding irritated.

"I was trying to be close to you," she countered. "What's wrong?"

"I'm tired. I didn't sleep very well last night, and it's been a long day."

"I can help you relax . . ." she offered.

"No," he snapped, and then softened his voice somewhat. "I just want to go to sleep."

"Fine, sleep well," she replied, feeling disappointed. She moved back to her side of the bed.

A few days later, it was Sunday and Ryker was down for his afternoon nap. Alyson had a beef roast with carrots and potatoes cooking in the Crock-Pot for dinner. She had put it in that morning before church but it wasn't quite done. Jared was looking through a clearance catalog from a hobby store in California, trying to decide what RC airplane to build next.

Alyson came up behind him and looked over his shoulder. She moved her head close to his, lightly moving her fingers through his hair.

"Find anything good?" she asked him.

"Oh, maybe. I think I have it narrowed down to two different models, but I'm not quite sure. One is cheaper except I need a different size motor than what I have. If I bought that, the cost between them would be the same."

"Ryker is asleep," Alyson told him.

"That's good. He needed a nap. Sundays are always hard on the little guy. Hopefully he'll sleep for a while."

"What should we do?" she whispered in his ear. "The roast won't be done for over an hour. Do you want to spend some time together?"

Jared moved his head away from hers. "Maybe later. I want to figure out which plane to get and fill out the order so I can mail it tomorrow."

"Oh. Jared—?" she hesitated, deciding whether or not to bring up the subject weighing on her mind.

"What?" He wanted to lose himself in the magazine and not talk.

"Is everything okay? Lately it feels like you're hardly ever in the mood for intimacy . . . it never used to be like this. Is it me?"

He put the magazine down. "Why do you keep bringing this up? I feel like you're pressuring me all the time. You act like you're obsessed or something." His tone was condescending.

Ouch.

Alyson blinked rapidly. "I'm sorry. I'm not trying to but . . ." She wished he would understand and not make her feel so defensive. She wanted to be close to him—that was horrible, all right. "I thought guys were supposed to want sex all the time. You don't act like you do."

He sighed with aggravation and looked at her pointedly. "I thought most girls didn't want it all the time, at least not good girls."

That comment upset her even more. "What's that supposed to mean?" she asked him.

"Well . . . it seems like you sure bring it up a lot." Now it felt like he was mocking her.

Do I? Before we were married he used to joke about us setting a new record. . . . That's a joke.

"No I don't. You just hardly ever want it. Maybe you're not a 'normal guy,' " she threw back.

His eyes flashed angrily, but he didn't say anything else.

Her friends complained to her about their husbands never leaving them alone. She had no idea what that would be like.

Jared thought once he was married, he would have a healthy outlet for his sexual needs. When the newness with Alyson wore off, so did his resolve to never return to his former habits. Pornography began to entice him again. The addicting chemical released in his brain during sex, could be released from looking at a graphic picture anytime he wanted. He could take care of it himself, which in some ways was easier, and what he was used to.

He loved Alyson, but the guilt he felt when he was with her, especially sexually, stopped him emotionally from letting her get too close. If he allowed her to take the blame, let her think she was the problem, it drew the attention away from him—exactly what he wanted.

Chapter Four

"You are braver than you believe, stronger than you seem, and smarter than you think."[5]

Ryker was two-and-a-half when his baby brother, Cade, joined the family. It was August of 1988 and the Clarkes were living in California. His delivery was easier and shorter compared to Ryker's and Alyson recovered quickly.

She worried about whether she would be able to love another child as much as her first. Cade was sweet and good-natured. His dark brown eyes were just like his dad's and he had the cutest little fuzz of blond hair. In no time at all, he had a place of his own in Alyson's heart.

Due in part to unsteady employment, Jared had enlisted in the Army several months before. He was hoping to increase his experience in aviation and use the GI Bill to finish paying for his commercial rating.

In September, the young family left California when Jared was transferred to Fort Rucker, Alabama for training as a Black Hawk helicopter mechanic. He had hoped to fly. Without a college degree, it wasn't an option.

Upon completing the training, Jared received new orders sending him overseas to Mainz, Germany, a port city on the left bank of the Rhine River. He left after Christmas. The rest of the family couldn't leave

Alabama until housing was available.

Jared moved into the single barracks on base and became situated at his new assignment. The first chance he could, he found out where his church met. The following week, he called Alyson to check on the family and give her an update.

"Hi, honey," Jared said when she answered the phone.

Alyson's pulse quickened. She was excited to hear her husband's voice. They hadn't talked very often since he left because it was so expensive to call. Hearing his voice was like being thrown a lifeline. She knew very few people in Alabama, didn't have a car, and felt lonely and isolated most of the time.

"Jared! Hi," she said excitedly, her day instantly becoming better.

"How is everything going?" he asked, glad she sounded so happy to hear from him. "How are the boys?" he added.

She let out a little sigh. "It's going well and the boys are fine." She hesitated while trying to keep her voice positive. "We all just miss you."

"I miss all of you too," he said warmly.

"Any idea how much longer it will be until we get housing?" she asked, hoping he would have good news.

"No, from what I hear it varies so much. Sometimes several places become available at once, and other times only one at a time."

"I see." She was disappointed. "So, what have you been doing lately?" she asked, changing the subject.

"Mostly working on the helicopters inside the hangers. It's been busy." He stopped to think. "A few of the guys and I went to dinner last night at this great restaurant. I had speisbraten. It came with salad, pommes frites, and rot kohl. Man, it was all so good. I can hardly wait to take you there."

"Speisbraten, what's that?" she asked. "I know pommes frites are French fries and rot kohl is red cabbage, right?" She laughed. "I guess some of my high school German is coming back."

"Good! It will come in handy when you're here. Speisbraten is a thin cut of beef rolled around a filling of diced bacon, onions, and some spices. The outside edges were kind of crispy, and the rest, super tender."

"That sounds good. You're making me hungry," she told him. Her stomach rumbled.

Jared changed the subject. "Did I tell you I've gone to church twice, now?"

"No. So how was it?" She was a little surprised, only because she assumed he had other things to take care of first; however, that was good news. She loved the fact that wherever they lived, their church was always there.

"The members are really friendly. No one has extended family here, so the relationships among them are close. It's all military personnel and their families. The meetings are in English, not German. The chapel we meet in is kind of small, otherwise it's the same. I found a ride to get back and forth until our car gets here."

"That's good. Who are you going with—another guy or a family?" she asked out of curiosity.

"Last week, it was a woman named Lisa. She was nice. I think you'll like her. I told her all about you and the boys."

Alyson felt a twinge of uneasiness. "Was it just the two of you?"

"Alyson." Jared seemed taken aback. "I wasn't the one that arranged it and her two little boys were in the backseat. They're close in age to ours."

She felt a little better, but part of her was jealous that this woman, who she didn't even know got to be with her husband, even if it was only a ride to church. She wanted so badly to be with him herself.

"Where was her husband?" she asked.

"I don't know," he replied as if it shouldn't it matter. "Maybe he had an early meeting or was out on a field exercise. I didn't ask her."

Alyson wished she hadn't changed the mood of their conversation by letting her insecurities escape; it had been going so well. She could tell Jared was annoyed.

"I need to go," he said. "We can't afford this call to be very long anyway."

"I agree," she told him, somewhat subdued. She did try to end things on a lighter note by forcing cheerfulness into her voice. "Thanks for calling me, Jared . . . I love you."

"Love you, too. Give the boys a hug and kiss for me."

"I will. I'll talk to you later." As soon as he said good-bye, she hung up.

Eventually the car arrived in Germany and within another few weeks, the boys and Alyson did, too. It had been almost two months since Jared left Alabama. They were tired when they landed in Frankfurt after the long hours of travel. When Alyson saw Jared and was in his arms, she felt much better. They had never been separated so long since their wedding. She was ecstatic it was over.

Ryker jumped in excitement as soon as he saw his dad and Cade squirmed in the stroller until Jared picked him up. Ryker chattered non-stop as they went through customs, claimed their bags, and walked to the car. It wasn't until he was buckled in his seat and distracted by the changing view outside his window that he stopped the incessant talking.

Alyson was intrigued by the new buildings, street signs, and landscape they passed, but what held her attention most was Jared's face. Her eyes drank in the sight of him close by and happy. He mentioned several times how much he had missed them and how glad he was they were back together. That warmed her heart even more.

After about thirty minutes of driving, Jared exited the autobahn and turned in to a neighborhood of half-timbered houses and narrow streets. He made a few more turns, and then parked the car parallel in front of what looked like a well-kept family restaurant.

"Where are we?" Alyson asked him.

"This is a place where the guys from the barracks eat often. The prices are good and the food is terrific. They serve traditional German dishes. Are you hungry? I wanted to take you and the boys out for dinner your first night here."

She nodded. "Sure, that sounds great."

Ryker piped up that he was starving. Jared winked at him. "Okay, kiddo, hang on for a few more minutes."

Cade had fallen asleep on the way and was startled when Alyson undid the straps of his car seat. She kissed his head as she lifted him out. He yawned, then his lips curved in to a smile. "You're such a good boy," she whispered in his ear.

Once inside the restaurant, they were seated promptly at a sturdy hardwood table with chairs on one side and a corner bench on the other. Only a few of the other six tables were being used. The waitress welcomed them in German before handing out menus.

Alyson hadn't expected her to speak anything else. Here she was sitting in a small restaurant in central Germany, but the sound of the words was strange. She was looking over the menu when Jared interrupted.

"Alyson, you need to try the schnitzel, it is really good here. That's what I'm going to get." He showed her where it was listed. It came plain or there was a choice of several different sauces, and it was served with salad and French fries.

"Jared, which sauce have you tried?" she asked while continuing to study the menu.

"I've had the rahm sauce—it's a cream sauce. And I've had the jager sauce, which is a darker sauce with onions and mushrooms. I haven't tried the others, but I liked both of those."

"They all sound good," she said, undecided and more and more hungry. The smells alone in the restaurant filled her with anticipation.

The waitress came to take their orders, so Alyson told her what she wanted. She decided to try the cream sauce. She wasn't sure what to get for Ryker. "What should we order for Ryker, Jared?" She couldn't find anything specific for kids. She knew he would love the French fries but wanted him to eat something else, too.

"You know what, the schnitzels are huge, he could probably share from ours—there would still be plenty," Jared explained. "Let's go with that."

He turned to Ryker. "What do you want to drink, son?" He gave him the choices.

Ryker decided on apple juice, and the waitress made more notes on her pad.

Jared ordered last. "I will have the same thing as my wife, except I want the jager sauce on mine, and we need an extra plate."

She nodded. When she came back with two salads a few minutes later, she brought a chunk of dark bread for Cade to chew on. He bounced up and down in the highchair when she handed it to him, immediately gnawing on a corner with his only two teeth.

The main courses arrived soon after they finished their salads. Alyson's eyes widened as the hefty oval sized platter was set in front of her.

"Danke shon," she said.

"Bitte," the waitress responded, smiling.

The schnitzel was a boneless pork cutlet pounded thin, breaded, and lightly fried, with a generous amount of sauce over the top. Alyson cut her first bite, making sure it was well-covered with sauce. She put it in her mouth, closing her eyes as she chewed. It was tender and the coating was lightly crisp, not greasy. She was impressed. When she made chicken-fried steak at home, a similar dish, it was almost always too greasy.

"You're right, Jared, the schnitzel is huge, I couldn't eat one all by myself."

He laughed. "I told you. It's great though, huh?"

She nodded and gave a portion to Ryker, putting it on his plate and cutting it into smaller pieces. She added a handful of fries and he eagerly started eating. She also put a couple of fries on Cade's tray.

By the time dinner was finished, everyone was full. After getting back in the car, it wasn't long before all but Jared fell asleep, still feeling the effects of jet lag. They dozed most of the way to Mainz. Jared woke Alyson up when they arrived.

Their new apartment was in a traditional neighborhood in the suburbs of the city, not on the military base. There were several specialty shops and even a few restaurants lining the streets intermixed with the homes. Many of the businesses had apartments built above them. Their apartment was above a printing shop.

Alyson noticed several European differences in the apartment—the electrical outlets were perfectly round, each room was separated with a door that had a large key hole, and the refrigerator in the kitchen was quite small. She asked Jared about the refrigerator.

"Shopping every day or so for food and fresh flowers is common, which is why it's so small," he explained. "When you go several times a week, you don't need as much storage space, obviously."

"Every day? You're kidding!" she said to Jared, thinking how much time that would take.

"Don't worry, we can get a regular sized-one from the base and have it delivered. There's plenty of room in the hallway."

Alyson looked when they toured the rest of the apartment and saw he was right. The hallway was roomy and quite wide between the two bedrooms. She was relieved. She disliked grocery shopping once a week as it was.

That night, Jared and Alyson slept on the floor of their bedroom using blankets and pillows on loan from temporary housing supply on base. Despite the fact she wasn't as comfortable as she would have been on a mattress, it was worth it to be with her husband. She did not think they had ever missed each other so much. Jared was warm and affectionate, making her feel overwhelmingly loved.

On Sunday they attended church in their new congregation. Alyson met Lisa, her husband, Jacob, and their sons.

"Thanks for helping Jared get to church before our car came. I know he really appreciated it," Alyson said to Lisa.

"Sure. It wasn't a problem. Jared was so happy when he heard he was finally getting housing. Whenever he talked about you and your boys, his whole face lit up."

"Really?" That made Alyson feel great.

Lisa nodded. "What do you think of Germany so far?" she asked.

"It's wonderful. I'm excited to be here. I still can't believe that I am." Alyson's eyes brightened.

Lisa smiled. "That's exactly how I felt at first."

Alyson liked Lisa right away. She wondered why she had worried in the first place, especially seeing her interact with her own husband and children. They appeared to be very close.

Less than a month later, the young women's organization at the church was reorganized and Lisa was called to be the president with Alyson as her first counselor. From then on, they spent a lot of time around one another, and their friendship developed quickly. It expanded to include their husbands and children.

The two families were together often—talking, laughing, eating, swimming, playing with the kids at the park, and frequently sharing a babysitter on the weekends to go out as couples. Lisa and Alyson talked all the time, either in person or on the phone and occasionally the subject was their husbands. From some of Lisa's comments, Alyson learned there were problems in her marriage. She listened to her concerns and tried to be supportive, but was surprised—she would never have guessed it.

The first year in Germany flew by.

Alyson was thrilled at the chance to live there and share it with her little boys, as well as her husband. They explored the many castles along the Rhine, visited nearby towns and villages, tried new foods, and learned local customs and traditions. They often went hiking on Volksmarches held almost every Saturday in different locations.

There was a small fee to participate and at the end of the trail you could purchase a miniature decorated medal with the name of that location on it. The medals were displayed vertically on wooden walking sticks.

They always bought one and eventually had quite a collection. Ryker loved the walks and proudly carried the stick each time they went.

The nearby parks were plentiful, and the boys and Alyson frequently spent unhurried weekday afternoons visiting them. Ryker and Cade played on the jungle gym or in the sandboxes, while she sat on a nearby bench watching them or reading a book from the library on base.

Chapter Five

*"Immorality and sexual innuendo are everywhere. . . . This perni-
cious evil is not out in the street somewhere; it is coming right into
our homes, right into the heart of our families."*[6]

Alyson glanced at the ticking clock on the wall behind her head, realizing it was time to start dinner. She put a pound of hamburger in a skillet
to brown and assembled ingredients for homemade spaghetti sauce. Once
that was simmering, she cleaned up the kitchen, carrying two empty cans
and a plastic wrapper over to the wastebasket. She was about to toss them
in when she noticed five or six pieces of paper wadded up on top of the
garbage.

Ryker had been coloring earlier in the afternoon. He was usually
eager to show Alyson his completed projects; she was curious as to why
this time he threw them away. She picked them up and smoothed out the
wrinkles, instantly concerned when she realized what they were.

The drawings were simple illustrations of female bodies without any
clothes on. Some were from head to toe and some only from the waist up.
Ink had been scribbled over the top of the drawings, maybe in a frustrated
effort to cover them up. The fact that Ryker had drawn them made her
very uneasy. Alyson wasn't sure what to do. She wanted to discuss the
situation with Jared, but he wasn't home from work. She put the pictures

47

on a shelf in her bedroom closet and continued to worry.

When she returned to the kitchen, the hamburger was fully cooked. She drained the grease and added it to the sauce. She put a pot of water on to boil for the noodles, started a green salad, and called to Ryker to come set the table.

She had already set out the plates, silverware, and glasses he would need. Those few minutes had given her a chance to reorganize her thoughts and, although at first she was hesitant to talk to her oldest son without his dad, she ended up feeling she should.

"Ryker, I found the pictures you made, the ones you threw away in the kitchen wastebasket. Why did you draw them and then scribble all over the top?"

His hazel eyes became guarded. "I don't know," he quietly replied.

She pressed on. "Have you seen pictures like that somewhere?"

He started placing each knife and spoon alongside the edge of the plates as if he hadn't heard his mother's second question.

Alyson tried again. "Sweetheart, Mommy isn't mad at you. It's okay. I was wondering if you could tell me about what happened."

He focused even more intently on his task. She walked closer to give him a reassuring hug, offering a silent prayer at the same time that he would be all right.

"Ryker, God has created each of our bodies. They are special and we shouldn't draw or look at pictures of them without any clothes on."

Even though by now he had finished setting the table, he kept his eyes downcast, nodding slightly at her explanation without comment until she finished talking. Then he suddenly found his voice, "Mom, can I go back to my bedroom to play?"

"That would be fine," Alyson told him. "Thanks for helping me. I love you."

She was placing the prepared food on the table when she heard the click of a key turning in the lock of the front door. She was glad Jared was home and felt some relief from her worries immediately. He would probably know what to do.

He came into the dining area and lightly brushed her lips with his. "Hi, Alyson, how's it going?" he asked her.

Once her hands were free, she turned and gave him a hug and a real kiss. "It's going good." She wouldn't bring up her concerns now. "How was your day?"

"Busy—as usual." He sighed. "We have an inspection coming up the end of this week and we're trying to get ready for that."

"Sounds fun," she told him with a touch of sarcasm.

"Oh yeah," he replied, rolling his eyes.

"I hope you're hungry. I made a lot of spaghetti." She glanced once more over the table to see if she had forgotten anything important. She hadn't put out the salad dressing. She went to the kitchen to get it out of the refrigerator.

"Yum, one of my favorites. Great, I'm starved."

"Good, it's ready. Do you want to go tell the boys?" She put ranch and Italian dressing on the table next to the bowl of salad. That looked like everything.

"Sure, I can do that." Jared walked to the back of the apartment to give them a hug and let them know.

Later that night after Ryker and Cade were asleep, Jared and Alyson were relaxing alone in the living room. He was reading when Alyson brought up the earlier incident.

"Jared, I found some drawings that Ryker had thrown in the garbage this afternoon when I was cooking dinner. I want to show them to you. Hang on, okay?" She got off the couch and went to the bedroom to get them. When she came back she handed them to him without further explanation.

He looked at each one and his eyebrows rose. "Wow, those are pretty interesting," he chuckled.

Alyson looked more closely at his face, not sure how he could find any humor at all in what Ryker had done. It annoyed her. "I don't think it's funny. He's four. Why would he be drawing pictures of naked women?" Frustration filled her voice.

Jared became serious after he saw her reaction. "I don't know. It does seem kind of strange. What do you think it means?" he asked her soberly.

His words didn't erase the fact that she could still see a touch of amusement in his eyes. She tried to ignore it. "I talked to him about it after I found them, and he wouldn't say anything, except he didn't know. I think the fact he scribbled over them and threw them away makes it obvious he didn't feel good about what he had done. And why would he suddenly draw them out of the blue? I've been thinking about it, and the only thing that makes sense is if he saw something like that first."

"Like what?" Jared asked her, sounding as if he had no idea.

"I don't know, you tell me," she said. A possibility was forming in her mind but she didn't know if it was credible.

Jared shrugged his shoulders. "You've talked to him, he wouldn't tell you anything. What more can we do?" He looked at her. When she didn't say anything right away, he went back to his book.

Why doesn't he seem very concerned?

In annoyance, she got off the couch from where she had been sitting next to him and moved to a nearby chair. She didn't care if it was childish. On the one hand he had a point; on the other, it was too important to let it go. Jared hadn't even talked to Ryker about it himself. Maybe he could find out more from their son. It felt to her as if he didn't think it was worth the bother. The memory she tried to push away earlier kept persisting.

Three to four weeks before, Alyson was going through the mail Jared brought home. Their mail came to his unit on base through an APO address subsidized by the military. This cut down on the expensive cost of postage for any mail transported overseas. Jared picked it up because it was more convenient. The base he worked at was about thirty minutes away from their apartment.

She found a graphic advertisement two pages long from a company selling adult products. She immediately threw it in the garbage, burying it underneath some other pieces of paper and an empty cereal box. She wanted to make sure the boys didn't inadvertently see it, Ryker especially. She forgot about it until a few days later.

Jared had been home about fifteen minutes and had placed the mail in a pile on the kitchen counter next to his empty containers from lunch, like always. As soon as Alyson had a chance to go through it, she did. Jared never bothered—he left that up to her. If there was something important he needed to see or address, she gave it to him.

Alyson was not happy when she was sorting through it and came across another similar advertisement for adult products. This time she took it to show Jared. He was in the bedroom changing.

"Jared, look at this." Alyson held it up in her hand. "This is the second time we've received this kind of junk. I don't understand why all of the sudden it's coming in our mail or how we could have gotten on this kind of a mailing list to begin with."

He glanced at it and shrugged his shoulders. "Hmm, I don't know. It's probably just one of those things."

"Well, I don't want to get any more. What if Ryker sees them?" She was worried.

"No, that wouldn't be good. I'll try to remember from now to glance through the mail before coming home. Usually I just grab whatever is in my box."

"Thanks," she replied, feeling a little better, but still not happy. The inappropriate advertisements kept weighing on her mind. She decided she would write a letter to make sure their address was removed from the mailing list and tell the company what she personally thought about their kind of business and products. She typed it up later that night and showed it to Jared.

"Will you read this?" she said to him.

"What is it?" he asked as he took it from her outstretched hand. He started reading it before she explained. When he finished he handed it back to her, smirking.

"What's so funny?" she said, looking at his face. She had hoped he would have been supportive of her efforts.

"Do you think it will make any difference to them what you think?" he wanted to know.

"Probably not, but it makes me feel better to do something and hopefully get us off their mailing list."

"Okay. If you put a stamp on it, I'll mail it for you tomorrow."

"I will. I'll put it on the dresser by your wallet and keys so you won't forget. Thanks."

She felt better, momentarily.

Could Ryker have seen one of the advertisements after all? If so, wouldn't he have drawn those pictures right away? Did another one come I didn't see?

Alyson looked at Jared and interrupted his reading again. "Do you think Ryker could have seen one of those advertisements we got in the mail a while ago?"

It didn't register with him.

She went on. "Remember, I wrote the company and told them to take our name off the mailing list? You mailed it right?"

Jared put down his book and looked at her. She thought for an instant a flicker of guilt flashed in his eyes, but it was gone so fast she wasn't sure she had not imagined it.

"Yes," he said a bit defensively.

"I was just asking." She was startled by his tone. Was there something she missed? Even if Jared had forgotten to mail it, he had said he would go through the mail more carefully before he brought it home—she hadn't seen anything else since.

"I'm worried. Ryker wouldn't have suddenly drawn those pictures for no reason." She wanted him to understand her concern.

Jared shook his head, and this time it was anger she saw in his eyes. Instead of giving her any kind of an explanation, he walked out of the room. She was now totally confused. Why was he so upset?

Jared walked to the back of the apartment and went in the bathroom. He shut the door, locked it, and turned the water on full blast. He cursed under his breath, and then splashed the icy cold water on his face. Now what?

He didn't mail the letter, but he was certain he hadn't brought any more advertisements home. The order he had placed with the company was for two videos, and they were safely hidden in a spot Alyson would never look. He only watched them at night when he was certain everyone was asleep.

His face paled.

A few nights ago Ryker had gotten up for a drink. He was pretty sure the door to the living room had been shut. Hadn't it? As soon as he heard a sound, he flipped the TV off instantly and looked. Ryker was standing at the door. Jared got a cup, filled it with water, and tucked him back in bed.

He assumed it was the sound of the door opening that alerted him. If it hadn't been closed, Ryker would have had a perfect view of the television. Who knows how long he could have been standing there watching before he heard him? He felt sick to his stomach. Poor Ryker. What had he done to his son?

He splashed more water on his face, shocking his nerves again to create a distraction from the emotion he felt building inside. Since he joined the military, many opportunities were wearing down his resolve, especially out in the field. Many of the guys brought porn and passed it around; it was more the norm than not. No one thought it was a big deal. How was he supposed to fight it when it was all around him? Was he losing the battle again? He hated being so weak. When Alyson came to bed later, Jared pretended he was asleep. He couldn't bear to look at her anymore that night.

The following Saturday afternoon, Jared was putting a few final touches on his newest model airplane when the cover of the latest issue of his RC airplane magazine caught his eye. It was sticking out from under a roll of red Mylar he was heat shrinking onto the frame of the last section of wing. He pulled the magazine out completely.

It displayed a model wearing a patriotic-colored bikini while holding a large airplane above her head. The colors of the airplane matched her swimsuit. He wondered. He picked it up and carried it to the bedroom where Alyson was folding laundry on top of the bed. He thrust it under her gaze.

"Alyson, maybe this is what Ryker saw that made him draw those pictures." His voice held unmistakable relief as if the mystery was now solved. "I found it on my shelf. Maybe I left it lying around the house the last time I read it, and he picked it up."

Alyson looked at it and shrugged her shoulders. "I don't know, Jared, maybe. But she is still wearing something. The pictures Ryker drew had no clothing on whatsoever and were pretty explicit even though they were very simple. He wouldn't have known that unless he had seen a woman undressed." She shook her head. "That explanation doesn't feel right to me."

"I still think this could have been it. Ryker's a bright little boy . . ." his words trailed off. He was going to say something more but changed his mind.

"I can't talk about this anymore, Jared. It makes me too frustrated. I feel so helpless. I never expected to worry about anything like this until our boys were much older. I want to forget it ever happened. Let's keep a closer eye on Ryker for awhile, okay?" She turned away to finish folding the laundry.

Jared left the room, carrying the magazine. He put it back on the shelf. He hated this. What if he leveled with her and spilled everything? Would she understand, or would it make things worse? He knew she loved him, but how much? Where would he start? Back to when he was a teenager and first started looking at pornography? Would he have to be honest about Mandy and Tara, too? He shuddered at the thought—there was no way. That was in the past, and he had started over. This was a minor setback.

He wouldn't let it ruin everything.

Over the next few months, Jared tried to do better, only it became even harder. The more he gave in, the easier it was to keep doing it, and the weaker his resolve grew. He became more confused in his relationship with Alyson. When she made little mistakes, she was too hard on herself, like if she yelled at the kids all day or had a bad attitude about someone at church. The pressure she put on herself spilled over on him. He could never measure up. They were so different. Maybe they were wrong for each other anyway.

Chapter Six

"When you get to the end of all the light you know and it's time to step into the darkness of the unknown, faith is knowing that one of two things will happen: either you will be given something solid to stand on, or you will be taught to fly."[7]

May 1990

Sunday morning dawned brightly, only a few fluffy, white clouds dotted the sky. When Alyson gave Ryker and Cade a bath their vigorous playing covered the tile floor of the bathroom in bubbles and splashes of water. Once they were both clean, she wrapped them in towels and helped them get dressed for church.

Jared was all ready to go. He took over putting on their shoes and getting them buckled in the car, while Alyson changed into a skirt and blouse. On the way out the door she grabbed her scriptures and the diaper bag. She was quiet on the drive to church, her thoughts preoccupied with the morning.

It was Mother's Day, but it didn't feel like it.

It was tradition that Jared served her favorite breakfast to her in bed— waffles and fruit. She did the same for him on Father's Day, except he got sausage and eggs. That morning it hadn't happened. No present tied with a bow or card written with flowery sentiments. No homemade, colored pictures with the boy's names scrawled shakily at the bottom where Jared helped guide the pen. From the very first Mother's Day when she was expecting Ryker, Jared had made the holiday a big deal.

Alyson couldn't figure out what was going on. They hadn't had a recent fight. Jared didn't seem to be in a bad mood, and he signed two cards last week to send to each of their own mothers—he shouldn't have forgotten. It wasn't so much that he hadn't made her a special breakfast or given her a gift, it was that he was acting as if it was another ordinary day. She only wanted him to acknowledge it or tell her what was wrong.

The chapel was close to full by the time the Clarkes arrived for the first meeting. They had barely sat down when it started. When the closing prayer was said, the mothers were asked to remain in the room a few minutes longer. Each of the women was presented with a carnation to recognize them on the holiday.

Alyson loved fresh flowers and accepted hers gladly. She had tried all morning long to stop worrying over Jared's lack of even a small sign of appreciation for her efforts with their children. Finally she couldn't take it. As they waited in the pew for the aisles to clear she asked him, "Did you remember what day it was today, Jared?"

"Yes, I know." He gave her a smugly arrogant look as if he was trying to tell her she had become insignificant to him. For a moment she felt immobilized, her cheeks flushed, and she had the ridiculous thought she should apologize. Tears burned behind her eyes. She needed to get away from Jared to compose herself.

What is going on?

Lisa was suddenly next to her, Jacob and their children close behind. "Hi, Alyson. Happy Mother's Day." She smiled brightly. "Did Jared make you breakfast in bed this morning or did he give you flowers?"

Alyson almost choked. Lisa did not seem to notice.

"No . . ." she barely got out.

"Really?" She seemed surprised and looked at Jared. He flushed slightly under her gaze.

"How about you?" she asked Lisa.

"Yeah, Jacob and the boys made me pancakes." She laughed. "They looked interesting," she looked at her husband and smiled, "but they tasted delicious."

"That was nice." Alyson's voice felt strained. By then, Jacob was close enough to her to shake her hand. He stuck his out, and she put hers in his briefly.

"How are you, Alyson." His smile was warm.

She smiled back, feeling more pulled together. "I'm good, Jacob. Thanks. How are you?"

By then the two oldest boys were starting to run circles around them and act silly. She reached for Ryker's hand.

"Come on, bud. Let's take you to your class." She was already holding Cade. Alyson said good-bye to Lisa and Jacob and ignored her husband. She gave Ryker a hug at the door of his classroom.

"Be good for your teacher, okay?" Before he answered, she hurried to her next meeting with the young women.

Lisa was no longer helping with the young women, but Alyson had remained in the presidency under the new president. She was glad she wasn't teaching today. She sat down, and one of the girls came up to her and asked if she could hold Cade.

"Sure, as long as he doesn't distract you from listening to the lesson."

"Okay," the girl agreed. "He's so cute."

Alyson gave her a distracted smile. After class was over, she went to get Ryker but Jared had already picked him up. She found them in the hallway and as soon as Ryker saw her, he handed her a card he made in class.

"Happy Mother's Day, Mommy," he said. "I made it myself."

She looked at the cover and then inside. "Thanks, sweetheart. It's beautiful." She hugged him and kissed his cheek. They walked out of the building in the warm sunshine to their car. When they left the parking lot, Jared glanced over at Alyson once but didn't say anything. She kept her eyes focused out the window all the way home.

Alyson changed out of her skirt before she started making lunch. When Jared came in the bedroom to change, she was finished and brushed by him without making eye contact.

She went to the kitchen and made tuna sandwiches with fresh fruit. Ryker came in to help her, When it was ready he told his dad. Jared brought Cade when he came and put him in his highchair.

While they ate, the conversation between her and Jared was minimal, centered mainly on the boys. Ryker told them about what he learned in his class. They finished eating and Alyson cleared the table while Jared washed Cade's hands and face. Ryker insisted on doing his own.

"Ryker, you and Cade can play for a little while in your bedroom before you have to take your nap," Alyson told them. They still had lots of energy after being at church for three hours. Ryker took the lead and went skipping down the hallway singing "Jesus Wants Me for a Sunbeam" as loud as he could. Cade was close on his heels going as fast as his little legs could carry him.

The scene made Alyson and Jared laugh. She went to her bedroom and got a cross-stitch project she had been working on and went back to the living room. When she'd left the room, Jared had been reading. When she came back he was watching television.

She moved the throw pillows on one end of the couch to make room for her project and sat down. She threaded her needle and had made three half x's when Jared turned off the television and went into the kitchen. He started looking through one of the cupboards. She found her spot again and pulled the thread to one side when the cupboard door he opened banged shut.

She jumped.

"Alyson, I can't find any graham crackers. Did you move them from their usual spot next to the peanut butter?" Jared asked her.

She sighed, how nice of him to talk to her—when he needed something. "That's where I always put them. We must be out. Write it on the grocery list on the side of the refrigerator and I'll buy some when I go shopping Tuesday. There should be some granola bars by the cereal if you want one of those."

"Okay, thanks," he mumbled.

Alyson decided Jared must have changed his mind about getting a snack because when he came back in the living room his hands were empty. He turned the stereo on to a jazz station and stretched out on the floor.

Alyson wondered why he was so restless; it was starting to get on her nerves. She stopped working on her project for a minute to decide if she should change one of the colors of thread. Then the doorbell rang. She put everything down and went to answer it.

Lisa was standing alone on the other side. She hadn't mentioned anything at church about coming over. Alyson wondered what was up.

"Hi, Lisa. This is an unexpected surprise. Come on in." She smiled cheerfully at her.

Lisa hesitated before walking a few steps into the entryway. "Hi

Alyson, uh . . . I need to talk to Jared."

"Jared?" she questioned.

"Uh-huh. Please." She nodded, avoiding Alyson's eyes.

"Okay. Is everything all right?" An uncomfortable knot began to form in her stomach.

Lisa ignored her question. "I just need to talk to him."

Confused and a little hurt, Alyson turned away to go get Jared and about collided with him. He had come up behind her.

"Hi, Lisa," Jared said. He gave her a small smile.

Lisa didn't say anything and the two of them stared at each other. Jared's face was expectant, and Lisa's dark eyes were serious.

Lisa broke the silence. "We need to talk." Her sharp, pointed words hung stiffly in the air, stabbing them all. Alyson looked at Lisa and then her husband. They both ignored her. Lisa turned to leave and Jared followed her. Neither of them told Alyson good-bye, gave an explanation, or even acknowledged she was still there.

The latch on the door clicked in place as it shut, and she looked at it bewildered. The knot in her stomach had turned into a boulder. She went in the living room and looked through the lace curtains to see if they were gone. They were. Every minute that passed after that felt like fifteen. She looked out the window frequently to see if they had returned.

"What are you doing, Mommy? Where did Daddy go?" Ryker asked, after coming in the room and watching her strange behavior.

"I'm looking out the window. Daddy will be home in a little while. It's time for your nap anyway. Please go pick up your toys."

"But I'm not tired," he whined. "I want to keep playing."

"I think you are," she said resolutely. "If you hurry and go lay down I'll read you a story first, whatever you pick."

"Fine," he said unenthusiastically. "What about Cade. Doesn't he have to take a nap, too?"

"Don't worry, he will. Come on, let's go." Alyson took his hand and led the way to his room. Once he was on his bed, she covered him up securely and kissed him on the nose. Before she finished reading him his favorite book, *Farmer Brown*, he was asleep.

Cade needed a drink, so she left him stacking blocks in the corner and went to the kitchen to get him some milk in a toddler cup. She finished pouring it, screwed on the lid and was surprised when she felt his hand touching her leg. He must have followed her.

"You silly goose," she said, and gave him his cup. She sat down on the living room floor and he climbed on her lap. He leaned his head on her chest while he drank. When it was all gone, she put him down for his nap. He didn't fuss at all. On the way back to the living room, she looked at her watch.

Jared had been gone an hour and a half. She was glad taking care of the boys had created a distraction. She went over to the window and moved the curtains out of the way to look one more time. Lisa's car turned into the driveway.

Finally.

Alyson watched her husband get out, close the passenger door, and wave to Lisa as she drove away. He took his time coming up the metal stairs to their apartment. When she heard the front door open, she moved away from the window to the doorway. The relief she felt at first over him being home was short-lived when she looked at his face.

Jared's jaw was set in a hard line and his eyes pierced her coldly.

"Jared, what is going on? You're scaring me. Why did you leave with Lisa?" Her last words escalated in pitch.

He stared at her, staring at him, and said nothing. A heavy, ugly feeling filled the room, soon becoming claustrophobic.

Jared started to talk, addressing none of her questions.

"Lisa and I have been seeing each other for a while." His slow and matter-of-fact tone would have been perfect for discussing the weather.

Lisa and you together? No way! She would never do that to me . . .

Jared went on. "A few days ago, in the middle of the afternoon, I was over at Lisa's. Jacob came home unexpectedly from work. When we heard the key turning in the lock, Lisa told me to hurry and go out a window in the back. I almost made it out completely, but my foot got hung up in a hedge below the window. Jacob came running around the side of the house and saw me as I was trying to pull it free."

Alyson could feel the pulse pounding in her ears and could only imagine what Jacob must have thought when he saw Jared sneaking out of his house. "What happened?"

"You could say Jacob was upset and surprised."

Gee, I wonder why?

"He asked me what was going on. By then Lisa had joined us. She told him to come back in the house so they could talk, but he wanted me out of there first. He told me to leave." He stopped talking and looked past her, remembering.

"And?" she questioned, feeling frantic. She needed to hear everything.

He refocused on her anxious face. "I talked to Lisa later. She told Jacob the truth about our relationship. Today he asked her if we had told you. She told him no, and he said it better happen right away or he would tell you himself. That's why Lisa came over."

"What is the truth about the two of you, Jared?"

"The truth is—I'm in love with her." He described how their relationship had progressed over the last few weeks, some of it right under Alyson's nose. She wasn't sure if she should laugh hysterically or start screaming. Had they slept together?

It was as if he read her thoughts. "We didn't have sex, but I wanted to." He added the final punch as if it could get any worse—it did. "Alyson, Lisa and I are soul mates. I've prayed about it, and I know it's true."

How dare he bring God into this as if He would approve.

"We are so much alike. I want to marry her." He continued and actually smiled at her.

The words cut right into her heart. How could she even begin to comprehend what he just told her? He was in love with her best friend? It was completely unreal. She had become part of a television soap opera.

"Jared, how can you even think you can justify breaking up two marriages for no good reason, to create a third?"

He looked at her as if he couldn't understand why she didn't get it. "Alyson, it's different if she and I are meant to be together."

Her brow wrinkled, trying to follow his logic.

He saw her reaction and added, "Believe me, I haven't made this decision lightly."

She wanted to shake him. She approached it from another direction. "Even if you don't care about me," she had to work to keep her voice steady, "what do think this would do to Ryker and Cade? Are they supposed to watch you suddenly leave and become a dad to their friends? They would never understand that."

Jared's response was quick, as if he had planned everything out. "I would tell them I would always be their dad, but I needed to live somewhere else. It might be hard at first, but they would adjust. Because I love Lisa so much I would be willing to make that sacrifice to be with her."

He was acting as if it should make perfect sense, and she should commend him for being so generous and committed, all in the name of true love. His rationalization was beyond her understanding. Could he mean what he was saying and cast them aside so easily? He had never told her, not even once that he was unhappy in their marriage or with her as his wife. Not once. Sure, their relationship wasn't perfect and they had issues, but who didn't?

She was overwhelmed by hurt and couldn't hold back the flood of tears any longer. They began to pour out of her eyes. "How dare you!" she said to Jared, her voice choking with pain. "How could you do this to me? To our children?" She was both angry and terrified. Was it somehow her fault? How could she fix it? What should she do?

Sobbing, she slid down the wall she was leaning against onto the floor, pulling her legs to her chest and wrapping her arms around her calves.

Jared looked at her in disgust and frustration as if her display was a weakness he wanted no part of. "It's time you grow up, Alyson. Time to learn how to take care of yourself."

That cruel comment wounded her even more. She came extremely close to hating him for it.

Who is this man?

When he left the room, she cried harder and couldn't stop until her eyes burned like fire and her energy was completely spent.

The next couple days were a foggy blur as she alternated from disbelief to anger and then to wrenching sadness. She wished she could turn back the clock. In the morning when she woke up, ending the respite of sleep, the weight of the situation settled on her immediately. She was besieged, wanting the pain that had shaken her so thoroughly replaced by the comforting innocence she used to know. There were times she wanted to hit Jared with her fists as hard as she could and times when she wanted him to hold her close with reassurance.

She called her parents. They were devastated when she told them, but willing to do whatever they could to help. Jared's parents were, too. Alyson knew she had to get out of Germany, as far away from Jared as she could, to figure out what to do. She called a travel agent and made arrangements to leave for Alaska as soon as possible. All the boys knew was that they were going on a trip to see Grandma, and they were excited.

She told the young women's president she was leaving because she and Jared were having problems. She told the bishop, the leader of their congregation, the same thing. She was relieved that neither one pushed her for details.

Jared didn't protest when she told him it would be for an indefinite period of time. They met with the legal office on base to sign paperwork for an official separation including fixing an amount for support. It would be taken out of Jared's paychecks automatically and sent to her.

When Jared dropped them off at the airport, he hugged and kissed the boys. "You be good to your mom, okay? Remember, she's in charge. Have lots of fun at Grandma's. We can talk on the phone while you're gone. I love you both." He turned to Alyson. "Be careful and call me when you arrive in Anchorage." He didn't try to touch her.

She was glad. "I'll call you." It was awkward. She didn't know what else to say. She still could not believe what was happening to them but was relieved she wouldn't have to see his face every day. It hurt too much.

She hadn't talked to Lisa since Mother's Day. She wasn't ready for that and most likely Jared had told her she and the boys were leaving. When they boarded the plane and she got the boys situated, playing contentedly with a new toy, she started to relax. However, when the airplane left the ground, she silently cried.

The boys did better than Alyson expected. They changed planes twice on the way to Anchorage, the layover at each stop minimal. On the last leg of the journey they were seated in front of an elderly couple. Several times during the flight Ryker pointed to the woman and said, "Hi, Grandma," or "Look, Cade, it's Grandma."

Alyson explained to him more than once that this wasn't the grandma they were going to see, but every time he caught sight of her he got excited. The woman ended up holding him on her lap and reading him a few stories. She told him he could call her grandma if he wanted.

Alyson's parents were waiting at the arrival gate when their plane landed. As soon as she saw them, she pointed and told Ryker, "She's your grandma."

"Grandma!" He ran to her giggling with excitement. He gave her a huge bear hug, and Grandpa, too. Elizabeth and Nate were smiling. When they looked at their daughter, their gazes held concern and sadness. Alyson had to fight back her tears. She was glad her sons were too young to understand the unspoken words hanging in the air. They were so excited to see her parents, they forgot about the absence of their dad, despite how the rest of the family were painfully aware of it.

Ryker told his grandparents all about the plane ride as they went down the escalator to the baggage claim area. The carousel was crowded with waiting passengers. When she spotted her luggage, she signaled to her dad, and he took them off the conveyor belt. Once all three pieces were accounted for, he led the way to the car.

Nate and Elizabeth lived on the outskirts of Wasilla in a secluded wooded area. Their well-kept yard was just beginning to turn green. Spring came late in Alaska compared to many other places. They had neighbors nearby but not so close as to interrupt their privacy, or the singing birds, chattering squirrels, and the occasional wandering moose.

It was several days before Alyson and the boys adjusted to the time change. After they did, time passed slowly. The constant awareness of the situation lessened Alyson's enjoyment of normal everyday things as she struggled to decide which direction to go.

Weeks passed but there didn't seem to be much of a change in Jared. The few times they talked, he was distant and kept referring to Lisa. It didn't give Alyson much hope that things between them would work out. By July she knew she needed to make some firm decisions. She was tired of being in limbo.

If she and Jared got a dissolution of their marriage, it would be less expensive than hiring attorneys and going before a judge. If they could amicably agree on everything, they could fill out a packet of paperwork and submit it directly to the judge. A short hearing would be held to ask a few questions and make sure they were in agreement. If so, their paperwork would be reviewed and signed, and they would be divorced in a few weeks.

Alyson had to go to the courthouse in downtown Anchorage, a two-hour drive round-trip, to get the paperwork. Once she arrived and found the right office, she was finished in ten minutes. On the way home she stopped at the post office and mailed one of the packets to Jared. He called her on the telephone several days later.

"Hi, Alyson. I got the papers you sent." His voice sounded panicked—unusual for him.

"Hi—you did? It seems like I just sent them. Wow, that was fast," she said.

He went on as if she hadn't spoken. "I was surprised when I opened the envelope and saw what it was." He hesitated. "I'm not ready to take such a big step."

His words were a shock. She hadn't seen anything up to then that would lead her to believe he felt that way. She wondered what changed.

"I'm arranging for leave to come to Alaska as soon as possible," he told her.

"You're coming here? Why?" She hadn't expected that, either.

"I don't want to get into it over the phone. I need to do it in person. I want to talk to you about all of this. Will you wait a little longer before you submit anything to the court?"

She was dubious. She had finally gotten off the emotional roller coaster she had been riding for weeks because she had made a decision—and she did not want to get back on.

He continued, "Alyson, things have been bad since you left. It's over between Lisa and me. Last night I—" his voice broke. "Last night I actually had a gun . . . in my mouth. I just couldn't pull the trigger." His words turned to sobs. "My whole life is falling apart."

His whole life? What about mine and our boys'? Since when is it only about him? Suicide? Is he telling me the truth?

Something that extreme was far removed from the man she knew. She didn't trust him, yet what if he did do something that foolish?

"Jared, I need to think about all of this—"

He cut her off. "Alyson please, will you wait until I can come?"

She felt like screaming at him. Not once had he asked her about what she was going through or how she felt. "You have no idea how much you have hurt me, Jared."

"Let me at least come and talk to you. Can you give me that much?" he asked.

She thought about Ryker and Cade and her resolve started to falter. "I guess . . . but no promises, Jared."

"I understand." His voice was subdued. "Thank you . . . I'll let you know as soon as I get my reservations made."

"Fine. Good-bye, Jared." She turned off the cordless phone and remained sitting on the bed in her room thinking and feeling shaken.

Jared arrived in Alaska in the middle of August. They had been separated for three months. He looked the same as always, but so much between them was different. Alyson was wary of letting him get too close.

Ryker and Cade were excited to see him and needed lots of his attention the first couple of days back together. When things calmed down, she and Jared had time alone to talk seriously. They drove to Anchorage to stay with Jared's parents for a few days while Alyson's parents kept the boys.

Jared had a lot less to say than she expected. He didn't spend time rationalizing what he had done by giving her excuses. She was glad. Rehashing everything would rip the partially healed scab off her wound and make it bleed all over again.

"I know I really screwed up and I've hurt you. What I did was wrong, period." He hesitated. "I don't know for sure how it happened. It wasn't as if I got up one day and decided to pursue a relationship with Lisa, fall in love, and break apart our family."

Alyson leaned back, trying to stay calm, not wanting to remember how she felt when Jared told her he loved her best friend.

"What can I say? I made a huge mistake. I know that. Please give me another chance, Alyson. Being away from each other these past three months has made me realize how important you and the boys are—" he stopped talking and looked her in the eyes.

She could see sincerity there, but could not believe it was real, not yet. She was plagued by the ache and disloyalty of his actions, unable to understand how and why it ever happened.

"No matter how I look at the situation, I can't find logical answers, Jared. It wasn't as if some dramatic thing happened in our relationship that was a catalyst to you betraying me. How did we go from being happy—not perfect, I know—but to you telling me it was over?"

"I don't know," he said, sounding irritated. She looked at him sharply. If he was going to be short with her the conversation was over.

He saw the warning in her eyes and changed his tone.

"I'm sorry, Alyson. Can we please pick up the pieces and start over? I promise I will do everything I can from now on to make it up to you and treat you the way you deserve."

She still loved him. He was a part of her life, a part of the children that meant the world to her, but she was scared. "How can we get through such an enormous obstacle in our relationship, Jared? How can I ever trust you again?" She fervently believed in commitment in marriage. Why should she take him back just because he asked?

"I don't know, Alyson. The only way is if we take it one day at a time. I don't expect you to trust me anytime soon. If you give me time to show you, one day at a time, and I prove myself, I hope at some point you can."

He rubbed his eyes and ran his fingers through his hair, feeling tired.

Alyson looked at herself honestly. How good of a wife had she been? Maybe some of this was her fault. Were there things she needed to work on? Patience? Perhaps being less emotional and more understanding? She knew there were. Maybe this time, if she tried harder to make him happy, to change, he would finally love her completely. Maybe once they got through this, their marriage could be better than before.

She agreed to try again. She didn't know how to believe in Jared or how long it would take until she could, but knew she could trust in God's help. His love would make up the difference.

When Jared returned to Germany, she and the boys stayed in Alaska until September, after Jared's next field duty was over. She watched the fall colors arrive and felt the crisp coolness return to the air before they left. Autumn was her favorite season. Regardless of why she changed her mind to go back to Germany and Jared, her heart was chilled with apprehension, just like the temperatures outside.

Chapter Seven

"Let me not pray to be sheltered from dangers but to be fearless in facing them. Let me not beg for the stilling of my pain, but for the heart to conquer it."[8]

Alyson's apprehension must have been a premonition. On the drive from the Frankfurt airport, their reunion rapidly grew contentious. She was sharing her concerns about rebuilding their relationship on a day-to-day basis looking for reassurance they would be okay and face everything together. That isn't what happened.

Jared reacted by shouting so loudly she jumped, telling her not to add more pressure to his life, that he was over his limit already. She didn't know what he was referring to and didn't like the fact he put her in the same category as something to be endured.

Her mind scrambled to make sense of his charged reaction. He wasn't acting like he wanted to be back together and certainly not as if he was glad to see her. Obviously he too was struggling, but why was she the target of his anger instead of his ally? Insecurity overwhelmed her, accompanied by fresh pain, and tears filled her eyes. The homecoming she had hoped for wasn't happening.

She stared through the car window at the shifting landscape, keeping her face turned so he couldn't see her tears. She shivered, doubting her decision even though she had barely returned. She prayed for more courage. Her choice to stick it out wasn't going to be easy.

After they got home, she kept busy unpacking and getting Ryker and Cade in their pajamas and to bed. She avoided her husband. In bed that night she faced the wall as far to one side as she could. When she fell asleep, she was physically and mentally exhausted.

The next morning started on a more positive note. Jared hugged her good-bye on his way out the door. Getting rest had helped them both. The hours flew by as she finished unpacking, did laundry, cleaned, and went grocery shopping.

For several days, Alyson found it hard to relax whenever Jared was around and felt as if she had to walk on eggshells. Constantly careful of what she said to him in order to avoid a fight, she could tell the rapport between them too precarious to handle even the smallest argument. It was a bumpy transition, fraught with personal insecurities.

Their relationship was different and uncertain. They couldn't fall back on the comforting routine their marriage used to have. In many ways, they were starting completely over again, and it was awkward. The chasm between them was wide and didn't heal quickly. How could it? Negative and distraught feelings often returned and had to repeatedly be pushed away.

God was Alyson's strength, her constant friend, counselor, and her support. She leaned on Him completely until she found her own strength again. He was always there and her faith in Him grew immensely.

Lisa wasn't suddenly out of their lives because Jared and Alyson were back together. They saw her and her family at church meetings or social functions they attended. That, in itself, made the situation extremely hard to put in the past.

One night Jared was working late and Lisa called. Alyson picked up the phone. Hearing Lisa's voice on the line had once been a pleasant and familiar occurrence, but now it was deeply uncomfortable, unwelcome, and disconcerting.

At the beginning of the conversation, Lisa made small talk about the boys, the weather, and other similar things. The entire time, Alyson was waiting for her to bring up the elephant they both knew was in the room but were pretending not to see.

"Alyson, the main reason I called is because there are some things I need to say to you about what happened between Jared and me." She'd done it. The elephant was acknowledged. Her words enveloped Alyson in silence. You could have heard a pin drop.

She started again. "I know I should never have let it happen. It was my fault and I knew better."

Alyson heard the regret in her voice. "Jared knew better, too, Lisa. He—"

Lisa cut her off. "No, Alyson. I mean . . . yes, he did, but I could have ended it right away." Her voice dropped. "I wasn't reading my scriptures or praying as I should. The problems between me and Jacob were not getting resolved, and I was down on myself. No matter what, it felt as if I couldn't do anything right to please him." She took a deep breath.

"It wasn't long before Jared started pushing me for physical things. I turned him down but he was persistent and I was attracted to him. I ended up giving in on some of the things he wanted to do. But when he told me he wanted to have sex, I told him there was no way I would go that far."

Her words sounded unreal to Alyson. "Lisa, didn't you feel guilty when you saw me? We were together all the time."

Lisa sighed. "Yes, I felt terribly guilty, and I didn't want you to be hurt. Really."

Alyson had a hard time believing that and her words conveyed her disbelief. "Of course, I would be hurt! You were messing around with my husband!" Emotion caught in her throat. "I thought we were close friends." What Lisa had done to her was incomprehensible.

Lisa hesitated. "I know, I know . . . it doesn't make any sense." She began to cry, fighting the emotion to stay composed. When she spoke again her voice was steady.

"There were a few times Jared came and I sent him home, telling him he should be with you. I knew it was wrong and wanted to stop several times but didn't. I liked the attention and the compliments. I wasn't getting any of that from Jacob." For a minute she couldn't speak. "I'm so sorry. Alyson, there is no excuse for what I did but I hope at some point you can forgive me." Her voice broke. This time she couldn't mask the tears.

Alyson wasn't ready—the hurt too fresh. She responded hesitantly, "I'm not there yet, Lisa."

Lisa was crying openly now. "I understand. Please know I am very sorry."

"Thanks for calling me," Alyson said quietly. "I know it wasn't easy . . ." She had to get off the phone before her own emotions overtook her. "Good-bye, Lisa."

Tears ran from her eyes as soon as she moved the receiver away from her ear. She grabbed a handful of Kleenex out of the box in the bathroom and went to her room. She laid face down on the bed, burying her head in the pillows and crying until she was spent.

Later that night when Jared came home, he didn't seem to notice she had been crying. She didn't mention the phone call. She hated to say Lisa's name around him unless it was absolutely necessary. It made her overanalyze his reaction, verbally and non-verbally, and it messed with her head.

Jared had another assignment in the field for over a week. Alyson didn't want to wait until he came home to get the mail. Going got her out of the house, and the road meandered through a picturesque village and fields of cherry trees.

She picked up a good-sized stack of letters, bills, and a couple of magazines held together with a rubber band and glanced through them quickly on the way back to the car. She noticed a couple of personal-looking letters addressed only to Jared and the name Kristine Barker written in neat cursive in the upper left hand corner.

It seemed vaguely familiar. She had met someone by that same name once, right before she left for Alaska. Kristine had come to their apartment with a girlfriend one afternoon, and Jared introduced them to their family. He told Alyson the women lived on base and were in his company. They seemed nice enough but her thoughts had been on packing. She remembered wondering why they came over. Why would Kristine send Jared letters?

She got back in the car, got the boys situated, and put the mail on the empty front seat. Once they arrived home and were inside the house, she put a cartoon video on for the boys to watch and opened one of the letters.

Kristine described in detail a weekend she and Jared supposedly spent together. It included graphic descriptions of them having sex. A horrible feeling crept over her but she couldn't stop reading, compelled to take in every word on the page. At the bottom of the letter, Kristine told Jared she would gladly spend another weekend with him whenever he wanted. The other envelope held a card.

Alyson could barely breathe.

The difficult decisions she made in the past several months concerning her marriage were in front of her again. She loved Jared and that was why she agreed to risk her heart on giving him a second chance in spite of her vulnerability and fears.

What have I done—has Jared been playing with my emotions? Did he actually cheat on me after all, in a worse way than with Lisa? He promised if I gave him another chance, he would do whatever he could to make it up to me. He said he was sorry—but these letters . . . Father in Heaven, please don't let them be true. I can't bear to go through something like this again!

She checked the calendar for the exact date Jared would be home from the field. It wouldn't be for several more days. This couldn't wait. She felt like tearing him apart. If the letters weren't true, she had to see his face, look him straight in the eye, and hear the words from his own lips.

She picked up the telephone receiver with a shaky hand and dialed the number of a girlfriend whose husband was in the field with hers. Jennifer answered on the third ring.

"Hello."

Alyson could barely talk, and when she heard her voice, she started crying.

"Alyson, is that you? What's wrong?" she asked.

She couldn't say a thing until she calmed down.

"Alyson, are you okay? What happened?" Jennifer was worried.

Alyson felt her concern but couldn't tell her what she had found. She was too humiliated. "I need Jared to come home right away," she finally got out.

"Why?" Jennifer wanted to know. "The guys still have almost a week before they'll be back. Can I help you?"

"No . . . but thank you." She began crying again, feeling desperate. "I'm sorry I can't tell you what has happened. I have to talk to Jared. He needs to come home as soon as possible. How can I get him home?" She felt frantic.

"I don't know if you can," her friend replied.

"He has to come. I need him." Her voice broke.

Jennifer must have realized that was as far as she was going to get. "I'll make some phone calls, okay? Whatever happened must be serious. Will you be all right until I call you back?"

"Yes, I will, but please hurry." Alyson felt emotionally panicked. While she waited, she walked in the bathroom and grabbed a handful of Kleenex to wipe her wet cheeks and eyes. The phone rang. It had only been five minutes.

She walked back to the phone and picked it up. "Hello."

A woman's voice answered, but it wasn't her friend. Before she had time to figure out who it was, the caller identified herself as the wife of the unit commander. She proceeded to try and find out herself why Alyson was so upset.

Alyson couldn't tell her either, just that she desperately did need Jared to come home. Something serious had happened, and she couldn't deal with it alone—the words in the letter kept replaying in her head. The woman told Alyson she would try to see what she could do, if anything, and then hung up.

Alyson called the bishop. She needed some religious counsel and knew she could trust him. She summarized what she had found. He agreed to rearrange his schedule and come over as soon as he could. She put the boys down for a nap and sat on the couch, trying to thumb through a magazine. She wasn't processing any of it.

It was less than an hour when the bishop and his first counselor rang the doorbell. She invited them in, and by the way they stared at her face, she must have looked a mess. Having them there made her feel calmer right away. She appreciated that they came over so quickly.

They sat on the couch, and she handed the bishop the wrinkled letter and the card stained with her tears. He unfolded the letter and, with his counselor looking on, started to read. The expression on both of their faces visibly changed. He glanced at the card.

When they finished, he handed them back to Alyson. No one spoke at first. She could tell they were shocked. She had been too, and both of them knew her family well. For the next few minutes, the only sound came from the steady ticking of the wooden cuckoo clock hanging on the wall in the room.

The bishop looked at her with sadness. "I'm sorry, Alyson. I can only imagine how you must have felt when you read these." He shook his head. "You do need to see Jared as soon as possible. I think you should also call your parents back in the states for their advice on handling this. Can we have a prayer with you?"

"Thanks, Bishop, I will. I really appreciate you coming over," she said gratefully. "I would like to have prayer."

"Who would you like to say it? It's your home," he asked.

"Would you please?" she said.

"Certainly," he replied. A few minutes later she walked with them to the door. The bishop turned to face her. "Alyson, if there is any other way I can help you, please call me." He gave her a reassuring smile and added, "I mean that. I'll check on you tomorrow after you have a chance to talk with Jared."

She nodded, making an effort to give him a brave smile in return. "I appreciate that. Thanks again to both of you for coming." She shook their hands and stayed outside, watching until their car backed out of the driveway and entered the street.

Back inside, she walked straight to the telephone. It took longer than usual to punch in the necessary numbers on the keypad, yet in a relatively short time, considering how far the connection was traveling, her mother answered the phone.

"Hi, Mom, it's Alyson."

"Alyson! How are you?" She was surprised to hear her daughter's voice. It was unusual for her to call during the day when the long distance rates were the most expensive

"I'm okay," she answered.

"What's wrong?" her mother asked, concerned.

Alyson told her everything, including that it was the bishop's idea that she call.

Elizabeth listened carefully without interruption. When Alyson was finished, she didn't respond immediately. Once she did, her voice was filled with concern.

"Alyson, I'm so sorry you have to go through something like this. I'm sure it was very traumatic to find those letters and even more so after you read them," she audibly breathed out. "But, no," Alyson could almost see her shaking her head, "I don't think they're true. My opinion would be that the woman who wrote them—did you say her name was Kristine? I think she was living out some kind of fantasy involving Jared."

Her words brought relief. Her mom had always given her sound advice before. "Really? You think so?" Alyson sighed deeply. "I hope you're right, Mom. I can't deal with one more thing involving Jared and another woman." Tears filled her eyes again.

"I understand. You've been through so much. Maybe this girl gets a kick out of sending these kind of letters to married men. I don't know. But I just don't think Jared would do something like that to you. It seems too far-fetched, especially since you so recently got back together . . . which was his idea. No. I don't think they are true."

By the time she finished, doubts filled Alyson again and she simply wasn't sure. The letters were so graphic.

"Thanks, Mom. I better go. This call is probably costing a fortune. I'll talk to you soon."

"Alyson, be sure and call me back after you and Jared talk. I'll be praying for you both."

"Okay, I will. Bye." She hung up the phone, wanting to believe her mom's explanation was right. She forgot to talk to her dad. His response might have been different.

Jared arrived late that night, hours after the children were asleep. When he walked in, Alyson was in the living room. As soon as she saw him, she started to cry.

"Alyson, what's going on? What's happened?" he asked her.

She cried harder.

Jared walked toward her opening his arms and Alyson stepped back, before he got too close. He moved nearer anyway and put his arm around her despite the fact that she was unresponsive and kept her body rigid. She continued to cry for several minutes, but Jared didn't let go. When her emotion was temporarily spent, she pulled back regaining her composure.

Jared looked closely at her face and red, swollen eyes. He asked her again. "Alyson, what is going on? What has happened?" Anxiety and worry shadowed his face.

The warmth of his voice began to disarm her. She picked up the letter and card from the coffee table and handed them to him. Her words tumbled out.

"I found these when I picked up the mail earlier today . . . "

Jared's face changed little, if any, as she went on. "I opened them after I recognized Kristine's name on the envelope. When I read the first one, well, to say I was shocked is an understatement. The details she wrote about you and her being together . . ." Alyson couldn't go on. She couldn't say it.

Jared listened without visible reaction, keeping his eyes on her face until she finished talking. "Oh, Alyson, I'm so sorry," he began, earnestly. "Kristine is a soldier in my company. She's single. She has acted for a while like she has a crush on me, openly flirting whenever she can and making sure I know she's available, if I'm interested. In the past few weeks she started sending me letters like the one you found. They were suggestive and talked about some fantasy of the two of us being together."

Fantasy? That was the exact same word Mom used.

"I was worried she might send another one while I was gone, but I didn't want to make you upset by saying something ahead of time, in case she didn't. I threw the other ones away hoping if I ignored them, she would stop."

"They're not true?" Alyson asked him.

"Of course not," he replied, his voice sounding sincere. "I'm really sorry you saw them and were hurt. I never wanted that to happen."

Alyson wanted to melt with relief and believe him. She looked in his eyes, pleading with her own to understand and not get angry when she brought up the past.

"Jared," she began, "I keep thinking of all we've been through and how ready I was to leave you after you got involved with Lisa." She noticed his body tensed, and she hurriedly went on, needing to say it but wanting to be finished. "You promised me we were beginning over in our marriage. You said you would do everything you could from then on to try and make up for what you had done to me. When I read that first letter, I lost it."

She could tell he didn't like the reminder about Lisa, but his voice didn't alter.

"I love you, Alyson! We got back together because I want our marriage to work. I still do. I messed up before, but that is the past and I'm trying to make it up to you. Please believe me, Kristine means nothing. She just has a crush on me."

A sheepish grin spread across his face. "Babe, what can I say, women want me." His attempted joke fell flat instantly when he noticed Alyson's eyes were filling with tears. He quickly became serious again.

"I'm so sorry. I'll tell her again I'm not interested. You and the boys are more important to me than anything else. Please don't cry anymore." He took her again into his arms.

Jared returned to the field early the next morning. It was hard for Alyson to have him go. She had hoped he wouldn't have to go back—the exercise was more than half over. Unfortunately, she wasn't that lucky. Once his commanding officer found out she was okay, he sent someone from the company to pick him up.

The telephone rang at nine-thirty. It was the bishop calling, concerned and wanting to know how things had gone. Alyson told him how Jared reacted, how he treated her, and what he said.

"Alyson, do you believe he was being completely honest with you?" His voice sounded somewhat baffled. "Did he answer every one of your questions in a way that alleviated all your fears and concerns? It is so important that you're certain."

She thought again about how the more Jared had talked last night, the calmer she became. His concern seemed genuine, and he held her tenderly while she cried, reassuring her with soothing words. His response even left her questioning if she had let her emotions get carried away. With embarrassment she remembered her close to hysterical reaction when she called her friend and later the bishop. On the other hand, it was understandable. Her trust in Jared was fragile considering what they had gone through, and the letter was so graphic.

"Bishop, I do feel a lot better despite everything. After Jared explained the situation with Kristine and that it wasn't the first letter she had written to him, it made more sense."

"Really? You're positively sure you believe him, Alyson?" His response sounded skeptical.

Do I believe Jared?

She felt an instantaneous nervous twinge create a small doubt, but in no uncertain terms could she let it stay to take root. She didn't have enough strength to go back to a place of daily fear.

"Yes, I believe him. But can I tell you I believe 100 percent that he was telling the truth? No. When he and I talked last night, he was so loving and open, it felt sincere. Afterwards, I felt so much better. If he was lying, wouldn't I have known? Wouldn't the confusion and fear have stayed with me?"

"I don't know, Alyson, Jared can be pretty convincing. Only you, as his wife, can make that decision. I still plan on talking to him in my office next week after he's home."

"I think that's a great idea. Thank you for all your help." Once he talked to Jared, the bishop might feel different, too.

"You're welcome. I'll talk to you again soon. Good-bye."

Chapter Eight

"I ask not for a lighter burden, but for broader shoulders."

The following Tuesday night, Alyson was at the church. She was now in charge of planning activities for the women in the congregation and was setting up for a Chinese dinner. She busily put plates, cups, and silverware on low tables spread throughout the cultural hall, while attempting to keep her wandering thoughts in check. She wanted to enjoy the activity without worrying about her problems.

She finished preparing the tables as women started to arrive. Several commented on the decorations and the delicious smells coming from the kitchen. Michelle, the president of the women's class, approached her.

"Hey, Alyson, everything looks great. How are you?"

She breathed in before answering with a smile. "I'm fine. I hope you're hungry tonight, we made a lot of food."

"That sounds good to me." Michelle studied Alyson's face, seeing past her brave smile into her eyes. Michelle touched her arm. "Alyson, how are you really doing? The bishop called me a few days ago and asked me to check on you. He sounded pretty worried. What's been happening? You look as if you've had a difficult week."

Alyson hesitated, but Michelle was someone she could trust. Speaking softly so the gathering women couldn't overhear, she gave her a generalized version of what she had been dealing with.

Michelle listened sympathetically, her eyes growing wider as the story unfolded. "Have you confronted this girl, Kristine, as to why she was writing Jared those kinds of letters in the first place?"

Alyson hadn't thought of doing that. "No, I haven't," she answered honestly.

"If I were you, I would go see her, look her straight in the eye, and ask her."

A flicker of fear ran through Alyson's body at the thought of a confrontation with Kristine. She was feeling so vulnerable. She pushed it away.

Why not go see her?

"You know, maybe I should. If she saw me face to face, it might have a bigger impact on getting her to stop."

"I agree. I think you should go talk to her right now," Michelle said.

"Now? How can I go now? I can't leave when everything is about to start. Tonight is my responsibility."

"Alyson, I think you should. I'll come with you. Don't worry about the dinner. I'll get my someone else to cover it. Everything will be fine. This is important."

"Okay, if you're sure." Michelle's response was definitely not anything Alyson saw coming. She felt a rush of adrenaline on the way to her car. Michelle joined her there a few minutes later.

"Everything is all taken care of, so don't worry, Alyson. Let's go."

The setting sun was creating a beautiful display of varying shades of pink and purple in the sky on the drive to the base. Alyson didn't enjoy it as much as she normally would have, thinking about what was going to happen. She reached the turnoff and took a left, driving past the entrance of the base. Her heart raced. She parked the car next to the women's barracks and turned off the engine, staying in the driver's seat.

I can do this.

Michelle reached over, squeezed her arm, and smiled reassuringly. They got out of the car and walked to the front doors of a plain, brown building. Inside a female guard was seated at a desk directly in front of the entrance doors. She looked up when they approached. Alyson gave her Kristine's name, and the guard paged her over the intercom. She and Michelle went back outside to wait on the sidewalk out front.

Kristine appeared about five minutes later and glanced around. After not seeing anyone else, she walked uncertainly toward them. She didn't seem to recognize Alyson at first and came closer. Her expression changed as recollection dawned in her eyes.

Alyson could tell Kristine was uncomfortable, but so was she. "I'm Alyson Clarke, Jared's wife. I found the last letter you sent him." It was a conscious effort to keep her voice steady.

The look in Kristine's blue eyes changed. It reminded Alyson of a stray animal suddenly caught in the net of a dog catcher and put inside a cage. She became angry again, remembering how she felt the day she picked up the mail. Kristine's obvious discomfort gave her some satisfaction.

Alyson asked her. "Was it true?"

In a barely audible voice Kristine said, "No."

Although that was the answer Alyson wanted to hear, it shocked her anyway. She couldn't understand how Kristine could have written the graphic letter in the first place.

"Why did you write it?" she asked in frustration, firing her next questions in rapid succession. "You knew Jared was married. You've been to our home and met our two little boys. What were you thinking? Do you have any idea the kind of problems a letter like that can cause in a marriage? Do you even care?"

Kristine's lost composure returned, this time answering defensively. "The letters were only meant as a joke. It wasn't supposed to be such a big deal."

Alyson was even more frustrated as Kristine casually dismissed something that turned her life upside down. She spat out her next words. "That is a horrible idea of a joke. How would you feel if you were married and someone did that to you?"

Kristine's face reddened.

Alyson knew her words sounded harsh. Her fear over her already tenuous marriage overshadowed everything else. She raised the volume of her voice in one last effort to make her point. "I want you to stay away from my husband." The words made her feel more in control, even though she knew she actually had none.

Kristine's eyes remained focused on both women.

Everyone was uncomfortable. Alyson was sure Kristine was anxious for them to leave. She turned away, traumatized despite her brave words. Michelle did too after giving Kristine one last look. They walked toward the parking lot.

"Thanks for being there, Michelle. Coming with me and missing dinner was definitely not a fair trade."

Michelle put an arm around Alyson's shoulders and gave her a quick squeeze. "You're very welcome. I'll be glad to help you any time you need . . . I'm sorry you have to deal with this. It really sucks. I wouldn't be handling it as well as you are if my husband got that kind of a letter. Let's just say it wouldn't be pretty."

Her last comment made Alyson smile. That was Michelle, forthright and never afraid to speak her mind.

Jared returned from field duty later that week and kept his appointment with the bishop. When he returned home afterwards, he didn't say much to Alyson about how it had gone, and she didn't want to press it. The next morning after he left for work, the bishop called.

"Hi, Alyson, how are you this morning?" he asked in a cheerful voice.

"I'm doing fine, thank you, Bishop. How are you?"

"I'm doing well. Do you have a few minutes?" he asked.

She glanced around. Ryker and Cade were playing happily with some toy cars. "Sure, what's up?" she asked, noticing a cobweb hanging from the ceiling.

"I wanted to talk to you about how the appointment went with Jared," he said.

"Okay . . ." she hesitated. Something in his tone made her anticipate she wouldn't like what he was going to tell her, and she wanted to be wrong. "He didn't say much about it to me."

"Jared and I talked for quite some time last night, and I asked him a lot of questions. He told me many of the same things he told you." The bishop didn't go in to any specific details. "I want you to know, I think he's lying."

Her hopes were instantly dashed. She hadn't expected his assessment to be so blunt and direct. It flooded her mind again with doubts about Jared. She was emotionally worn out and slumped against the wall behind her.

"You really think so?" she asked.

"Yes; I'm sorry, Alyson. What are you going to do?" he inquired.

She wanted the whole experience to disappear like a bad dream and once she was awake, any memories of it, too. She didn't want to go back to the fear and panicked uncertainty she had dealt with when she read the card and letter. She wasn't even finished dealing with how draining the whole experience had been.

"Bishop, I really appreciate all you've done to help me and Jared. I want to talk with him again and then get back to you."

"Okay, Alyson, that sounds good. I'll talk with you then."

She followed her usual routine the rest of the day, keeping her conversation with the bishop in the back of her mind. When Jared returned home from work, they ate dinner. Once the boys were occupied coloring she brought up the phone call. She was not looking forward to discussing the bishop's call, especially since she and Jared were getting along well.

"Jared, the bishop called me this morning."

"What did he want?" he asked, immediately sounding cross. His instant negative reaction made her apprehensive to continue.

"Basically, he said he had talked to you last night and asked a lot of questions but when he was done, he felt like . . . you weren't telling the truth."

Jared looked at her intently.

"He did, huh? You know what, Alyson, I don't really care if he believes me or not." He shrugged his shoulders and went on, "Bishops can make mistakes like the rest of us. Do you agree with him?"

That was what worried her. She had a lot of confidence in the bishop. His assessment carried weight. "I didn't say I believe him, but why would he say that? Do the two of you not get along?" she asked, trying to find an explanation that made some sort of sense.

"I thought we did. Look, I'm tired of rehashing this. Either you believe me or you believe the bishop. I'm your husband, I would hope I get your first loyalties, but whatever, you have to decide for yourself." He shifted his weight from one foot to the other impatiently, looked at her, and left the room.

The thoughts that tempted her consideration were so horrible and vile that the only way she could cope with them was to ignore them completely. She loved Jared and knew he loved her, too. Things had not been easy since they had reunited and were a long way from being healed; however, they were trying. She knew going in that it would be a long and difficult process and hard work. If she quit now, she would be haunted the rest of her life, wondering whether or not they could have made it work the second time. How could she face her children someday if a broken home could have been prevented? She had to stay focused on them. Not her fears.

When she called the bishop the next day, he sounded amazed by her decision but he put his personal feelings aside quickly and reiterated that it was her choice. He did recommend she and Jared discuss things with the stake president, the leader over several congregations, who could give them additional counsel.

Alyson scheduled the appointment with the stake president's secretary, telling him the soonest available time would be great. He set up the appointment at the stake president's home for the following Friday afternoon.

When she and Jared arrived, his wife led them to a quiet room at the back of the house, shutting the door as she left. They sat on the comfortable chairs, casually glancing around the room while they waited for the stake president to come in. Neither Jared nor Alyson had met him before.

When he entered the room, they stood up, and he shook their hands warmly, verifying their names. He gestured to them to sit back down and then offered a prayer before they began the discussion. He asked several questions about the letters, the situation, and their feelings.

Jared and Alyson took turns answering, and he listened carefully, his gaze traveling back and forth between them, as if he was trying to visually gauge their responses, which might or might not have lent credibility to their words.

They stopped talking when there was nothing else to add and the stake president seemed satisfied with what they shared. He opened his scriptures and read a few relevant verses, encouraging Jared and Alyson to put the situation in the past and not bring it up anymore. She and Jared agreed, and the meeting ended.

On the way out of the room, the stake president added that he would give their bishop a call to let him know what happened. They thanked him and left.

Alyson occasionally dreamed of Jared cheating on her. The women's faces kept changing. She would wake up with a sense of dread. Jared would hold her and tell her it would be okay; it was only a dream. When doubts about the situation nagged at her, she tried to follow the stake president's advice. She placed her fears in God's hands.

The Clarkes spent one more year in Germany before the military began downsizing. Jared was to be released early with an honorable discharge. They did as much traveling as they could that last summer. Ryker started kindergarten a few months before they returned to the states. Cade was three.

They landed on American soil in Pittsburgh, Pennsylvania in November and Jared was officially discharged. It was Thanksgiving Day when they arrived in Florida. Jared had enrolled in a flight school near Sanford to finish his commercial and instrument ratings. He completed the courses in less than three months.

They then drove to Seattle, moving in with Jared's sister, and he applied for several flying jobs. He looked for two months without success. They returned to Alaska. Construction had picked up during their absence, and Jared was offered a drafting job with a raise in salary. They purchased a home the following year.

Chapter Nine

"God will not give me anything I can't handle."[10]

November 1999

"Good morning," Jared said softly as Alyson opened her eyes. "How do you feel?" he asked with concern.

"Like I'm going to throw up." She smiled faintly. When she lifted her head off her pillow, she got dizzy.

"I brought you some peppermint tea and some toast." He set it down carefully on the night stand next to her. "I'll get Ryker and Cade off to school this morning before I leave for work."

She pulled Jared closer to give him a hug. "Thanks, honey. You're great. Remind me again how worth it this will be."

"I promise, it will. Remember how long we tried to get pregnant? Remember how many months you cried when it didn't happen? Next summer you will be holding a sweet new baby—maybe even a little girl."

Alyson smiled bigger this time. She could hardly wait. Cade would be seven when this baby came. She and Jared planned on having four children but when their marriage fell apart, it took several years before either of them wanted to think about having a third.

Things had changed so much since then. She hardly ever thought about that horrible time anymore. She knew Jared loved her, and their marriage was stronger than before.

"Bye, Mom," Ryker said, coming in the room. He was in fourth grade and had turned nine the month before. He gave her a hug. "I'll see you at lunch."

She worked at the boys' elementary school two hours a day during lunch and recess. It got her out of the house and the extra money helped. "Okay. Did you and Cade brush your teeth?" she asked, wondering if she had put toothpaste on the grocery list downstairs. They were almost out.

"I did. Cade is in the bathroom brushing his right now."

"Oh, send him in before you leave. Have a great day today, and don't chase too many girls at recess! I'll be watching."

"Mom." He rolled his eyes in mock embarrassment.

"Fine, I'll try not to notice if you do." She smirked. "Love you."

Cade came in the room a few minutes later with a big smile that showed his missing front teeth. He and Ryker were both born with blonde hair, but Ryker's had darkened by age three. Cade's still hadn't.

"Bye, sweetie," she told him.

He hugged her and kissed his cheek—that was Cade, very loving. "Don't forget to take your library book back today. It's due."

"Dad already reminded me. Bye, Mom." He waved when he reached the doorway of the bedroom. In a few minutes, Jared and the boys' voices faded. She heard the front door close, and the house was still.

Alyson rearranged her pillow and closed her eyes, hoping to get a little more sleep. She dozed for a while. The next time she opened her eyes, the clock radio on the night stand next to her said ten. Time to get ready to go.

She showered quickly, knowing if she stayed in even a minute too long she would become light-headed and weak, something she had dealt with in all her pregnancies. Before she left, she ate another piece of toast and put a few saltine crackers in a plastic bag in the pocket of her coat. If she let her stomach get empty, she would throw up for sure.

She had one dizzy spell at work. When she got home after lunch, she laid down for a nap before the boys arrived from school.

She was using a midwife for this pregnancy and planned on having the baby at home, something Jared was behind 100 percent. She was due the end of June.

On the afternoon of July 3rd, 1995, Alyson started having contractions.

Jayden arrived a little after midnight. He wasn't the baby girl she had hoped for but after a few minutes of holding him it didn't matter. He had ten perfect fingers, ten perfect toes, and a head of black hair.

In the spring of 1997, almost two years later, Jared and Alyson were relaxing for a few minutes after breakfast. Jared was sitting at the table reviewing the sports section of the local paper. He stopped and looked over at her.

"Do you have specific plans for today?" he asked.

"Not really," she told him. "I need to do some laundry, and I want to do some baking, but both are flexible. Why?"

"The weather is perfect to go flying. Ben has been asking when we could try out his latest RC airplane. He just finished building it and my P-51 Mustang hasn't been flown since I fixed the right wing. I want to check out the balance on it." He folded up the newspaper and moved it aside. "I know the boys would enjoy watching and it would be great if you came, too. We could make it a family activity. What do you think, do you want to come?" His eyes were bright with anticipation.

She liked Ben, one of Jared's coworkers. "How long are you planning on being gone?"

"Maybe for an hour or a little more, depending on how the flights go. We only have one airplane each to fly this time."

That would leave her the afternoon for doing the things she had planned. "Sure, I'll come. How soon do you want to leave?" she asked.

"Can you and the boys be ready in half an hour?"

She nodded. "That should work."

"Great! I'll give Ben a call and have him meet us at the flying field, then get my stuff loaded in the car." He left the room and Alyson picked up the remaining cereal bowls from the table and took them over to the kitchen sink. She gave the table and counters a swipe with a sponge and glanced around. Satisfied that the quick clean-up was fine for now, she went upstairs.

Ryker and Cade were already dressed and only needed to brush their teeth. When they finished brushing, Alyson had Ryker help Jayden get ready. Once the boys were ready, they went downstairs to play until she was. She showered, did her hair and make-up, and changed into jeans and a light sweater. Grabbing her things, she went downstairs.

"It's time to go, guys," she said to the boys. "Everyone get your shoes on and head to the car."

When they got to the flying field, it took some time for Jared and Ben to get their planes fueled and ready to go. Once they had, they flew several flights. Ryker, Cade, and Jayden followed their dad around, making comments and asking questions. Alyson chose the softest spot of grass she could find to sit on that still had a good view. She was six months pregnant and had a hard time being comfortable anywhere for long.

They had decided to try one more time for a girl and this was the first pregnancy she had a sonogram—she had to know before the baby arrived. When the technician had told her two months ago it was another boy, she couldn't believe it. She was depressed for at least a week after, but had come to terms with it since. For whatever reason, having a little girl was not in God's plan for her. Now she was anxious to have this new little boy and never be pregnant again.

Jared and Ben flew their airplanes until the gas ran out. Once they had landed them and shut off the engines, Jared turned toward Alyson.

"Wow, Alyson, you must be good luck. Neither of us crashed. Usually we do way before the gas runs out."

Ben nodded his head in agreement. "That's right. I can't remember how long it's been since I made that many flights in a row. You must be good luck."

She laughed at their silly comments, not completely sure if they were teasing or serious. She didn't come flying with them very often. Once the cars were repacked, they decided on McDonald's for lunch. They would get it "to go" and take it to a park to eat. Alyson and the boys stayed in the car while Jared and Ben went inside and ordered.

Alyson decided to balance her checkbook while she waited, but she couldn't find a pen inside her purse. She opened the glove box to look for one. In the process of moving the contents around, a yellow credit card receipt fell onto the floor mat. She looked at it when she picked it up. It was for the rental of a post office box at a place called Mailboxes, Etc. Jared's signature was at the bottom. The amount charged on the slip was a hundred and fifty dollars.

Why would he have a post office box? Our mail comes to our house.

Alyson began to feel apprehensive. When Jared got back in the car, she asked him about the receipt on the way to the park.

"The post office box isn't mine," he snapped. "Why would I need one?" He looked at her as if he couldn't believe she could be so dumb.

Alyson's face colored slightly. Shrugging her shoulders, she said, "But it was on your credit card."

"I got it for Ben. Why are you so worried about it? He paid me cash the next day to cover the charge." He was clearly annoyed with her.

She wasn't sure why and asked him another question anyway. The uneasy feeling inside her persisted. "Why would Ben need one?"

Jared gave her an irritated look. "Ben needed to get it because he and his wife separated, and he moved out. He and I were going to lunch and stopped there first. Ben filled out the form but when he went to pay for it, he discovered he didn't have his wallet. I helped him out and put the charge on my credit card. He paid me back before the bill came in the mail."

"Oh. I didn't realize he and his wife separated. How sad. They haven't been married very long." She wanted to say something else, and then changed her mind. Eventually the bad feeling left; however, doubts lingered in her mind.

Later that summer at a barbecue she was surprised to see Ben and his wife together. Jared told her they had worked things out.

Chapter Ten

"If life gets too hard to stand, kneel."[1]

February 1998

Valentine's Day was next week and the church was having a dance for the adults. Jared and Alyson thought going might be fun. Alyson planned on cooking an especially nice dinner first and wanted to make a new dessert recipe she had been saving for a special occasion just like this. She was still trying to decide what to give Jared for a gift, something other than chocolate or cologne, but so far she hadn't come up with anything exciting.

While waiting for Ryker and Cade to come home from school, she sat down at the kitchen table with a women's magazine. It was the February issue and full of romantic ideas. One of the articles caught her eye, describing a creative gift the author had made for her husband. She had cut out several small strips of pink paper, one for every week of the year. On each one she had written a reason why she loved him then folded them and put them inside a decorated glass jar. It sounded perfect to give to Jared.

The front door suddenly burst open; Ryker and Cade raced in, dropped their backpacks in the middle of the floor, and hurried to the kitchen for a snack. The noise level inside the house rose instantly. While they rummaged in the refrigerator, they told her about their day at school.

After they finished eating, Alyson was encouraging them to start on their homework when someone knocked at the front door. On her way to answer it, she picked up five-month-old Alex, who had started to cry. He had joined their family the previous August. He had been playing on a flannel blanket at her feet that was now strewn with toys. She was pretty sure he was hungry.

While she bounced him on her left hip, trying to calm him, she opened the door with her right hand. Immediately, an icy blast of cold winter air hit her face. Her neighbor Trisha, from across the street was standing on the porch.

"Hi, Trisha, come on in. It's freezing outside." Alyson quickly closed the door. Trisha and her husband, Dave, both members of their ward at church, had moved to the area a few months before with their two small children. Two weekends earlier, she and Jared had invited them to see the latest James Bond movie. Afterwards, they stopped at a twenty-four hour restaurant for dessert.

On the way home, Jared needed to stop at his office to pick up some papers he had forgotten earlier. Everyone came inside. Upstairs in the drafting area, he proudly pointed out two of his model airplanes hanging above his desk. Trisha had asked him a lot of questions about the designs.

Since that weekend she had been extra friendly—especially to Jared. Several times when Jared arrived home from work, she would be out in her yard, usually shoveling snow, and would try to engage him in an animated conversation from across the street. When he came inside he often was chuckling to himself. It bothered Alyson, but she was so sensitive to things like that, it was probably nothing. Jared talked to everyone.

"Hi, Alyson, how are you?" Trisha smiled when she came in. "Do you have an egg I could borrow? I started making banana bread, and realized I didn't have enough."

"Of course, hang on a second."

She got a carton of eggs out of the refrigerator. With only one hand free because of Alex, she handed Trisha the whole thing.

"Thanks, I really appreciate it." She opened the top and took out one egg, and then handed the carton back to Alyson. Alyson returned it to the refrigerator.

"By the way, are you and Jared going to go to the Valentine's dance next week at the church?" Trisha wanted to know.

"We've discussed it but haven't decided for sure yet," Alyson replied. "Are you and Dave going?"

"Probably not, Dave hates to dance." Trisha sounded wistful.

"Would he come just to socialize?" Alyson asked.

"I'm not sure. If you and Jared decide to go . . . maybe." Trisha hesitated, then abruptly changed the subject, shocking Alyson momentarily. "A few months after Dave and I were married, he told me he felt he made a mistake in marrying me. He told me he wanted a divorce." Her eyes were pensive.

Alyson focused more intently on her face.

Trisha's unexpected declaration made her uncomfortable. She could only imagine how hurtful that must have been. If Jared had said that to her right after they were married, she would have been devastated. Dave seemed like such a nice guy.

"He said that? Wow—I'm sorry. What did you tell him?" Alyson asked.

"No," Trisha answered curtly. "I told him he could forget it because I would never give him a divorce. I reminded him we made vows to each other in the temple and I was going to stand by them." Her voice was firm.

That had to have taken guts.

"How have things been between the two of you?" Alyson asked. "Do you think Dave is happier now? I mean, obviously you stayed together and had kids and everything."

"He's never brought it up again," Trisha told her. She added, "It's been hard for me to forget it though. What about you and Jared? Are you happy?"

How did the conversation go from borrowing an egg to talking about her marriage with Jared? She felt a flutter of apprehension in her stomach. No way was she going there. She purposefully kept her answers vague.

"Well, you know every relationship has its ups and downs, but I would have to say—yes, we're happy."

"Oh . . . that's good." Trisha sounded disappointed, possibly sad.

Alyson hoped it was the latter. She wanted to end the conversation with Trisha as soon as possible. Alex started to fuss again, reminding her he was still hungry. Alyson inwardly cheered for the distraction.

"I need to feed him . . ." she said, her voice trailing off, hoping Trisha would realize she wanted her to leave.

Trisha got the hint. "I need to go, too. I left my daughter watching cartoons. I'll talk to you later. Oh—thanks again for the egg."

"No problem. Good-bye." Alyson was relieved to shut the door behind Trisha.

Valentine's Day arrived and Alyson finished the gift for Jared that afternoon. It hadn't been as hard as she thought it would be to fill in fifty-two slips of paper, once she got going. She carefully folded them and put them inside the decorated jar she had ready. She was anxious to see his reaction that night when she gave it to him. She would love it if he gave her something so personal.

Ryker and Cade helped her cut out red, white, and pink paper hearts after school. They wrote little notes on them or drew pictures and taped them to the upstairs door of the master bedroom, hoping to give their dad a pleasant "heart attack" when he found them.

For dinner, Alyson was making lemon basil chicken, one of Jared's favorites, with rice, green salad, rolls, and creamy orange-chocolate mousse for dessert. She had fed the boys grilled-cheese sandwiches and tomato soup earlier so she and Jared could have a quiet dinner alone.

Alyson checked the time and glanced outside the kitchen window, noticing the sun had already set. The outside lights of the surrounding neighborhood houses were reflecting off the snow-covered branches of the trees and the blanket of white covering the yards. There were even a few stars twinkling in the sky above. Now that darkness had arrived, it wouldn't be much longer before Jared came home.

The boys were in the family room, absorbed in various activities. The room had light peach walls and overstuffed furniture and doubled as a playroom, one wall lined with books and toys. The door to the family room was closed so the boys' playful noise didn't disturb the rest of the house.

Alyson wanted things to be calm and settled when Jared walked in. When he did, everything was ready. She gave him a warm hug at the front door and, as soon as he took off his coat and shoes, they went to the dining room together to eat. Alyson had the lights turned off and candles lit on the table. The flames danced on the wall, creating a romantic mood.

They talked in hushed voices while they ate, and it was nice not to hear any loud noises coming from the family room. When they were finished, Jared pushed his chair back from the table with a contented sigh.

"That was a wonderful dinner tonight, Alyson. Thank you."

"You're welcome. Did you save room for dessert or do want to eat it later?"

"Later would be better. My stomach needs to rest first." He raised his arms above his head and stretched. "Wow, it's been a long day! We have another deadline coming up next week for our current project, so I'll probably have to work late several nights." He stopped, and then changed the subject. "Do you want to go to the church dance tonight?"

Alyson yawned. "I don't know. It sounds fun, but it's freezing outside, and I'm not sure anymore if I feel like getting dressed up to go—it's been a long day. How about after we put the kids to bed we have our own dance together?" She smiled.

"Sounds great to me. I would rather stay home, too. I think I'll go upstairs first to change out of these clothes and spend some time with the boys before they go to bed." Jared left the kitchen.

Alyson looked around at the cluttered table and counter but decided the dishes could wait. She wanted to be upstairs to see Jared's reaction to the surprise. She hurried up, reaching the top stair as he got to the end of the hall by their bedroom.

He opened the door and flipped the light switch up, flooding the room with light. She came in behind him but walked past to sit on the edge of the bed. He turned back to shut the door. His hand was resting loosely on the knob when he discovered the decorated hearts taped across the wood surface. He glanced over the words, back and forth.

"Did you do this?" he asked, his face showing little emotion.

"The boys and I did it together. They were very excited for you to come home and find it." She smiled widely.

"Hmm, it looks nice. Thanks." His voice lacked excitement. He went to the walk-in closet and changed out of his work clothes into a T-shirt and loose-fitting pants.

Alyson mentally calculated the time she and the boys had spent cutting out, writing on, and decorating the door with the hearts. She was disappointed. She decided to give him the Valentine gift she made for him, hoping his reaction would be different. She got it off the dresser from underneath a sweater..

"Jared, I have something else for you. This one is only from me." She walked to the end of the bed where he had sat down and handed him the jar. "On each of the slips of paper inside I've written a reason why I love you. There is enough for you to read one every week for a whole year."

Jared raised his eyebrows and turned the glass jar around on all sides. "Wow. There's really enough for a whole year? How could you come up with so many reasons?"

Alyson laughed. "It didn't take me as long as you would think." She lowered her voice. "I wanted to give you something different this year, not something from the store, something special. I found this idea in a magazine. Thanks for all you do, honey. I love and appreciate you."

She stood up to give him a hug and noticed his body felt stiff, as if her words had made him uncomfortable. She had no idea what was wrong. She stepped back to look in his face and dropped her arms. He stood up and set the jar on the dresser.

"Is everything okay?" she asked him, concerned.

He shrugged, made eye contact briefly, and then looked away. "Yes— thanks for the gift. I'm going downstairs to see the boys or do you want help with the dishes?" His words were subdued.

"No, it's okay. The boys need some time with you. When I'm done, I'll come and let you know." She had a hard time talking around the lump that had formed in her throat. She followed him downstairs to get started on the kitchen.

Jared appreciated Alyson's thoughtfulness—sort of—but it magnified the guilt inside him. He hated that. He tried so hard to stay away from pornography and had done really well over the past several years, only indulging a few times. He worked hard on his relationship with Alyson. He didn't want to hurt her and the boys, but lately the intensity of his need was worse.

When he got his own computer with Internet access at work, everything changed. It was insane how many adult sites there were and, at first, he ran into them when he wasn't looking. There were varieties of porn he had never seen before that created new fantasies in his head. What used to turn him on didn't give him the same feeling. The Internet made it so easy to get it back, sometimes even stronger. He frequently made excuses to go to work early or stay late several times a week. He couldn't help himself. He was like a piece of metal drawn to a magnet, strongly, quickly—inevitably. It couldn't be stopped.

He had been losing weight and working out, and restlessness was building up inside him. He needed some excitement. Since he had tightened up physically, women were giving him more attention. It was easy to pique their interest—just smile and be friendly. They would start talking about their feelings, especially those who felt their husbands weren't giving them what they needed. He knew what to say to make them feel better about themselves and they would look at him as if he was some kind of knight in shining armor. It was gratifying to know he was helping them.

Lately, Trisha, from across the street, had been giving him lots of attention; he thought it was amusing but he liked it. Dave was gone a lot with school and work. She was just lonely. Jared could get her laughing hard, and she always thanked him for brightening her day.

He had been thinking lately about Mandy—she was the very first one. He wondered how his life would be if he had married her instead. She had pretty red hair like Alyson, but her personality was completely different. She had liked experimenting and getting close to the "edge" like he did, and she was laid back and spontaneous.

For Alyson, it was more important to do the right thing, even if it wasn't as exciting. When they married he had thought that was what he needed in his life. He wanted to be a stronger person and be closer to God, but he had made so many mistakes. Why keep banging his head against a brick wall? All it gave him was severe headaches. He wanted happiness in his life, not constant guilt and feeling like a failure. He wanted to feel good.

The next morning Alyson prepared the boys' lunches for school, making sure their backpacks held their homework. She called a reminder to them to hurry and brush their teeth since it was almost time to leave.

When Jared came into the kitchen, Alex was sitting in his highchair, chewing on the rubber-tipped spoon he was using to eat his cereal. Jayden was at the table munching on toast spread thickly with raspberry jam.

"Hey, little buddy, where's my bite?" Jared asked Jayden, tousling his dark hair and making him giggle. Jared kissed Jayden on the cheek, and then gave Alex a kiss on the top of his head.

He turned to his wife. "Good morning, Alyson. By the way, I got these for you for Valentine's Day, but forgot to give them to you last night." He set down three compact disks on the counter.

She glanced at the artists' names, recognizing only one of them. "Thanks, Jared." She gave him a tentative smile, still uncertain about last night. "You didn't have to get me three; one would have been plenty." She liked to have music on when she did the housework. It would be nice to have something different to listen to. She noticed all three compact disks were missing the cellophane wrappers.

It was eight in the evening two weeks later after a heavy snowfall. Jared went outside to put the trash can by the curb for pick up in morning. Alyson was helping Jayden clean up a puzzle he left on the floor when Jared went outside.

"Thanks, Jayden. Next time I want you to remember to put the pieces away yourself after you're finished, okay?" She handed him the puzzle box with a picture of two puppies and a red ball on the top.

"Okay, Mommy," Jayden said. "I will." He took the box into the family room and put it on the shelf next to the bucket of Legos. When he came back, Alyson took his hand and they walked upstairs. She wanted to get him ready for bed. She got his pajamas out of the drawer and helped him put them on. She didn't turn on the bedroom light because Alex was in the crib, already asleep.

"Jayden, go brush your teeth, and I'll tuck you in bed after you're done," she whispered. He nodded and headed to the bathroom. Jared hadn't come back in the house yet. The window in Jayden's room faced the street. She opened the blinds and looked out.

Trisha, snow shovel in hand, was talking to Jared in front of their house, their faces so close the heat of their breath combined into one frosty upward swirl. The streetlights shone above them, and she could see they were laughing. She slid open the window and could hear the sound of their voices but couldn't make out any words.

She watched the two of them together with growing concern. "Jared!"

Alyson loudly called. She hoped it didn't wake Alex. Instantly their talking stopped, and they turned toward the sound of her voice. "I need you to come here, please," she replied, not knowing what to say, but wanting to stop the pounding of her heart and the panicked feeling that was gaining momentum.

Alyson felt frantic to get them away from each other and didn't know why. Jared continued talking as if he wasn't in a hurry to end the tête-à-tête, despite her request to come in. When he finally did, she met him downstairs, and she wasn't calm.

"What is going on between you and Trisha, Jared?" she asked angrily.

Instantly his eyes lit up defensively. "What is your problem, Alyson? We were only talking."

"How do you think the two of you looked standing that close, face-to-face in the middle of the street in the dark?" she retorted.

"Exactly. It would be ridiculous if we were doing anything where anyone could see. Why are you so insecure?" he shot back.

"How did this become my fault, Jared?" He was manipulating her. Even she was surprised by her own reaction. The bad feeling she had took a long time to leave. The rest of the night, Jared treated her as if she had done something wrong.

Chapter Eleven

"*Though no one can go back and make a brand new start, anyone can start from now and make a brand new ending.*"[12]

April 1998

The envelope . . . Alyson's mind cleared as time shifted back to the present. She felt an opening of understanding settle. Her life was about to change. She had arrived at a significant crossroad and only *she* could choose which path to take. If she opened the envelope, she would be on a path facing darkness and pain, not knowing the outcome. She was as certain of that as if she had been told by a tangible voice. Yet choosing to open it was the only way she could find the complete truth.

On the other hand, the path she was on was familiar and well traveled. This path assured her that the future would change very little from the past. By not opening the envelope, she would at least have the security of knowing what to expect. But there would be no answers or freedom from the persistent and nagging doubts and confusion she'd dealt with repeatedly throughout her marriage.

Her shaking increased as she examined each possible outcome, but beyond everything she considered, she couldn't keep living the way she had. That scared her too much; she had to face the unknown.

Turning the envelope, she partially raised the flap from its glued position, straightened the metal brad, and opened it completely. Putting her hand inside, she pulled out the papers that were there. The words on the first sheet caused her heart to plummet.

Jared's most recent betrayal was in her hand—a letter addressed to some woman in his handwriting. It said she had intrigued him from the first time they met, and he was interested in pursuing a relationship with her. He said he was married, but it wasn't an issue. If anything, that would make things more exciting. They could have a wild time with no worries or strings attached. As soon as she called him at his work they could make plans. He had signed his name at the bottom.

Alyson's whole body was overcome with hurt and shock. She felt sick to her stomach. The other paper had a differet woman's name on it. It was a picture of a sunset Jared had painted using watercolors—something he was good at. In the upper left hand corner, he had written a romantic verse in calligraphy. Alyson recognized the words from part of a song on one of the CDs Jared had given her for Valentine's Day. She set the picture down and picked up the letter again, reading it once more, hoping she had misunderstood. It was as clear as it had been the first time.

Tears rapidly filled her eyes and overflowed, making a wet path down her cheeks and falling unheeded onto her lap. She shoved the papers back in the envelope, not worrying anymore about being careful. More emotions flooded her, anger striking first, and then wrenching pain. She started to silently pray for help.

How can something like this be happening again? The man who wrote these letters, the man I sleep with each night, the man I've rebuilt my trust in, my husband, and the father of my four sons, has once again broken my heart. How could Jared do this to me after everything we have gone through—have I ever known him at all?

When she finally remembered her errand, she dried her eyes with the back of her hand, not caring that her mascara had likely left black smudges. She locked the car door and went inside the store for the diapers, ignoring the curious looks coming from other customers.

A rising tide of tears filled her eyes again as soon as she made it back to the car, got in, and shut the driver side door. Before more tears erupted, she took a few deep breaths and regained some control. She couldn't fall apart.

On the way home, she decided she and the boys would drive to her parents' home that night, an hour away. She would tell them they were going on an adventure to Grandma's. She couldn't even think of looking at Jared at the moment, not to mention talking to him. She had to get away. She wanted him to worry for a change when he discovered they had left, if he even cared.

Back at the house, she told Ryker and Cade to quietly put pajamas and clean clothes for the next day together in a bag and grab their pillows. She checked on Jayden, discovering with relief that he was feeling better after his nap and his small dinner had stayed down. She got a few things for herself from her bedroom and the upstairs bathroom, moving even more carefully this time. Thankfully, Jared stayed asleep. She also packed a few items for the two youngest boys.

Alex moaned, but didn't cry when she lifted him from the crib, taking his special blanket next to him on the mattress. Alyson's mom had a crib set up in her guest room. She hoped he would adjust as she wasn't up to dealing with a cranky, tired baby all night on top of everything else.

They piled into the van as soon as they possibly could, each carrying something. Before she left, she double-checked the front door to make sure it was locked. Ryker sat in front with her. From Anchorage they headed northeast on the new Glenn Highway toward Wasilla. During the drive, Alyson's mind dwelled on the earlier trauma of the letters. Her tears started again.

Ryker heard her masked efforts not to cry out loud. With growing concern, he turned his eyes to hers. "Mom, what's going on?" he finally asked. "Why are we going to Grandma's this late without telling Dad?"

She glanced in the rearview mirror and saw that everyone else had fallen asleep. She could talk openly with her oldest son if she wanted. Yet how could she possibly tell him what she had found or what was really going on? She chose her next words carefully.

"Ryker, I can't go into it right now. I found some things of your dad's that have really confused me, and I needed to leave for a while to figure out how to deal with them." Her answer seemed to satisfy him. She was grateful he didn't question her any further.

"Okay, Mom, but please stop crying."

Her parents' home was completely dark when she pulled in the long, graveled driveway, except for a dim glow coming from the front porch light. Alyson figured they had probably been in bed for about an hour. She hated to disturb them. She got out of the car and walked to the front door, knocked loudly, and then tried the doorbell. No response. She had to think of something else.

She bent down and picked up a few small, smooth stones from the driveway and tried tossing them up, one at a time at the master bedroom window. She didn't want to throw them too hard, yet needed enough force so the noise would wake them up. It took her three times of actually striking the glass before her mom's sleepy face appeared to her view.

She glanced down to the driveway below, saw Alyson, and slid the window open, exposing several inches of screen. "Alyson? What are you doing here? What's going on?"

"I'm sorry to wake you up, Mom. Can the boys and I stay here tonight?"

"Of course, I'll be down to let you inside in just a minute."

Alyson woke up her three oldest children and told them they were at Grandma's. They climbed sleepily out of the car and she somehow managed to get Alex out of his car seat without him waking up. They were all standing tiredly on the porch when her mom opened the door. Elizabeth immediately took Alex from her arms and brought him inside.

Once Alyson's arms were free, she was able to grab Jayden's hand so he wouldn't trip over the small rise going into the house. He was barely awake. She also picked up the diapers and a bag of clothes Ryker had moved from the car.

Ryker and Cade came behind her and Jayden, walking slowly as they tried to force open their heavy eyelids and readjust to the light. Within ten minutes, all four children were settled comfortably in spare beds, already asleep.

Alyson sat down tiredly on the living room couch. "Thanks so much, Mom. Would it be okay if we talked?"

Elizabeth looked at her daughter with concern and nodded. "Of course. Alyson, what has happened?"

She started to tell her but had trouble getting out any understandable words. They were facing each other, one lamp on beside them to break up the room's darkness, but the darkness Alyson felt internally wasn't as easily dispelled. Emotion choked her throat. When she gained sufficient control of her voice, the shrill ring of the telephone interrupted her. She knew it was Jared.

Elizabeth stood up and went to the kitchen, facing Alyson. She lifted the telephone receiver to her ear and when she said hello, her eyes went to her daughter's.

Alyson shook her head, mouthing "no."

"Yes, she's here. They are all fine. No, she doesn't want to talk right now. Okay, I'll tell her." She hung up the phone, walked back to the love-seat, and sat down.

"Alyson, Jared said he will be out in the morning so the two of you can talk. He sounded concerned about you."

"Fine. Let him worry," she said angrily.

Elizabeth's eyebrows rose.

Alyson couldn't contain how upset she felt over what Jared had done. She had believed the dark days in their marriage had ended for good, long before. Now, she wondered if she had been naive to ever go back to him.

Her mom's words interrupted her thoughts. "What is going on?"

Alyson started explaining Jared's odd behavior earlier that night after he had gone to bed, his anxiety over an envelope, and the unmistakable impression she received. Then she backed up and told her other things which had happened recently. Finding the letters gave them more significance—like a floodgate opening in her mind.

"Have I ever mentioned Mandy to you, Mom?"

Elizabeth's eyes looked momentarily blank. "Is she the girl Jared met on his mission?"

"Yes, that's her. Last Christmas we got a card from her in the mail. I thought it was really strange to suddenly hear from her out of the blue. I don't even know how she would have gotten our address. Jared acted thrilled to hear from her. A couple of months later she sent a letter addressed only to Jared. I opened it because he wasn't home. Mandy said she had been thinking about him a lot and she wanted to know if he was happy in his marriage. She included a picture of herself, one of those glamour kinds of shots, and asked if they could start writing to each other—she's married with three children."

"What did you do?" Elizabeth asked.

"I told Jared about it—cautiously. I waited until we were lying in bed that night, talking, and brought it up. He acted flattered. I was not amused. I asked him if he thought it had been an appropriate thing for Mandy to do in the first place. He agreed it wasn't. He told me he would contact her and let her know he was very happy with me."

Alyson's mouth was dry. She went to the kitchen for a drink of water. Standing by the sink, draining her glass, she looked at the clock on the microwave—it was past midnight. She was exhausted but her mind continued to overflow. She turned her head to look at the dark night through the large, unobstructed picture window and noticed the shining stars. The sky was clear and peaceful. She wished she was.

Elizabeth was waiting for her to continue. Alyson sighed and resumed talking.

"Things haven't been normal lately, Mom, especially with Jared. Remember last month when the boys and I came out to spend a few days with you and Dad during spring break? Jared called me the first day during his lunch and told me he just wanted to say how much he loved me—that was all."

"I do remember that. I thought it was unusual, too. He hardly ever calls when you're here."

"I know, and something else doesn't make any sense. Last month he came home in the middle of the day, twice in one week to tell me he needed to see my pretty face, kiss me, and say he loved me. He also sent me flowers for no apparent reason. He rarely gives me flowers, even when it's a special occasion. The last time was when I had Alex, only because I hinted I wanted some." Tears filled her eyes.

"When I found those letters in the car tonight, I lost it. I don't know what to think anymore. I was devastated when he got involved with Lisa all those years ago. He promised me, if I gave him another chance he would do whatever he could to make it work between us—I can't go through something like that again—" She was openly crying now.

Elizabeth came over and put an arm around her daughter's shoulder. "I know you're confused, Alyson. Things don't sound right to me either, but whatever is going on, your dad and I will help you deal with it. So will your Father in Heaven. Try to get some rest and hopefully tomorrow, when Jared comes, you'll get your questions answered to your satisfaction. Until then, remember how much I love you."

Alyson wiped at her eyes. "Thanks, Mom." She gave her a hug. "Thanks for being here to listen to me—good night." Alyson spent the next hour tossing and turning in bed before she finally fell asleep.

Jared arrived early the next morning. He searched Alyson's face for answers as she got in the car, but she would barely look at him. She could tell he wasn't sure what was going on. They drove to a small lake in a quiet clearing ten minutes away from her parents' home. He pulled off the main road onto the shoulder and turned off the engine. There were lots of trees surrounding the lake and both sides of the road.

Alyson felt the movement of Jared's body shifting toward her. She kept looking out the window at the view, bright in the morning sunlight, not wanting to start the difficult conversation. She sensed Jared's discomfort and uncertainty as the time ticked past.

Jared cleared his throat. "Alyson, I'm not positive why you left but I can understand why you might be upset. It's about Trisha, right?" He quickly went on, "I don't even know why it happened. It was a stupid mistake. She was always showing up wherever I was, hanging on my every word, even calling me at work."

Alyson turned her startled eyes to his, "What are you talking about?"

Jared swallowed audibly, looking confused. "Well, isn't that what you're upset about? I'm assuming she decided to tell you what happened between us and that's the reason you left last night, right?"

"No! That isn't why." Her heart began to race.

Oh, no! What next?

Her marriage was crumbling before her eyes. "What *did* happen between the two of you, Jared?" Her voice was getting louder, overwhelmed by the new information.

Jared colored. "Well, uh . . . there was one night that she wanted me to come over while Dave was working late . . . you thought I was, too."

Alyson sucked in a breath.

"Trisha and I got to talking—actually more than talking—we did some kissing too, but it wasn't that great. She's just . . ." His voice trailed off when he saw the expression on Alyson's face. To say she was horrified would be an understatement,

Her concerns about Jared and Trisha had been right-on. He had manipulated the situation, saying she was insecure. He'd totally played her—she wanted to scream. Why was he putting her through this kind of garbage? How could he care at all if he could do this to her?

Jared's voice broke into her thoughts. "I'm sorry, Alyson. It should never have happened. If you didn't find out about it, then why did you leave last night?"

She looked at Jared before explaining, wondering why he couldn't see what she thought was obvious. "Remember the envelope you left on the front seat of the car yesterday?"

It clicked. Surprise and anger entered his voice. "You opened it? I told you to leave it alone."

Ignoring him, Alyson went on, her words coming out in a frustrated rush. "Who are those women you were writing to? I can't believe you said our marriage wasn't an issue. You are planning on having a wild fling with no worries about a long-term commitment or consequence? What about our commitment and our family? That verse in the corner of the picture was from a song on one of the CDs you gave me for Valentine's Day."

Her voice grew louder as shock and disbelief seeped out in her words. Things were much worse than she thought. "I don't even think I know you anymore!" she added.

Jared lowered his voice to a normal speaking level. "Alyson, those women were two overly friendly waitresses I met at lunch with Ben. They came to our table repeatedly while we ate, even when we didn't need anything. They asked a lot of questions including where we worked. The next day I got a call at the office from one and she asked if I wanted to meet her after work. She suggested going to a bar for a drink. I didn't go, but she's called twice since then. The letter and the card. . . . well I got carried away, they were attractive women."

"Were you really going to give them those things? I mean, what is going through your head? Were you planning on cheating on me? I don't even know what to think, Jared—I can't believe this." Alyson was overwhelmed with negative emotions.

She threw out another question, hoping he would see how far he had crossed the line. "How would you feel if I did something like that to you? How would you like to read in a letter I was planning on cheating on you, Jared?"

"Alyson, I don't know why I did it. Like I said, I got carried away. You deserve someone a lot better."

"Why can't you see? I don't want someone else—I want you. How could you cheat on me again after all we've been through? You promised it would never happen again. How am I supposed to trust you?" She had to stop to catch her breath. She couldn't hold back the tears any longer.

Jared's voice rapidly raised in irritation. "Look, I'm sorry. It was stupid! I'm not going to deliver the letter or picture. I'll tell the secretary at work to not accept calls from any females other than you unless they're business related, and I won't talk to Trisha. Okay? Besides, she already talked to the bishop and told her husband. She agrees it never should have happened. Can we go home and forget this whole thing?"

How could he turn his defensive anger on her again? She wanted badly to reach him, to make him understand how much he was hurting her, but he wouldn't listen. The more he hurt her, the more he pulled away, when what she needed was for him to pull her closer.

Jared's words gave her little relief. The letter haunted her, yet at the same time his explanation dripped off his tongue like honey, coating her in its stickiness and muffling the strong emotions of her initial reaction. She needed to think.

Do you divorce your husband for writing love notes to other women? How about for kissing a neighbor? Does a "sorry" make it okay?

Alyson felt so confused—why couldn't he be faithful? She was so tired of being wounded by him.

She needed time to figure out what to do. She needed more answers.

Chapter Twelve

"We must embrace pain and burn it as fuel for our journey."[13]

Alyson was working on dinner and noticed it had gotten dark outside. She went around to each window on the main floor to close the blinds. At the last one, Ryker called her from the family room.

"Mom, can you come here? I was getting ready to put in a cartoon for Jayden and I saw this on top of the VCR. Do you know what it is?" He handed her a video that wasn't labeled.

When the black plastic made contact with her hand, a burning heat shot through her. She wanted to immediately let go.

"Ryker, can you please take the other kids out of the room for a minute so I can find out what is on the tape," she asked him.

He gave her a questioning look, but didn't say anything.

Alyson was pretty sure she knew exactly what kind of video it was. Hoping she was wrong, she pushed it into the VCR and it started playing immediately. She reeled at the explicit image of the couple that came on the screen. She pushed stop, overwhelmed by a dark and awful feeling in the room. She knew the tape was Jared's.

When she took the video out, she noticed there was a small label on the back with the name of an adult company on it. She was so glad Ryker brought it to her before putting it in himself.

"What was it, Mom?" Ryker asked, looking at her intently.

"Let's just say it isn't good—I need to make a phone call." She went upstairs to her room where she could talk privately and called the bishop. She told him what Ryker had found and asked if he could possibly come over later to talk with Jared. She couldn't deal with this situation by herself. She was completely maxed-out.

After dinner the doorbell rang. Jared answered it and sounded surprised to see the bishop. He invited him to come inside.

"Hi, Jared, how are you?" he said as he came in.

Jared shook his hand. "I'm fine, what's up?"

"Alyson called me earlier and asked if I would come over. Didn't she tell you?"

Alyson was standing in the kitchen, watching. Jared's eyes went to her face, studying it intently for a moment. "No, she never told me." He was bewildered.

She hadn't told him because she wasn't in the mood to hear any more of his excuses.

"Is there somewhere we could talk alone, Jared?" the bishop asked.

Alyson jumped in. "I'll go upstairs and you can talk here." She excused herself and went to her room. In a shorter time than she expected, Jared was calling her name. "I'm coming," she said, going back downstairs. She came in the living room and saw Jared and the bishop sitting on the couch. She sat in the rocking chair.

The bishop began, "Alyson, I talked to Jared about the tape and I think the two of you need to get some marriage counseling to help you with this. The ward's funding can help cover the cost. What do you think?"

"I'm fine with going," she said, relieved that he'd offered something substantial, not only his opinion.

"I'm fine with it, too," Jared agreed.

Alyson hadn't expected that. The bishop filled out a referral slip and gave it to her.

"You can call either of these two numbers," he pointed, "to make an appointment. You should be able to get one fairly quickly. After you go a few times, I want the two of you to meet with me again at my office. Do either of you have any questions?" He looked at Jared first. They shook their heads.

"Then I'm going to go. If anything comes up in the meantime, feel free to give me a call—either of you."

"Thanks for coming over, Bishop," Alyson told him with a smile. She shook his hand.

"No problem," he replied.

Jared walked him to the door and saw him out. After he had gone, Alyson tried to talk to Jared about the tape, but he refused, telling her he wouldn't get into it until they met with the counselor.

They had their first session one week later. The tape was brought up, but after the counselor listened to Alyson's concerns, he briefly asked Jared about it and then moved on to something else. It made Alyson frustrated. Jared acted relieved that it wasn't pursued.

There it was again, the incessant ringing of the telephone.

Alyson dreaded answering it. Creditors were calling repeatedly, saying Jared was behind on payments, his late fees were increasing, and when could they expect a check in the mail? She had complained to Jared about it several times, and he kept telling her he would take care of it. However, the calls continued.

For most of their marriage, she had handled the budgeting and paid the bills. In the past year she gave the responsibility to Jared; it had become too stressful for her. Jared worked full-time, had two part-time jobs, including one she, Ryker, and Cade helped with every Saturday, and money was still tight. She wasn't sure why.

The phone rang again. She answered it, hoping it was someone she wanted to talk to. It wasn't and the man's voice on the other end was unfamiliar. He asked for Jared.

"No, I'm sorry, he's at work. May I take a message?"

"Is this his wife?"

"Yes, it is."

"Great. I'm with Valley Mortgage. I'm calling to remind you your monthly payment is overdue. You need to bring your account current immediately to avoid further late charges."

His words didn't make sense. "Valley Mortgage, you said?"

"That's right."

"There must be some mistake because the mortgage for our home is carried by someone else, and I know our house payment was paid two weeks ago." She had mailed several things when Jared had asked her to, and the payment was one of them.

"I'm not talking about your regular house payment, ma'am, I'm talking about the second mortgage you all took out six months ago, which is now overdue."

Alyson was growing more frustrated. "We don't have a second mortgage on our home; you must have the wrong number."

His voice picked up speed. "You do have a second mortgage. I have the paperwork in front of me. You borrowed over fifteen thousand dollars, and we initially paid off several credit cards. We sent a check for the rest."

There had to be a mistake. "Whose name is on the loan?" she asked him.

Papers shuffled in the background and when they stopped, the man repeated hers and Jared's full names, social security numbers, and current address.

She drew a quick breath and blurted, "I've never signed any documents with your company—ever. There is no way you have my signature on anything. Someone must have forged it. The loan can't be legal and my husband has never mentioned any of this to me."

Bingo. A warning light went off in her head. She suddenly felt nauseous.

When the man spoke again his voice was filled with impatience. "Look, lady, I don't know the kind of relationship you and your husband have, but both of your signatures are on the loan. You did receive several thousand dollars and are behind on paying it back. Have your husband give me a call as soon as he gets in. I'll work it out with him."

The phone clicked in her ear.

Jared actually forged my signature? You've got to be kidding. How did he do it? Where did the money go? If our credit cards were paid off, why are we getting so many calls?

The nausea intensified. She had to find out what was going on. How was she supposed to deal with the fact that the debt she already was stressing over had increased by over fifteen thousand dollars. It was unreal.

She reached for the Yellow Pages, flipping through the sections until she found the one she wanted. The receiver was still warm when she picked it up and dialed the number. It didn't take more than a minute to get the information she needed. She hung up and then called Jared at work.

"Hi," she said when the secretary answered. "This is Alyson, Jared's wife. Is he available?"

"Sure, one minute," she replied pleasantly. All of a sudden, Alyson could hear jazz music in the background. She waited for Jared to pick up and her thoughts wandered. Should she make tacos or chili for dinner? Before she made up her mind, Jared's voice interrupted.

"Hi, Alyson, how's it going?" he asked.

"Hi, it's going good. Can you meet me somewhere on your lunch break in a little while?"

"I guess, if it's really important. Ben and I were going to go flying at lunch, but we can go tomorrow instead. Why?"

"I just need you to meet me somewhere. Here is the address. Say in about thirty minutes?"

"Alyson, why do you need me? Can't you go alone?"

"No, you'll need to sign something, otherwise I would."

He sighed with irritation. "Can't it wait?"

"No, it can't." Her voice was firm. "Jared, I need to get off the phone. The boys need something to eat before we leave. I'll see you soon." Alyson moved the phone away from her ear and thought she heard Jared say something else. She hung up anyway. She couldn't let him change his mind.

She made a quick lunch for Jayden and Alex and a sandwich for herself. Soon they were on their way. Once she pulled in the parking lot and parked, she kept an eye on her rearview mirror watching for Jared. She waved when she saw him pull in. He parked close to her.

While she waited, she got the boys out of the car. As soon as he met them, they walked together to the building and took the elevator up to the third floor.

"What are we doing here?" Jared asked, looking around.

"We need a copy of our credit history, yours especially. I couldn't get it without paying the required fee and having your signature," Alyson explained.

Jared scowled.

She tried to placate him. "Hon, I know it isn't a fun way to spend your lunch break, but aren't you tired of being hassled by so many calls? If we have the report in front of us, we can prove we're being harassed and won't have to keep dealing with them. I know you're as tired of it as I am."

Jared looked at her intently, as if trying to figure out why it was so important. He shrugged his shoulders. "Well, maybe you're right. Let's hurry and get it over with." Twenty minutes later their name was called and Jared walked up to the counter. He gave them a check and, in return, was handed a thick packet of papers stapled together. He looked through them slowly on the way back to his seat, scanning each page before moving to the next. He didn't say a word.

Alyson barely resisted the impulse to grab them from his hands and look at it herself. She was on pins and needles.

When Jared got to the bottom of the last page he set the packet on his lap. He didn't look at Alyson.

"What's wrong?" she finally asked. "What does it say?"

"It isn't good," he answered, shaking his head. "Let's talk about it at home."

Alyson couldn't wait that long. She took the papers off his lap and was surprised he didn't protest. There were several pages of notations showing account after account with different companies, some closed, several with large, outstanding balances.

She recognized the names of a few companies—ones who had pestered them with phone calls—and she could see why. Her heart sank. She found the page that said "Valley Mortgage" and the initial debt was listed over fifteen thousand dollars, plus interest for several late payments. Seeing the facts about their finances in black and white appalled her.

They left the building, not speaking, somberly lost in their thoughts. She knew Jared still had time before he had to return to work. She situated the boys inside the van, shut the passenger door and turned to talk to him.

"The report has several of the credit card companies that have been calling us. You kept telling me they had the wrong Jared, that it was a mistake. Why were you lying to me?"

Jared didn't say anything.

She went on. "Earlier today I received a call from Valley Mortgage concerning a late payment on a loan against our home that has my name on it. How could you have actually forged my signature? You know, I could press charges if I wanted." She was so frustrated.

Finally he answered, his voice low. "I didn't want to tell you about all this because I knew you would worry. I thought I could get things worked out without you ever having to know. I originally got a couple of extra credit cards, for backup or an emergency. Occasionally I used them for surprises for you and the boys. Somehow things got out of control. I was basically getting cash advances from one card to pay off the minimum balance on another.

"Jared, how could this have happened? You work several jobs and money is always tight. It's not as if we are buying lots of extras."

"Alyson, remember when the engine went out on our old minivan and it wasn't worth trying to replace?"

Her eyes widened. "Are you telling me you bought the new van on a credit card?" she asked, dumbfounded.

He nodded. "I had no choice. We purchased it from a private owner. He wasn't going to finance it for us—we had to have a car." He shrugged his shoulders. "I don't know how it's gotten to this point. I thought my ideas would work to get us better set financially, only the problems increased and we got farther behind. I took out the second mortgage to consolidate the credit card debt—the high interest rates were killing us. Before I knew it, I had to use credit again to pay regular monthly expenses like utilities and food."

"This doesn't make sense to me, Jared. You put in a ton of overtime, you're gone late almost every weeknight, and the man I talked to from the mortgage company said they paid off several credit cards and sent a check for the remainder. What did you do with all that money, Jared?"

"First of all, it wasn't that much and that was six months ago. The money is all gone now."

Alyson was tired of the head games. "The man was lying to me about the amount; is that what you're saying? Why is everybody else always lying when I ask you to explain things? We have to sit down and go over our finances and we'll probably need some help. This whole thing is way over the top, Jared. I'll see you tonight." She climbed into the car, over-whelmingly frustrated, waiting to back out until after she saw Jared leave. She prayed as she headed home.

Oh, God, I'm so worried. Please help me deal with all these challenges. I want to believe in Jared, but confusing things are happening that I don't know how to handle. Please direct me to answers and the truth, so I can feel peace again.

Later that night, Alyson was underneath the warm covers of her bed reading her scriptures, something she could rely on to bring her comfort. She felt she was being guided to be patient. God knew she was hurting—the answer she kept getting was to love her husband and have faith.

When Jared came in the bedroom a short time later, he was ready to talk. Alyson thought the discussion would be on finances, but he brought up something else.

"You know how I fly clients on sightseeing trips to the Knik Glacier and Mt. McKinley?"

She nodded.

"On one of my recent flights I met a man from Fairbanks. He's been looking for an airplane to buy and he asked me questions about my flying background during the trip. Today I got a phone call from him at work, and he said he found a good deal on a Cessna 180. It's in Washington. He asked me if I would be willing to go with him to pick it up and fly it back. He would pay for my expenses, including the time I would lose at work." He stopped to let his words sink in.

"Alyson, it would be a way to log more hours, gain more experience and it would be totally fun. We would fly commercially to Seattle, pick up the plane, then fly it back to Anchorage—probably three to four days round trip. What do you think?"

She hesitated. "How well do you know this guy? Seattle to Anchorage in a small plane is a long flight. Do you feel ready for that? You'd be dealing with different flight patterns and weather changes on a route you're not familiar with."

"I know him well enough. Alyson—it would be great! Before I left I would review the maps to find the safest route and plot the whole trip. You know I file current flight plans anytime I go anywhere, and I watch the weather closely. This trip wouldn't be any different, just longer. I'll discuss it with your dad, too. He's flown that route commercially and could give me insight regarding alternate airports or terrain issues, in case I needed to make an emergency landing. I really want to do this, Alyson."

His answers implied he had thought the trip through carefully, except an uneasiness nagged her. She wasn't sure if it was based on her own fears over his safety or something else. She had made up her mind years before when she fell in love with a man whose life dream was to be a pilot, to put his safety in God's hands. She couldn't panic every time he left the house to fly or she would drive herself crazy.

The memory of losing her own dad in an aviation accident at age seven gave her firsthand experience of a tragedy like that, at least from a child's perspective. She didn't want to dwell on "what if."

"Jared, I would like to think about this some more. I'm not feeling good about you going for some reason. Can we pray about it?"

He sighed, not encouraged by her response, and then said, "Fine." He agreed to wait on making a final decision. He turned off the lamp on his side of the bed and Alyson felt the mattress shift as he rolled over. She was frustrated that he had forgotten the earlier trauma over the credit report.

"Jared, we need to talk about our financial situation."

He sighed louder this time. "It's late. I'll call tomorrow and get an appointment with a debt consolidation agency. Maybe they can help us."

Chapter Thirteen

"As individuals consume pornography and then become consumed by it, they descend into darkness, and the 'light of Christ' is driven out of their souls."[14]

Alyson walked to the mailbox, reviewing in her head what needed to be done the remainder of the day. Ryker and Cade had a few more weeks of school before summer vacation. She needed to get some activities planned that would keep them busy.

Inside the mailbox were several envelopes and a postcard. She looked through them on the way to the house and noticed almost all were bills. She decided, stressful or not, she needed to refamiliarize herself with how much they owed and to whom. Jared had made an appointment for the next week with an agency she hoped would help get them through this mess. She and Jared also discussed the flying trip again. It hadn't gone well. She prayed about it but still didn't have a good feeling. When she told him, he got upset and said she needed to be more supportive, then surprisingly enough, he reluctantly agreed not to go.

Back inside, she sat down at the desk in the corner of the family room and opened the mail, sorting the bills in appropriate piles, with the ones due soonest on top. When she opened the ones for the credit cards, she checked each charge to make sure the transaction amounts matched the saved receipts.

Some of the charges on the Visa she didn't recognize, and one she had no idea what it was for. It was made at a place called NiteShades. She thought she might have noticed a charge to the same place on the previous month's statement.

It a few minutes she located it and saw there were two charges on that one, made two days apart. One was for fifty dollars and the other one was for a hundred. The newest statement had another charge for fifty.

She flipped the calendar on the wall back to March and looked again at the charge dates from the oldest statement. They were made when she and the boys were at her parents during spring break. Noting the next date in April, she saw the charge was also made on a weekday. She made a mental note to ask Jared about them when she got a chance. She finished paying the bills and left them on the desk, needing stamps.

A few days later she got Ryker and Cade ready for school, gave them a hug, handing them their lunches as they left. Returning to the kitchen, she was almost finished with the breakfast dishes when Jayden came in to ask if he could watch his favorite morning show.

Alyson followed him into the family room to turn on the television and noticed the forgotten bills on the desk. She took them back into the kitchen and set them on the counter by her purse. The post office was on her list of errands. She would mail them then.

She wiped down the counters and rinsed the dishcloth, squeezing out the excess water before draping it over the spigot to air dry. She noticed the sound of the shower upstairs had stopped. Jared was getting ready for work. She still hadn't talked to him about the credit card charges and decided she'd better do it before she forgot again. First, she went back to the family room to get the statements.

The bathroom door upstairs was closed. Alyson knocked. "Jared?"

"Come in," he said.

Warm, moist air enveloped her when she entered the room, her reflection hazy in the steam-covered mirror. Jared stood to her left with his back facing her, a towel at his waist. His hair was damp, the sides neatly combed, and he was holding the blow dryer in one hand, a brush in the other.

"Jared, I just remembered I had some questions I needed to ask you from the other day when I worked on the bills. Some of the charges on the last two Visa statements might not be right." He freed his hands and turned to face her, and she showed him the papers, pointing to the specific charges in question.

"See, it says NiteShades, then the amount? There were three charges total. Do you know what those were for?"

He shook his head, sounding unsure. "I don't know. What's Nite-Shades?"

She expected a different answer, thinking he would clear up the mystery. "I thought you would know since the charges are on your card. I checked the calendar and noticed the first two were made in March when the boys and I were out in Wasilla with my parents."

"Maybe there was a mistake and the card was charged incorrectly," he offered.

Alyson wrinkled her forehead. "You didn't lose the card, did you?"

"No, I don't think so."

Her voice betrayed frustration when she spoke again—tired of more problems. "So you're sure you don't know anything about the charges? It seems unlikely if there was a mistake that it would have happened three different times, and you know what else? There were several, long distance phone charges made to a number in Washington state. Who do we know there?" She still hoped there was a simple explanation.

All of the sudden Jared's face rapidly deepened in color and his dark eyes flashed. He lifted one of his hands and leaned his body toward her threateningly close. His words exploded. "I told you, I don't know! If you don't trust me, this marriage is over right now!"

Alyson stepped back in shock, feeling almost certain he was going to strike her even though he never had before. She had never seen him this angry and tried to fathom how the last thing she said could have elicited such an extreme reaction.

"Calm down, Jared. I have no idea why you're getting so upset—unless you're hiding something." She reacted to his escalated anger by throwing back words that logically made sense, but only added to the heat of his mood. He looked at her, fuming.

Alyson had hit on the truth, and it rang loudly between them. She was completely unnerved; another corner had been turned in their struggling marriage. She left the bathroom and went downstairs to check on the boys. Several minutes later Jared left for work, slamming the front door behind him.

She decided she couldn't and wouldn't let it go and picked up the telephone to get more information. She found the number she needed on the credit card statements and dialed. On the third ring a female voice answered.

"Hello, NiteShades."

"Hi." Alyson tried not to sound as nervous as she was. "I have a couple of questions. The last two statements on our credit card show charges from NiteShades and I'm trying to find out what they were for." Her words produced a lengthy silence, then audible hesitation before she received a reply.

"Uh," the woman cleared her throat. "Do you know what kind of services we offer here?"

"No, that's why I'm calling. I'm trying to figure out if there has been a mistake; neither my husband nor I know what the charges were for. Somebody might have used our card without authorization, but we're not sure."

"I can't give you any information over the phone," she said. "You'll have to come in person to look at the signature on the receipts."

The problem kept growing worse. "Okay. What are your business hours and your address?" Alyson jotted down the information, thanked her, and hung up. She couldn't go that night since Jared was working late. Tomorrow was Friday, and they usually went out on a date, only after what just happened she had no idea what to expect. The woman on the phone had told her NightShades was open all the time—strange.

When Jared came home late that night they avoided what happened that morning despite how heavily it weighed on them both.

On Friday night they went out as usual. Alyson pretended everything was fine, waiting until she had more information, and Jared played along.

They went to dinner at their favorite Mexican restaurant. Alyson ordered chicken enchiladas and Jared ordered a shredded beef chimichanga. They ate at a leisurely pace, the discussion dancing deliberately away from anything contentious. Once they finished, Jared stood up to go pay the bill. Alyson handed him a coupon to make the price of their dinners two for one. On the way home, Jared asked her if there was anything else she wanted to do that night.

"Actually, there is." She internally braced herself. "After you left for work yesterday, I called that NiteShades place and asked them about the charges on our statements. They said we needed to come in person to verify the signatures. The address they gave is close to here."

Jared slammed his fist on the steering wheel and pulled the car over, jerking Alyson's body forward as he pushed hard on the brakes before shifting to park. She looked at him as if he was out of his mind. The incident the day before roared between them again.

"I am not going into that place with you! If you want to go, you can go yourself!" he shouted. His angry words bounced around the car's interior. Alyson was momentarily speechless, and then Jared jumped out of the car and took off at a brisk pace facing oncoming traffic. The feeling in her gut reconfirmed she had to continue pursuing whatever this was about.

She sat in the car watching the distance between them increase in more ways than one, not sure what to do as the next few minutes ticked slowly by. Finally she made a decision and slid over to the driver's side of the vehicle, turned the ignition until the engine engagedm and drove in the direction Jared had gone. He was cutting across a deserted parking lot. Alyson made a left-hand turn and stopped the car next to him, rolling down the window.

"Come on, Jared. We need to go there together; please get back in. Where are you going anyway?"

He looked at Alyson with tired, bloodshot eyes. His skin was pale. The anger was gone from his face, replaced with resignation. "Fine," he said, "but I'll drive."

The first time Jared went to Nightshades, Alyson was at her parents. He went before work, early enough to avoid being seen by someone he knew. By the time his lunch break arrived, he couldn't stand it anymore. Hating himself and in shock that he had actually followed through with the fantasy he had been living over and over in his mind, he called Alyson to tell her he loved her.

Despite that, he went back and did it a second and a third time, trying to satiate the fire of sexual hunger it ignited. He knew it was wrong, yet part of him liked it anyway. The second time, he sent Alyson flowers with a romantic note, and the third time he went home during lunch to hold her, see her face, and reaffirm that she could still look at him with love in her eyes.

Now, the inevitable had come. There wasn't any point in running. Either it would be horrible, or by some insane luck it would be okay, but it had to be faced. He knew without a doubt Alyson wasn't going to back down, and whether or not she had his cooperation, she was obviously determined to find out what he had done. She was stronger than he had known—her determination impressed him and at the same time, he was terrified.

Alyson slid over to her original seat and Jared climbed back in on the driver's side. In less than ten minutes, they were parked in front of their destination. When Alyson glanced around she recognized the area with mounting concern, becoming uneasy. She had heard about these kinds of places.

"I can't believe I'm going in here with my wife," Jared said, under his breath before he got out of the car.

"Let's get it over with quickly," she replied, her thoughts mirroring his. She couldn't believe she was going in either and hoped no one they knew would see them. Jared's office was close by.

He opened the door for her. The dimly lit interior was an immediate contrast to the outside brightness and a dark feeling permeated the small building. Alyson could feel it, and she wished she could be anywhere else but there. The thought to run back to the car was tempting, but she knew she had to finish what she came to do.

There was a dark-colored heavy curtain covering the doorway they pushed aside to walk through. Directly in front of them sat a young woman, about twenty, behind a small opening with a counter, like a check-in desk at a motel.

She stood up at once and came around the side of the counter. She was dressed in tight jeans, heels, and a clingy, sheer blouse with a neckline that showed a generous amount of cleavage. Alyson tried to act as if she didn't notice what the girl was wearing even though its immodesty made her uncomfortable.

"Can I help you two?" The woman asked uncertainly, looking first at Jared and then at Alyson. Off to Alyson's right, another girl stepped forward, dressed similarly. She scrutinized them, too. An anxious and expectant feeling surrounded both women.

Jared stood there, saying nothing.

Alyson knew it was up to her. She began to talk, trying to ignore her taut nerves, desperately wanting the whole encounter to be over with so they could leave. "I called earlier about some incorrect charges on our credit card and was told I needed to resolve it in person."

Both women visibly relaxed.

"Oh, yes, I remember. I was the one you talked to," the first woman said. "What dates were the charges for?"

Alyson gave her the two in March and the one in April and Jared's full name, exactly the way it was on the credit card.

She checked through the file of receipts locating the right ones within a few minutes

"Are you Jared?" she asked, looking at him.

He nodded.

"I need to see your driver's license," she explained.

He removed it from his worn leather wallet and handed it to her. She held it close to her face to see it clearly in the dull light of the room. She carefully compared it with the signature on each receipt.

"They look like the same signature to me," she replied, staring pointedly at Jared, and then Alyson. There was a long, awkward silence.

Alyson asked to see both signatures, and she held them side-by-side. She agreed they looked identical. She didn't say anything else, because as the huge impact of what that meant began to sink in, she felt like she was falling into a gigantic black hole. She was frantic to stop her descent and not feel the grief assaulting every cell in her body. Unfortunately, she was surrounded by empty space and crashed to the bottom, weak and in shock.

Jared didn't bother to look at the signatures and continued to protest they couldn't be his.

"Why don't you have a seat over there," the woman told him, referring to a nearby couch. There was a small table next to it, holding a dim lamp and few magazines. He sat down without protest.

"Come with me," she told Alyson, gesturing with her hand to follow her. She led the way to another room toward the back of the building. It was cluttered with clothes and a dressing table, with makeup and assorted perfume scattered across its surface.

"You can sit there," she told Alyson, pointing to a chair near the door. The other woman came in behind her. Two pairs of concerned eyes looked at Alyson, and it would have been comforting if she hadn't felt so out of place.

The first woman spoke. "Each 'package' that is purchased lists the number of the girl who is with that client. We called the girl we think was with your husband so she can see him. If she recognizes him, you will know for sure he was here. She's on her way over right now. I'm sorry . . ."

Alyson sat numbly, trying to take it all in. These two women used their bodies day after day to make a living—something she couldn't understand—yet they cared about her feelings. They seemed more normal than not.

"What exactly did my husband pay for?" she asked her. "I mean, he didn't actually get . . ." Her voice trailed off, not able to bring herself to say it. She knew her question sounded naive, but she had to ask it anyway. She watched the woman's eyebrows shift questioningly, and then her face softened.

Alyson went on. "The charges were for different amounts, two for fifty dollars, one was for a hundred. What would the difference be for?" She was so far from comprehending what Jared had done.

The same woman vaguely explained that the higher amount was for an hour with a girl and the lower amount was for thirty minutes.

Alyson's imagination ran wild with all she didn't tell her, emotions building with each new bit of information. She was too stunned to cry. Despite the unreal circumstances in which she was meeting the two women, they were considerate and nice, and she figured they probably didn't deal with wives very often.

Time crawled as they waited. Alyson's thoughts mounted in twisted fascination to see who her husband had been with, wondering if she was prettier or thinner than she.

"How could he act like such a jerk?" she said out loud, shaking her head, not knowing how to begin absorbing the experience.

The second woman spoke. "I know how you feel. My boyfriend

cheated on me with a dancer from a nightclub. I was so angry I wanted to kill him. You're right," she said, nodding her head in agreement. "Men can be such jerks!"

Alyson wondered at her logic when she worked in a place like this; at the same time, she appreciated the woman reaching out to her in the only way she knew how. And in spite of her hurt and anger, part of her was sad for Jared—sad he had been deceived into thinking a place like this would bring him something he wanted.

The door opened, and in came the girl they were waiting for. Her coworkers explained why they had called her in and introduced her to Alyson by first name only. Alyson talked to her briefly and studied her appearance, trying to comprehend that Jared had been with her. The woman acted uncomfortable and Alyson didn't blame her; she was, too. It was awkward, but the woman was as nice to Alyson as the other two had been.

They left the room in a group.

The woman Alyson just met separated herself from them and walked over to where Jared was sitting. He was trying to appear relaxed as he looked at a magazine. When he looked up as she approached, his face completely changed.

She moved closer to get a better look at him. Once she was satisfied she turned to Alyson and said, "I definitely remember him, probably on at least two occasions. I'm sorry." It was a strange moment. How could Alyson respond when there simply were no words?

Jared abruptly stood and walked toward his wife, deliberately keeping his eyes away from any contact with hers, or the other three women. Alyson thanked the girls for their help, and then she walked out quickly, leaving behind the man who was becoming a stranger. He had wounded her in the worst possible way.

She climbed stiffly into the passenger side of the car and with unsteady hands pulled the seat belt across her body. The heavy silence inside the car was stifling on the drive home. Alyson was completely overwhelmed, except she did feel a tiny amount of relief. She now had some concrete answers.

Jared's angry behavior in the bathroom yesterday and his flight earlier that evening from the car made sense, as well as the phone call in March during spring break at her parent's home, the flowers "just because" and his unexpected visit home in the middle of the day to "see her pretty face."

The dates matched up—except the experience she just endured shook her to the very core. Something of this nature was beyond her wildest imaginations. The rapidly growing transparent picture she saw of her husband and his deception was nightmarish and surreal.

"Do you want me to pack my bags and leave tonight?" he questioned somberly.

Her thoughts raced. Part of her wanted to reach across the growing chasm between them and have him hold her in his arms. She wanted to feel his warm breath on her cheek, his reassuring kisses on her lips, and hear him say he loved her. She wanted him to comfort her, to push away the black tide of expanding pain that was starting to consume who she was. She wanted him to make her world feel safe again.

Another voice in her head yelled loudly and unrelentingly that it was impossible. Jared couldn't make it stop. The blistering heat she felt inside was coming from him. He was the cause of her shattered heart and dreams. The pain and overpowering feelings inside her were horrible. Was she ready for him to pack his bags and get out? Everything was out of control and happening too fast. At least the women he did who-knew-what with were strangers—he couldn't love them. Did that make it better? Her mind was still looking for a way out, as ridiculous as that was.

"No, Jared, I don't want you to leave tonight, but you have to sleep downstairs. I don't know what to do right now. Later, you need to tell me exactly what you did with that girl."

Bewilderment covered his face.

"Okay." He hesitated. "I would understand if you told me to leave, but why do you want to know the details, Alyson? Why would you want to hear that?"

Her words were high-pitched. "Because I would rather know everything you did than be fixated on wondering. I don't expect you to understand—I don't—you just need to tell me." Her voice broke and she was filled with overwhelming sadness. "I've tried to give you what you needed physically in our marriage. How could you go to a prostitute, Jared? How could you take something so sacred, that we promised only to each other and cheapen it by giving it away so carelessly? How could you betray me like that?" A choking sob caught in her throat and released a deluge of tears.

"I don't know, Alyson. I don't know," Jared said to her, close to tears himself. "The thought of doing it got stuck in my head, and it wouldn't go away. I don't know what's wrong with me." His voice cracked as he fought to regain his composure.

It was different for her when Jared was like this; he seemed reachable. How did he come to this point in his life? How did they?

That night she lay in an empty bed, crying and aching all over. She felt so far away from Jared, even though he was only one floor below. This was worse than anything he had ever done to her. She got out of bed and knelt down to pour out her heart in prayer. She told God everything she was feeling, how much she hurt, and how confused she was. By the time she finished, her knees were sore, yet she had no doubt of His great compassion. He was hurting with her.

Chapter Fourteen

"If your partner remains involved in pornography, it does not have to destroy you or your children. . . . Whether we move ahead alone or with our partner, we must move ahead. There is a place of peace waiting for us."[15]

The next week was a blur. During the day, time alternated between fast forward and pause; during the night, Alyson's mind replayed her dilemma again and again until she sank into an exhausted sleep. She couldn't stop reviewing the years she and Jared had been together—how had it progressed to this point? Her mind erupted like a volcano filled with rising, burning red lava that couldn't be contained. It covered her and she became immersed in doubts and fears.

The inner turmoil didn't change her responsibility to care for her family and home. She watched everyone around her continuing on with their normal lives—hers had been changed forever. She felt isolated—wondering how her life could ever be "normal" again. She kept a smile pasted on. In reality, she was totally falling apart inside.

She and Jared continued seeing a marriage counselor. In some ways, going confused her even more. On the way to the car, Jared would ask her if they were going to make it and say he didn't want to lose her. His words caused tiny seeds of hope to sprout inside her until his rage returned and she felt the familiar constriction of raw pain hit her again. He was acting like two different people and, as she discovered more, she knew without a doubt he had been living two different lives.

They had to file for bankruptcy, the debt was so out of control there was no other way out. She was embarrassed and felt guilty. How could the debt have snowballed into an avalanche only to be erased through an order of the court? It went completely against what she believed in. Because of Jared's decisions, hers became limited. She hated it.

She wrote in her journal in the middle of June:

I go from feeling things will be okay and loving Jared, to feeling as if I can't bear life anymore with him in it. I know I need to have faith; God hasn't ever failed me before, so I'm sure He won't now.

Jared has a long history of patterned behavior that has repeatedly caused problems in our life. He says he wants a new heart, he says he wants to change, but his actions are staying the same. I don't know half the time what has ever been real in our marriage, and I am confused.

At some point didn't she need to take care of herself? How much did she have to take? There were times she wanted to get as far away from him as she possibly could and be numb to anything relating to him. Other times she caught glimpses of the man she fell in love with and couldn't imagine her life without him.

One afternoon she was dusting the large bookshelf in the family room and accidentally knocked out a loose page in Jared's journal. It fluttered to the floor. She went to slip it back in when the date caught her eye—it was written the night they investigated the charges on the credit card—the very night things drastically changed.

Jared had begun the entry saying he would spend the rest of his life doing everything he could to make up for what he had done to her. Reading that made her cry and added more confusion. She was struggling to make a definite decision. The occasional softening in Jared made her think that perhaps they could get through this, but such times became practically non-existent as the summer days went on.

She knew her prayers for help were being heard, but couldn't quite find the courage to take the final step. The thought of ending her marriage—getting away from the horrible negative energy, the times she didn't know if Jared was lying or not, and the endless stress—made her feel relieved and free. But when she thought about becoming a single mother, trying to provide for her children, facing an uncertain future and the stigma of being divorced in a family-oriented church—she was frightened and dreaded the loneliness.

Then she got a phone call.

The boys were all in bed, and Jared wasn't home. She was sitting on the couch in the family room watching TV. The late summer sky hadn't completely darkened yet and the deepening colors of sunlight cast a softened golden glow on the walls of the room. The show, a hospital drama, only half held her attention. When the telephone rang she pushed the mute button on the remote control.

"Hi, Alyson." It was her brother Reid. He knew how unstable her marriage had become and was calling to check on her. "How is it going?" he said in a voice warm with concern.

"It's going okay—I'm trying to get through one day at a time." Her voice was subdued.

"That's all you can do sometimes, huh? I'm sorry, Alyson. This has to be really tough . . ." His voice trailed off.

She lightened her tone. "What's up with you?" she asked, her eyes moving around the room. She noticed a few toys and books that had been left underneath the coffee table.

"Not much, same old thing. Get up at 4:00 AM, trade stocks until the market closes in New York, eat, hang out with my daughter, watch TV, eat, go to sleep, and do it all over the next day."

Alyson laughed as she picked up the toys.

Reid went on, "Sometimes I even throw in laundry, vacuuming, or a trip to the grocery store, only on the exciting days of course."

"That does sound exciting!" She replaced the books on the shelf. Nothing else in the room looked out of order.

"Alyson—how are you really doing?" he asked her, searchingly.

She hesitated about how open to be—but maybe his male perspective might help.

"I'm confused about what to do, Reid. Jared has hurt me in ways I never could have imagined. We've been married almost fourteen years—how can I throw all that away? I don't want to be a divorced, single mother—how can something this horrible have happened? Jared went to a prostitute—I saw her with my own eyes; I talked to her. She told me she had been with him, and yet it's incomprehensible. What did I ever do to him to deserve that? I've tried so hard to make him happy—if I could hate him, it would be so much easier—or if he had died, even that would be better than this. I feel so humiliated, so degraded, why was I not enough for him? What is wrong with me?" She started to cry. "I still love him and I know that's crazy. I have four boys—I'm almost thirty-two—no one else is going to want me. I don't want to be alone the rest of my life."

"Alyson, listen to me. You didn't do anything to deserve this. Sure, you weren't perfect—nobody is—and you made mistakes—everyone does. But that does not justify what Jared did. He has the problem—not you. Nothing you could have done deserves the way he has treated you.

"I know him. We spent a lot of time together when you weren't around, going fishing or duck hunting, for example. He flirts with women all the time. He doesn't act married. It always surprised me, but I figured it was harmless—just the way Jared is—obviously it wasn't.

"You won't have any problems finding someone else. Thirty-two isn't old, and your boys are good kids. Any guy would be lucky to have a wife like you. Trust me, I know. I hear what my friends say about you. I know what guys are looking for. You keep yourself in good shape, you're a good cook, a good mom—you'll probably have guys lined up to ask you out."

Alyson laughed. "Yeah, right! I doubt that," she said sarcastically. She hadn't expected to hear her brother say so many nice things about her. It made her feel good, even though she had a hard time believing him. If she was so great, why did Jared cheat on her?

"Alyson, I respect and admire you, and even though you're my younger sister, I look up to you—you've been a good example to me."

"Thanks, Reid, that means a lot. I'm glad you called. I know what I have to do." Her voice caught as the finality of her words sunk in. The right answer had come as clear as day. The doubts hadn't faded and the fear hadn't left, but she felt a calming peace, a feeling of assuredness that was unmistakable.

"Are you okay, Alyson?" Reid asked. She had become so quiet.

"Oh—sorry, yes, I'm fine. Thanks again for listening. You've helped me more than you probably know. I love you—good-bye."

"Love you, too. Good-bye, Alyson. Let me know if you need anything," he added sincerely.

"Okay, thanks. I will." She hung up the phone. The sun had set, leaving the room in deep shadow. An overwhelming surge of emotion filled her eyes with tears—her marriage was over. The longing for things to be right with Jared had not vanished, but the unrest was gone. She didn't know how she would cope with all her worries and fears except by completely relying on God. He had the answers.

With her mind made up, she knew she had to move quickly before doubts crept back in. The next morning before Jared left for work, she told him they needed to talk when he came home. The day dragged as she worried about the best way to tell him.

That night after dinner, they left the boys at home watching a movie and walked to the park. The early evening was warm—the surrounding foliage and trees vibrant green. It was perfect weather to be outside. On the way, they passed children playing, a family having a barbecue, and others mowing their lawn or working in their gardens. Ordinary things happening on an ordinary evening. Alyson felt like an outsider looking in, barely remembering what ordinary things felt like. Each step was leading her closer to an experience she never, ever, wanted to have.

There was no playground equipment at this park, just two open clearings with a carpet of thick grass surrounded by trees and a few scattered picnic benches. It was deserted. The grass looked cool and inviting, but Alyson didn't sit down. She couldn't. Jared turned to her, waiting expectantly. He didn't make a move to sit down, either.

She thought she was ready to begin her carefully rehearsed words, but the setting, the beautiful weather, the warm sun—it all felt wrong. There should have been a biting wind blowing and whipping her hair wildly across her face, crashing thunder with occasional streaks of lightning ripping across the dark sky—the same way her dream with Jared had been ripped apart. She should have been freezing instead of warm and when she said the fateful words, "I want a divorce," angry clouds should have burst with a cacophony of raindrops and sting them both with biting cold.

When she did find her voice and said the painful words to finalize the inevitable tearing apart of her family, the sky remained blue, the sun kept shining, the birds kept singing, and the air was still warm. Jared's face barely flinched with surprise or noticeable concern.

It was eerie.

He nodded. "Alyson, I don't blame you one bit. If I were you, I would want a divorce too. You'll be free to find a guy that will treat you the way you deserve."

She stared at him. She thought about living through the last several months—the tears, the pain, the disbelief and inner turmoil, the loneliness, the doubts about herself, and the many prayers she had said asking for help. The choice to end her marriage had been a huge, life-altering decision and all Jared could say was, "I don't blame you a bit."

That wasn't what she expected. Why wasn't he protesting and pleading with her to reconsider and making promise after promise he would keep this time? Why weren't his eyes filled with unshed tears?

She thought that was what she wanted.

On the other hand, she didn't have the energy to deal with him creating an emotional scene, throwing out apologies and words to convince her he would do anything to be a better husband, or try to confuse her with soft-spoken expressions of kindness. His immediate acceptance had lifted a heavy burden from her, and she no longer had to worry that he would make things harder than they already were. It was the best way.

"Okay . . ." she hesitated, "I guess we need to figure out how to tell the boys and go from there."

"Yes, I agree," he said with a faint smile. "We do need to work some things out. Do you want to go back home and talk there, or what?"

They had only been gone a short time and the boys' bedtime was still a ways off. Alyson felt an urgency to work out the details, and it would be easier if the boys weren't close by.

"No, I don't want to go home yet. Let's go somewhere else," she told him.

"Okay . . . we could go get fried ice cream?" Jared suggested.

Alyson loved fried ice cream and their favorite Mexican restaurant was five minutes away, only they weren't celebrating. This was so weird.

"Uh . . . sure, I guess . . . but in light of the discussion we've been having, going out for dessert seems strange, don't you think?" Her tone was uncertain.

"I know, but we can go as friends, right? We've always been good friends. We can talk while we eat. I also want to say, don't close your mind to the possibility of us getting back together at some future point, if I can straighten out my life."

Alyson started to protest. She couldn't live her life anymore hoping he would change, but Jared stopped her. "Just think about it, okay, as a maybe?"

Why did he keep confusing her? "I don't know, Jared . . ." she said hesitantly. She was 99.5 percent certain it would never happen. She was glad he had said the words, but she couldn't trust them, she couldn't exist on a "maybe" or "what if." She had to rebuild her life.

They walked home to get the car. After driving to the small restaurant, they parked and got out. Jared opened the entrance door for her as they went inside like always—a small thing but even that was different because their relationship had changed so much. The rules had all been rewritten, and nothing felt normal.

While they ate, they awkwardly got back to the conversation of the divorce. They decided they would tell the boys together tomorrow after school, agreeing to stress that it had nothing to do with anything they had or hadn't done. They would reassure the boys of how much they both loved them.

Jared said he would move out as soon as he could find an apartment nearby that was somewhat affordable. Until then, he would continue sleeping downstairs. The discussion included how often he would see the boys, financial issues, and what items he would take and what things Alyson would keep. It was only the beginning of all they would have to work out. They did it calmly.

After they finished eating, they headed home. During family prayer that night, Alyson looked at each of the boys' faces and could barely contain her sadness. The next day their safe and familiar world was going to abruptly alter, and there was nothing she could do anymore to prevent it. She spent another sleepless night.

A few days later she made another entry in her journal:

Going through this has made me a different person as well as my children. They could barely comprehend that their dad and I were splitting up when we told them. Their tears came quickly and they asked "Why?" over and over. It was heartbreaking and we tried to reassure them how much they are loved. Alex isn't even a year old. He'll never remember us together. And Jayden is very attached to Jared. He won't understand why he can't see his daddy every day. It hurt so much to see the pain and sadness in my children's eyes. On top of what I already feel, it is almost unbearable.

Jared found an apartment that would be available to move in at the end of the month. Meanwhile, he was in and out of the house, coming and going at different hours. Alyson was glad it was temporary. She was ready to have him gone.

One evening he came in as she and the boys were finishing dinner.

"Hi, Dad," Ryker, Cade, and Jayden chorused.

"Hi, everybody." He walked around the table to give each of them a hug. Alex was playing in the mess he had created with his food on the tray of his highchair. He got a kiss on top of his head.

"Hi, Alyson," Jared said to her after.

"Hi. Did you want some dinner?" she offered.

"No, thanks, I had a big lunch and I'm still full. I came by to pick up a few things and I'm leaving." He went upstairs.

Ryker and Cade started to clear the table and Alyson put the leftovers away. She remembered there was something she needed to ask Jared and couldn't do it in front of the kids.

"Boys, I need to run upstairs to talk to your dad for a minute. I'll finish cleaning things up when I'm done." She left the kitchen. When she came into the master bedroom, Jared was putting things in a suitcase. She asked him a question about a money issue.

"I'll take care of it. I'm sick of dealing with everything," his voice rose in irritation. He launched into a tirade of how difficult things were going for him, how tired he was of everyone giving him unwanted advice, how busy he was at work, how little money he had, and that he constantly felt stressed.

Alyson's thoughts ran along with his words, mentally checking off the similar things she was dealing with, taking away a few of his, and adding some of her own. She nodded her head with understanding. "Yep, no kidding. Things are stressful for me, too."

"Alyson, no, you don't have any idea what I'm dealing with," he snapped. "Your stress is nothing compared to mine." As if to prove it he yanked on the zipper in frustration trying to close the suitcase and snapped off the tab. "Just great," he muttered, throwing the broken piece on the floor.

Alyson looked at him, speechless, not believing he had the audacity to make that statement after the stress his actions were causing her and the boys. "Oh, really? Then you are clueless." Her temper flared.

He shook his head. "Whatever. You don't even know half of what has gone on for years in our marriage—you have no idea what I'm dealing with."

His words caused a shudder down her spine, knowing they held some truth. She was back, uselessly hitting against the same brick wall. Why had she thought since their relationship had fallen apart, that the insurmountable barrier he stood behind would too? She felt helpless and angry.

"Then why don't you tell me, Jared? Everything you have done has affected our life together—everything. Why do you keep hiding things?"

"You don't understand, and I won't tell you." The determination in his words was clear.

Do I really want to know, anyway?

Most likely the honesty she craved would bring additional pain. Maybe it would be better never knowing.

Jared stared at her face intently, his dark eyes serious. She glared back at him, fighting with herself to stay quiet. She knew responding hotly might make her feel better at first, yet that would only continue the pointless arguing.

Jared broke the silence. "I've got what I needed, Alyson. I'm going to go." He turned toward the door and walked out of the room. After a few steps, he unexpectedly stopped and faced her again. She hadn't moved.

His stance was more relaxed. "I will tell you . . . I've decided to write it all down someday . . ."

Alyson's eyebrows rose.

Jared continued, " . . . for the boys. I want them to see where the choices I made led me and how much I lost."

His words startled her. That was the closest thing she had ever heard to a complete confession from him. She was concerned what that knowledge would do to their children.

"Are you going to write down everything? You really want them to know all of it?" she asked. She thought about the parts she knew, especially with the prostitute. Why would he want their sons to know that?

He nodded his head. "Yes, I do—when they're older. If that prevents them from making the same mistakes I did, then I want them to know everything." He added quietly, "Maybe you can read it, too." Jared looked away and Alyson saw regret and sadness in his eyes. An ache filled her heart as she watched him leave the room carrying his suitcase.

"Good-bye," she called after him. A couple of minutes later the front door opened and closed. He was gone. Two days after her thirty-second birthday at the end of July, they filed divorce papers with the court.

Chapter Fifteen

"If forgiveness eludes you and you feel stuck in your pain and anger, I encourage you to return to the grieving process. . . . Forgiveness comes as a gift when we've completed healthy grieving."[16]

August 1998

Alyson never thought Mandy would call her. She and Jared were separated. He had his own apartment and the divorce would be final some time next month. She was trying to deal with the day-to-day emptiness and grief over her changed life, so when Mandy called she was thrust back into the heat of emotion.

"Hello," she answered, ending the annoying ringing of the phone.

A voice she didn't recognize spoke. "Is this Alyson?"

"Yes, it is. Who is this, please?"

"Hi. This is Mandy calling from Washington. Do you know who I am?"

"Hi—yes, I do," she said hesitantly.

Why is she calling me?

"Look, I know you probably didn't ever expect to hear from me, the other woman," she chuckled, "but my life is falling apart, and I need to get some answers from you about Jared. Can I talk to you?" she implored.

"Sure—I guess I have a few minutes." Alyson wanted to say no, but curiosity got the best of her.

Mandy began again. "Last spring, Jared started writing to me. He said he kept thinking about our past relationship and wanted to know if I was happy in my marriage. He asked me to write back and send a few pictures of myself."

Alyson remembered the day Mandy's letter came in the mail and the conversation it started that night. When she and Jared discussed it, he specifically said she was the one that initiated the contact.

"Jared said you wrote him first," she told Mandy.

"No," she protested humorously, "he definitely wrote to me first, but I doubt he would have told you that. He said when you found my letters you were upset. We decided to stick to emailing after that. Do you remember when he told you about an opportunity to fly an airplane from Washington to Alaska?"

"Um . . . yes. Why?" Alyson asked, wondering how she knew that or why she cared.

"Well, actually," Mandy paused, "that was a story he and I devised together so he could come here to see me. But since you were so against it, we had to figure out how to arrange it another way."

Alyson blinked away tears. She had gotten a bad feeling when she prayed about that trip and decided it was because Jared wouldn't be safe. That wasn't it—there had never been a trip like that in the first place.

Mandy continued, interrupting Alyson's thoughts. "Did you know Jared was out of state most of last week?"

She recalled with frustration the day she had waited for him to show up at the house to help Ryker and Cade with a new paper route. They wanted to earn some spending money. Jared had some experience and promised to help them until they could handle it on their own. On their third day, he never showed up. He had always been reliable and she worried that something happened to him. She ended up scrambling to get the papers delivered. They were late.

She couldn't reach him at his apartment and called his office. The secretary informed her he was out of town, acting surprised she hadn't known. They weren't living together, and she never expected him to check in. He could have called to say he wasn't coming. Ryker and Cade lost the paper route.

"Yes, I heard about it after he left," she said to Mandy.

"Well . . . he was in Washington with me. My husband and son were away at scout camp. It was the perfect time for him to come."

"Oh."

Is she expecting me to say how wonderful when all I feel like doing is screaming and then throwing up?

"Where did Jared stay?" She knew it was a dumb question.

"With me. It worked out great," Mandy said.

Alyson drew in an audible breath, implications filling her mind.

Mandy continued talking as if she read Alyson's thoughts. "Nothing happened between us, Alyson," her voice trailed off. She laughed nervously before finishing the sentence. "Well—except one morning I was in the shower and Jared surprised me by getting in, too—but we didn't do anything."

A slow burn started at Alyson's feet and crept up her whole body. She and Jared were still legally married.

Mandy went on, "I never got completely over him, and I realized that even more when I saw him again."

Alyson knew Jared's magnetic personality well.

"What about your husband?" she asked. "Does he know about all of this?"

Mandy's answer surprised her. "Yes, I've told him. I don't know if I can stay with him. He's a wreck over the situation. We have been married almost as long as you and Jared. Like I already said, I never got over my feelings for Jared. He was my first love. Over the years I've thought about him, wondering how he was, what he was doing, and how it might have been if we had gotten married."

"Has he told you why we're getting a divorce? I'm not sure he's capable of being faithful to any one woman." Alyson couldn't figure out why Mandy thought it would be any different with her.

"He told me some of your problems, mainly that you were wrong for each other. He admitted he hadn't gotten over me, either. When he was here, he showed me pictures of your house, your cars, and the airplane. He must really be doing well."

That made no sense. Why would she be envious of their small starter-home and their cars, although paid for, were old.

"Jared doesn't have an airplane, Mandy," Alyson told her.

"What do you mean?" she asked with hesitation. "In one of the pictures, he was standing in front of it. It was white, with a blue stripe down the side. Isn't that his plane?"

"I'm telling you, he doesn't own an airplane. When he flies clients, he rents a plane by the hour from a flight service downtown off of Merrill Field."

"I don't believe it! Do you drive a gray Toyota Forerunner and does your two-story house have a big yard surrounded by lots of trees?" Mandy asked, trying to hang on to some level of hope.

"You described my parents' house and one of their cars." In a softer voice Alyson added, "I guess he's been lying to you, too." An awkward silence filled the distance between them. Jared's dishonesty was too familiar.

"I can't talk anymore," Alyson said. "I need to be somewhere in about twenty minutes."

Mandy was probably reeling from disbelief and frustration. How could Alyson help her feel better when Mandy was talking about a relationship with a man who was still Alyson's husband? It was flawed logic. She was overwhelmed herself from dealing with the lies he told her—the ones about Mandy for example.

Alyson ended the call. She'd had enough.

The next time she saw Jared was when he picked the boys up for the weekend. She casually mentioned Mandy had called her.

His eyes widened, and his face flushed.

"Why did you show her pictures of my parents' home and car, pretending they were ours?"

He had a hard time meeting her questioning gaze.

"You told her they weren't?" he asked, his face heightening even more in color.

"Did you think I would lie for you, Jared? Why did you tell her you had your own airplane?"

"I did . . ." he said.

It was Alyson's turn to look startled.

". . . for about a month. I used the cash I got from the second mortgage to buy it."

"You're kidding me, right? You bought an airplane and forgot to tell me about it? Were you ever going to mention it?" She was incredulous.

"Alyson, there were times I wanted to show you and take you flying. How could I all of the sudden bring it up? It wouldn't have worked to casually mention it during dinner, right after I asked you to pass the salt or something." His mouth turned upward slightly.

"As more time went by, it would have been even harder to explain—I had to sell it. I couldn't afford the tie-down fees, the gas, and insurance. It's not that great to finally get something you've always wanted and not be able to talk about it or share it with friends and family."

She shook her head in disbelief. "Jared, you really had an airplane?" She imagined how he must have felt.

His face relaxed considerably, and he smiled widely. "Yeah. It was a really nice, too. Well, I've got to go—see you later." He walked out the front door toward the car where the boys had been waiting. Alyson waved to them through the window and blew four kisses. Five minutes later she left to join a friend for dinner, her countenance lighter.

Mandy called Alyson two more times the next week and was on the phone again Saturday morning. Every time Alyson talked with her she felt drained.

"Hi, Alyson. This is Mandy."

"Hi . . ."

Why does she keep calling me?

"Did Jared tell you he has the church court tomorrow?"

"Yeah, he did." Alyson was anxious to have it over so she could stop worrying about what would happen.

"Do you think he'll tell them everything?" Mandy asked her. "I told him he needed to."

She hadn't given that a lot of thought. "I don't know. Hopefully he will—otherwise, what's the point?"

"I agree," Mandy said, then hesitated. "Alyson, I told my husband I wouldn't talk to Jared anymore so we could work on our marriage, but I've been calling him after everyone leaves the house. I don't know what to do. It's like he has this hold over me, and I can't stop thinking about wanting to be with him. Other times, I tell myself getting involved with him again would be a huge mistake." She sighed.

Alyson didn't get it. "How can you think of trusting him, Mandy? He cheated on me. What makes you think he wouldn't do it to you, eventually?"

She responded unconcerned. "Oh, we've talked about all the other women he has been with, but he says that since I was the first one, no one else ever measured up. That's why he said he wants me back."

Alyson's throat tightened, blocking any immediate response. "You and Jared slept together?" she asked, nearly choking.

"Yes." Mandy sounded indifferent.

Her words chilled Alyson like frozen water.

Mandy went on. "You probably know how he and I met on his mission. We were attracted to each other but were only friends. His companion told the mission president we were more than that. The mission president talked with Jared. He didn't believe nothing happened. He sent Jared to another mission—he only stayed a few days, angry over how he had been treated."

Her story matched Jared's, so far.

"He wanted us to spend time together before he went home, so he came back to Utah to my grandmother's house. We spent four days together and that's when it happened, several times. When he left for Alaska we were talking about getting married. We wrote letters back and forth and talked on the phone several times a week. All of a sudden something changed. I never knew what. Jared stopped writing. He wouldn't answer my letters or return my phone calls. After several weeks, I knew it was over. My heart was broken. Eventually, I heard he was marrying you."

Alyson hurt for herself and for Mandy as a young girl, who had lost her virtue and her heart to the same man who had broken her own. Jared had left out a major part of the story when he told it to her—their marriage started with a lie. He told her he was morally clean—a virgin—and how well he played it on their wedding night. The whole time it was an act. She felt stupid and used. Did he laugh inside at her innocence and trust? Would this nightmare never end?

Mandy continued, "Jared told me how Tara broke his heart, his relationship with Lisa, and about Kristine. He said you found Kristine's letters describing their weekend fling, but he convinced you it hadn't happened—he said she meant nothing to him anyway."

The new information slammed into Alyson. Luckily she was already sitting down.

"He also told me why he went to NiteShades. If he and I get back together, I promised him he would never have to go to a place like that to get what he needed."

Disbelief gripped Alyson's thoughts. Mandy had recited Jared's indiscretions as if she was reading off a grocery list, crossing things off as she went. Why did she have to hear all of this from her? She asked Jared more than once to tell her the truth—like the saying goes, the wife is always the last to know.

She had no idea what had been real in their marriage or what he had lied to her about. She could feel herself sinking in cold, wet blackness. She had to make it stop. What good would it do to go back there and be crushed again with pain? She had to calm down and be rational. She could let her anger become all-consuming, but it wouldn't change what happened. The divorce would be final soon, and she didn't want to live her life with a heavy, constricting chain of resentment around her neck, choking everything she was.

She could argue with Mandy for hours and defend herself, but she already knew in her heart what the truth was. God knew how hard she had tried to make her marriage with Jared work. She had to let it go and leave it in God's hands. He would continue giving her the strength she needed.

She found her voice. "Be careful, Mandy. If you want Jared, that's your choice. It's completely over between us, but I hope you don't get hurt again. I'm trying to move on with my life and whatever you and he work out is between the two of you. I need to go."

"I understand, Alyson. I hope things work out for you and the boys. I'm sorry. Thanks for listening. Your perspective has helped me more than you know. I have to make up my mind. Good-bye."

Alyson hung up the phone and fell to her knees, desperately needing the comfort and reassurance of prayer.

Chapter Sixteen

"Let all bitterness, and wrath, and anger, and clamor, and evil speaking, be put away from you, with all malice: And be ye kind one to another, tenderhearted, forgiving one another, even as God for Christ's sake hath forgiven you."[17]

A few days later Alyson was reading Jayden a story about trucks when the phone rang. He scooted off her lap so she could stand up. "We'll finish the rest of it in a few minutes, okay? You save our place."

"Hello, Alyson." It was Jared.

"Hi, how are you?" she asked, sensing immediately something different about him.

"The church court was this morning. It's all over. I told you I would call."

"Really?" She felt anxious. "How did it go?"

"I was excommunicated," he said soberly.

That was what she had been expecting. "I'm sorry, Jared."

"Alyson, there was so much love in that room that it overwhelmed me. It was humiliating to stand before all those men, neatly dressed in white shirts, suits, and ties and say out loud all the things I did wrong. But I did and I confessed everything. Those men listened to me quietly, not with eyes filled with judgment like I had feared, but with compassion, even tears. It was amazing. Once I got it all out, the huge burden I have been carrying around for so many years was gone. All the mistakes I had made became crystal clear, and the guilt and sorrow hit me full force."

Alyson's heart ached from his words.

Jared went on. "In the Bible, Luke 11:24–25, is a story about a man possessed with an evil spirit. The Lord cast the evil spirit out, but it sought for another place to dwell. When it couldn't find one, it came back to the man, but the evil spirit found the house swept and put in order.

"It's been more than twenty years since I started looking at pornography and because I did, I let Satan's influence in, just like the man in the scriptures did. Pornography and lying has ruined my life in so many ways."

Jared's confession was as stark in Alyson's mind as a flash of white lightning in a coal black sky. She started to cry.

"If I had any idea from the first picture I saw—the hold it was going to have over me—what it would do—I would have run as fast and as far away as I could possibly get. I've tried over and over and over to stop, and when I confessed everything, I put that burden at the Lord's feet and swept my house clean. He is the only way I can ever be free." Jared's voice cracked. "I am so sorry, Alyson, for how I have hurt you and for what I have done to our boys . . ." He struggled to stay composed. "I have destroyed our marriage and torn apart our family—but I understand why it has to be this way. I have to face the consequences of what I've done. I don't even know who I am and I need to find out—I've been making wrong choices for so long. This morning, I literally felt the arms of our Savior, Jesus Christ, around me. Never in my entire life have I felt anything like that. I know without a doubt He loves me. The feeling was so strong that it's hard to find words to describe it. When I drove away from the church, I felt stronger and more at peace than I have for years and years."

The emotion Alyson heard in his voice tugged at her heart. If only he could have been honest with her in the beginning of their marriage, things might have turned out completely different.

"Jared, I'm proud of you for having the courage to do the right thing I can only imagine how hard it was." She waited. "Mandy called me again and told me about the two of you and the truth about Kristine and the others. Why wasn't I ever enough for you, Jared?"

An awkward silence descended.

Jared took a deep breath and let it slowly escape. "Alyson—I'm sorry. It wasn't about you. I kept looking for someone to love me and after awhile I messed up so many times it didn't seem to matter what I did. I always felt guilty, especially at night, and sometimes when I looked at you I couldn't deal with it except by trying not to care. It hurt too much."

"I always loved you, Jared. Why couldn't you see that?" Alyson asked him.

He didn't say anything.

"You told Mandy you wanted to marry her. Why did you ask me?" she questioned him.

He breathed in again. "After I came home from my mission, it was different. I could date anybody I wanted and there were a lot of pretty girls. Mandy was so far away, the attraction for her faded, and she was a huge reminder of the way my mission ended. When I first met you—so young and pretty—everyone that knew you said you were a good girl, a nice girl. I felt proud to have you on my arm wherever we went, and I wanted people to believe I was the same kind of person because you were with me."

Alyson wasn't sure if his comments should make her feel flattered or used.

"What was it I always told you? You make me smile my biggest smile, was that it?"

"Something like that," she replied. It hurt to remember.

Jared continued, "Because you were young, I think it was easier to convince you what a great guy I was. When I proposed and you said yes, I wanted to forget the mistakes I had made before I met you and start a new life together. I told myself after a few minutes inside the temple on our wedding day, everything would be okay.

"I tried to stay away from pornography. The times in our marriage when I succeeded were good times. I felt happy and we were closer, but it didn't last. I pushed you away because of the guilt; I didn't feel worthy of your love. I thought something was wrong with me. The cycle kept repeating and we both were caught in it. I thought real love would come with approval, recognition, popularity, or from adoring women. I couldn't see that repentance and the Savior were the only way. I thought I had messed up so many times that I was already lost, and I didn't think it mattered anymore what I did. It became easier to give in to worse temptations— like going to the prostitute."

Alyson cringed.

"That created even more guilt—I hated myself. Then I did it again—to stop the pain. I know it doesn't make any sense."

She felt her heart break all over again. "I always loved you, Jared—why couldn't you see that? You ended up destroying the very thing you wanted but thought you hadn't found."

In the second week of September, the official, signed papers from the judge arrived in the mail. Alyson's marriage to Jared was over. Looking at them hurt more than she expected. She was a divorced, single mother.

Her emotions had gone through a torrential storm. There were moments when pouring rain submerged her so quickly her breath came in gasps, until a break in the clouds gave her temporary respite, only to be met suddenly with another downpour, flooding everything around. The cold runoff left her shaking.

She assumed she would feel relief when the papers went through, knowing she could rebuild her life, but she felt a bittersweet pain that tore a fresh wound in her fragile heart. She knew she had made the right decision to end her marriage, and her family was blessed, yet the hurt overwhelmed her again.

Over the next several weeks, sadness hit her in waves as she mourned the death of her marriage. The peaks could be so overwhelming at times that Alyson felt she couldn't stand the pain or loneliness one more minute. She prayed for help as many times a day as it took to keep from falling apart.

Some of the hardest times were missing the day-to-day things. Jared wasn't there to share something funny one of the boys did or said and laugh with her. He wasn't home every night for dinner to appreciate her cooking and talk about the day—his spot at the table was permanently empty. He wasn't there to keep her feet warm in bed—they were always cold. He wasn't there to go to the kitchen with her for a midnight snack, and he wasn't there to hold her hand during church. The everyday sharing of adult companionship she had enjoyed for so many years was gone.

At the end of September, Jared, was hired by a regional airline in Barrow, the northernmost town in the state. His dream was finally coming true. Alyson was sincerely happy for him; her only apprehension was knowing the responsibility of their children would rest more heavily on her shoulders. However, Jared's absence ended up being a blessing in disguise for her emotional healing.

She decided to homeschool Cade that fall for fifth grade. Part of the program included the loan of a brand new computer to use at home.

Chapter Seventeen

"*Humble yourselves in the sight of the Lord, and he shall lift you up.*"[18]

October 1998

The fast approaching winter lent a bite to the early October air. Alyson was glad to be inside her cozy bedroom. It was late and she had on her favorite satin nightgown, lined with warm flannel, and soft-gray slippers. Her bedroom was dark. She was sitting in front of the computer because she couldn't go to sleep.

She wanted to check out some websites a friend had told her about. When she started surfing, something caught her eye. She came across a few dating sites to meet other members of her church. It piqued her curiosity. One of the sites advertised finding a pen pal, a new friend, a prospective date, or, for the serious romantics at heart, a possible love interest for the future. It made her wonder what she was looking for.

She couldn't imagine becoming involved in a serious relationship so soon after her divorce, but she liked the idea of a getting a male perspective from someone who would understand her situation. Alyson registered for the site, logged on, and began reading some of the posted letters.

She had heard about the new trend of Internet dating but wondered if there truly were happy endings. She scrolled through many pages of letters, narrowing her focus to a specific age range of men. Different impressions went through her mind. As she read several posts, a few sounded possibly interesting until one in particular caught her eye. When she read the words she got a warm feeling. The description of what the man was looking for in a woman gave her goose bumps.

The letter said:

Andrew (divorced, thirty-something) Posted March 1998
United States: Salt Lake City, Utah
Looking for: Pen Pal, Sister, Friend, Dating Connection, (All)

I am 6'0', 170 lbs, brown hair, and blue eyes with an active and easygoing personality. I enjoy keeping physically and mentally fit and being with others who feel the same. Those in their twenties or early thirties provide mutual attraction.

I am proud to be the father of two wonderful children, ages four and nine, who are happy, bright, and energetic. They have asked for someone nice to kids that will love them always, not leave all the time and, preferably, someone pretty.

I ultimately seek someone who is able and willing to place God, spouse, and children first in her life. In return I promise complete fidelity within marriage, frequent hugs, a compassionate ear, and to remember her birthday, anniversary, and Christmas. I want her to be my best friend and lead our family with me.

I would be happy to exchange photos with you. Please write me at beardad@bigfoot.com.

Alyson decided to write him. A nervous energy urged her forward as her fingers began to move across the keyboard. A rough draft emerged fairly easily, but she didn't send it until she did some rewriting.

Date: Wednesday, 7 Oct 1998, 10:41 PM AKST
Subject: A new adventure

Dear Andrew,

Hello! Yes, you could say this is a new adventure, writing to a stranger via email, but why not? Life is a series of new experiences, right? I came across your message tonight, and it touched my heart when I read it.

I live in Anchorage, Alaska and have recently gone through a difficult divorce myself. That is something I never planned or wanted in my life.

I was touched by your description of what you are seeking in a future wife because those standards are my own, and I say that with sincerity. But, to be honest, I am only looking for a friend.

Our church is, as you know, family-oriented and being a single, divorced mother certainly doesn't fit the mold. Things get difficult dealing with my own emotions and those of my boys.

Now for a bit about myself—I am 5'5", 32 years-old, with blue-green eyes and auburn hair a few inches past my shoulder.

I have many interests, including musical pursuits of piano and singing. I love to read, cook, tole paint, and do interior decorating and crafts. I enjoy drama or mystery movies, eating out, long walks, and listening to jazz, classic, pop, and some country music.

I have four boys, I know—WOW! Their ages are 13, 10, 3, and 1. They keep me busy, but are such a blessing in my life. I have been lucky and have never have had to work outside the home as my ex's and my own priorities were the same—day-care wasn't an option for our children even if it meant living on a tight budget.

How have your kids dealt with the divorce?

It's been the hardest on my three year-old. He doesn't understand like his older brothers. It has been challenging trying to deal with him, just like so many things in my life right now.

Yet, things are getting better. Time really helps, and I have felt a lot of love and support from people close to me.

Do your kids see their mom a lot?

I have full custody and my ex just got a new job flying in the Bush, so the boys won't be seeing him as much as they had been—another challenging adjustment. Divorce is so unfair to kids.

Well, I wasn't planning on this being so long. It would be nice to get a male perspective on things and you have my email address if you want to write back. Have a great day!

Sincerely,

Alyson

By the time she finished writing, it was close to midnight. Responding to Andrew's letter had taken her way out of her comfort zone. The Website contained pages and pages of posts, and over the next few days she responded to a few more but Andrew's was the only one she read that gave her a special feeling.

She checked her email inbox daily for a response, wondering if she would even get one and she drove herself nutty by analyzing everything she had written.

Then . . . he answered. Alyson's stomach filled with butterflies when she clicked on the mail icon and began to read:

Date: Saturday, 10 October 1998, 3:44 PM MST
Subject: Re: A new adventure

Your letter has intrigued me since it arrived and I have reflected upon it frequently. I apologize for not writing sooner; it left me not knowing how to reply. First, thank you so much for your kind words. I was moved when you described how you felt and hope that in some way I could be a blessing in your lives.

My marriage lasted (legally) for over twelve years. I worked to keep my marriage intact but she made a different choice. The children, especially my daughter (I attached a photo), have had a lot of difficulty with the events and still have many questions which I cannot answer without disparaging their mother; they will have to wait to understand in the future.

I try to establish some order in their lives, give lots of hugs, and create as much opportunity as possible to give them control of theirs. I have found that they will frequently place their hand on mine just to know that I am there for them.

Now a bit on the lighter side…

You sound beautiful! I would love to see your eyes. You also appear to have a great number of talents; your children will benefit greatly from your efforts with them. I think it is great you have chosen to remain home with them; my ex would not.

The children are officially with their mother about half of the time; about half of that they are sent to sitters in the evenings.

We are currently in the process of adjusting our time together upwards.

They often do enjoy time with her when she chooses to spend time with them.

I would love to hear back from you.

Have a wonderful evening,

Andrew

Adjusting the mouse, Alyson clicked on the attachment and watched a picture of an adorable little girl fill the monitor screen. Her big eyes were blue and golden brown curls framed her face. Alyson's eyes started to water as she looked at the picture, a strong emotion of longing touched her heart. She had always wanted a daughter, and Andrew's was adorable.

His email had been wonderful and she appreciated the compliments he had given her. But she was wary, wondering if the words were sincere, especially the part when he said she sounded beautiful.

He has never seen me. How can he say that?

Her past experiences with Jared left her cynical toward flattering words given easily away. She couldn't deal with that again. She thought about the way she first felt when reading his post and because of that, decided to write him back and see how things went. She might have misread something; and besides, she was lonely. His next response came faster this time.

Date: Sunday, 11 October 1998, 5:18 PM MST
Subject: A kinship

Hi Alyson,

Thank you for your wonderful letter. I composed a well-thought-out letter to share with you and went to attach a photo and it died prior to getting to you. I will try again, a little more succinctly, to share it with you . . .

Alyson's first fears about his compliments faded into the background as they continued to write back and forth. She, too, felt a connection with him. He seemed to personally understand what she had been through. Her days stayed hectic, filled with the children and adjustments she was dealing with, but the emails from Andrew gave her something to look forward to. They added brightness to her days.

They exchanged pictures with one of their letters. Alyson watched his download on her screen and became momentarily breathless. She saw a clean-cut, handsome man with gorgeous blue eyes, wearing a suit and tie with an arm around each of his children. They were all smiling and sitting close together in front of bushy green trees with sunlight filtering through the leaves, and below in the grass were tiny scattered orange flowers.

For some reason, Andrew told her he wasn't able to open the pictures she sent. His emails were warm, open, and interlaced with humor. His confident personality and the great love he had for his children was apparent in his words.

He and Alyson shared things about themselves, past marriages, heartaches, extended family ties, and experiences from their childhood. She didn't think the relationship would ever be more than a friendship since they lived over two thousand miles apart.

Chapter Eighteen

"Trust in the Lord with all thine heart; and lean not unto thine own understanding. In all thy ways acknowledge him, and he shall direct thy paths."[19]

Alyson wasn't sure at first how she felt about the idea. Her friend, Caren, had invited her to come on a trip with her in November, only a few weeks away. She was going to Lawrence, Kansas to see her parents who were serving a church mission at the Haskell Indian Nations University. Caren was bringing her two youngest children and planned to do some sightseeing in Missouri and Illinois. She had a free companion ticket and thought it would be even more fun if Alyson came along.

Alyson was torn. It sounded tempting; however, she was concerned about leaving her boys for over a week after everything they had been through in the recent months, and Alex was only a little over a year old. She mentioned Caren's offer to her mom the next time they talked on the phone. Elizabeth volunteered readily to take care of the boys. She agreed Alyson needed a break, and some fun. That was the final encouragement she needed. She would go.

One afternoon, a week later, Caren was talking to her on the phone about the trip and going over the itinerary. "Mark these dates on your calendar, Alyson. On the flight down there is a layover in Salt Lake City and from there we go on to Kansas, arriving mid-evening. Oh, can you hang on?" Caren said.

"Sure—no problem," Alyson replied

"I have to go check on one thing," Caren explained.

When Alyson heard Caren say Salt Lake City, the words had jumped out at her. That city had taken on a new meaning for her in the past few weeks. She began to wonder . . .

"All right, I'm back," Caren said, interrupting her daydreaming just as it started. "I had to double check one of the times . . . Where were we?" she asked.

"Caren, I want to tell you something first," Alyson began hesitantly. She hadn't talked to anyone about Andrew yet.

"Sure, what's up?" Caren got quiet.

"I haven't told you, but I've been writing to a man who lives in Salt Lake City for almost a month. I met him online and—"

Caren interrupted her. "Really? He lives in Salt Lake?" she asked.

"He does." Alyson sighed. "It would be so neat if we could meet in person. I can't believe we're flying through Salt Lake." Her mind raced full speed ahead. "Caren—do you think it would be possible for me to leave on an earlier flight with the way the tickets are set up?" She felt like crossing her fingers and her toes.

"I would think it could be adjusted if the earlier flight had room. I'll check with the airlines and see what I can find out." She stopped. "Do you really like this guy, Alyson?"

"Oh . . . I think so . . . I don't know. I hardly know him. We haven't been writing for very long. When I first came across his letter I had this feeling. He's divorced with two children and has gone through some of the same experiences I have. It's been great getting his perspective on things. I don't know for sure if he would even want to meet me." She started twisting a long strand of her hair around the fingers of her free hand.

"Alyson, that's exciting! I'll call you back as soon as I find out, okay?" Caren replied enthusiastically.

"Thanks Caren, that sounds great." Alyson hung up the phone thinking of the possibility of meeting Andrew in person. It gave her goose bumps.

She had promised Cade she would make chocolate chip cookies today and had been assembling the ingredients when Caren first called. She picked up where she left off, getting the eggs and butter out of the refrigerator, and the vanilla and chocolate chips from the cupboard. She already had the dry ingredients measured and sifted together. The dough was made, and she was putting the first pan of cookies into the preheated oven when the phone rang.

"Hi, Alyson," Caren said cheerfully. "Good news! I talked to the airline, and everything is worked out. You leave the night before on the redeye flight out of Anchorage and arrive in Salt Lake City by seven forty-five. Our flight to Kansas doesn't leave Salt Lake until four-thirty that afternoon. You will have almost a whole day to spend with Andrew."

"Really? Are there any extra charges?" Alyson said, holding her breath.

"No, none at all. They didn't give me any hassles, either." Caren replied.

"Good, I was a little worried; I'm surprised it was so easy. Now I have to find out if Andrew even wants me to come." Maybe it wasn't safe to get too excited—yet. The timer went off for the cookies. "Caren, I have to run; thanks again and I'll call you later."

She sent Andrew an email that night about the trip asking if he would be interested in spending the day with her in two weeks.

Date: Saturday, 24 October 1998, 5:27 AM MST
Subject: Two weeks and counting

Alyson,

Definitely, come on down! Sounds great; I was beginning to wonder if we would ever meet in person. Because of a trade for Halloween, it appears that I might be able to choose whether the children are with us or not. If they are not, we could speak more freely, and there are additional things we could do. On the other hand, I am sure they would enjoy meeting you, and perhaps vice-versa? Both are good options; you tell me which you would prefer that day.

Two weeks and counting,

Andrew

Andrew called Alyson on the phone the following Sunday afternoon. After discussing the pros and cons regarding his children coming or not, they decided on a compromise. They would spend a few hours with them in the morning and the rest of the time alone.

The day of her departure came closer, and Alyson grew more nervous.

Andrew was basically a stranger. What if he wasn't the person he portrayed? It couldn't hurt to double check. She would be spending the whole day with him. In one of his emails, he mentioned the name of his parents and the name of the area where they lived—Alyson tracked down their phone number.

She wasn't excited to call but decided a few minutes of discomfort on the telephone was a small sacrifice to stay safe. She took a few deep breaths and dialed. A woman with a German accent answered the phone.

"Hello?" she said.

"Hello, is this Elyse?"

"Yes, it is, who is this?" she sounded uncertain.

"My name is Alyson; I live in Alaska and have been writing online to your son, Andrew." She made herself talk more slowly. "I'm coming to Salt Lake in a few weeks to spend the day with him. Since I don't know him really well, I wanted to ask you a couple of questions."

"Oh, okay. That sounds like a good idea." Her voice held surprise. "What would you like to know?"

Alyson decided one question would cover everything. "Is Andrew honest?" she asked her.

Elyse did not hesitate. "Oh, yes. You don't have to worry about Andrew. He's a good guy and is just looking for a wife!"

The openness of her last words left Alyson momentarily speechless and even more anxious to end the call. "Oh?" she said. "Well, thank you for talking with me . . . have a good day."

"You are welcome. I hope you have a nice trip. If you and Andrew have time when you're here, we would love to meet you," she added.

"Okay—thank you, again." Alyson felt a lot better when she hung up the telephone, certain Andrew's mother would have leveled with her if she needed to be concerned regarding her son.

She mentioned the call to Andrew the next time they talked. He responded with silence. It became uncomfortable, and she started to wonder if he was upset.

"You called my mother?" He did sound a bit irritated. "How did you get her phone number?" he asked.

The tone of his voice caused her to feel defensive. "I did. I wanted to make sure I was doing the right thing meeting you and spending the whole day together. We don't know each other very well, and I needed reassurance it would be safe. Too many scary things happen nowadays," she said.

His voice relaxed. "You're right. That probably was a good idea. You're the first girl to call my mother to check up on me," he said, laughing.

The tension was gone.

Andrew continued, "All right, I'm curious. What did my mother say about me?"

Alyson was tempted to make something up, but she didn't. "The only question I ended up asking her was if you were honest. She said I didn't have to worry about you because you were a good guy—just looking for a wife," she explained.

He laughed again, louder this time. "I guess that's true."

Chapter Nineteen

"Only if you have been in the deepest valley, can you ever know how magnificent it is to be on the highest mountain."[20]

The day Alyson was leaving arrived. After her mom left with the boys, so did most of the distractions. Her packing went much faster. Her flight out of Anchorage left at midnight. As soon as she finished, she tried to get some sleep.

She ended up spending the next hour tossing and turning in her bed and must have adjusted her pillow at least ten times. Reading didn't help. Eventually she decided she was too excited and nervous to get any rest and might as well get up. She showered, dressed, did her hair and makeup and it still was at least an hour before it was time to leave. She walked around the house, absently straightening up anything that looked the tiniest bit out of place. That used up another fifteen minutes.

She played a few songs on the piano, checked to see what was on TV, and ate a granola bar, checking her watch about every five minutes. She brushed her teeth in the bathroom, rinsed out the sink, wiped off the counter, and then walked into Ryker and Alex's room. She picked up a pair of dirty socks off the floor and a book that was partially sticking out from underneath the crib. She even spent five minutes rearranging their stuffed animals—she never did that.

Finally it was time to go. She took her suitcase and carry-on downstairs to the front door, turned all the lights off, and double-checked the locks.

When her brother Michael pulled in the driveway to pick her up, she felt like shouting "hallelujah!"

Her flight wasn't crowded. After takeoff, a few overhead lights stayed on, illuminating a handful of people reading or talking softly. The majority of the passengers slept with their seats reclined. She fell asleep during the second half of the flight until the early morning light streamed through the small oval windows of the plane and woke her up.

When the large 727 aircraft touched the ground at Salt Lake City International Airport on schedule and taxied to the arrival gate, she wanted to clap her hands and shout hooray—almost. The captain welcomed the passengers, giving a brief local weather forecast as well as the current time. Once he turned off the "fasten seat belt" sign, the center aisle quickly filled with disembarking passengers. The volume of noise increased significantly from chattering voices, clicking overhead storage bins, and the bustle of carry-on luggage being reorganized and moved.

Alyson read a magazine, waiting to leave her seat until the aisles became less crowded. Once they were clear, she gathered her belongings and exited the plane. Despite the early morning hour, the terminal was filled with crowds of people. She scanned the faces around her searching for Andrew, hoping she would recognize him easily from the pictures he sent. She didn't see him right away. Off to her right she noticed two children looking through the large windows at the incoming and outgoing tarmac traffic. Alyson was certain they were Andrew's children.

She approached the young girl first, noticing her sleepy eyes and tousled brown hair.

"Hi." Alyson smiled. "Is your name Kate?"

"Yes," she said.

"Where is your dad?"

"He's right over there." She turned her head one direction.

Alyson looked and saw him walking toward her, he had watched the whole exchange. Andrew looked exactly like his picture except his blue eyes were more prominent in person. He had a muscular build, and was wearing a navy blue silk shirt and loose-fitting Levi's. "Alyson!" he exclaimed. "You made it. How was your flight?"

"Hi, Andrew," she said, extending her hand. "It's great to finally meet you in person. I already met your daughter, and this is Eric, right?" Her gaze shifted to the young blue-eyed boy with light brown hair standing next to his dad.

He nodded, his eyes studying Alyson's face and hair before glancing over the rest of her. She was wearing a pale yellow sweater and jeans.

"Remember the JPG pictures you sent me of you?"

"Yeah. You said you were going to work on them and never said anything later. I assumed you eventually got them open."

"Well," he laughed, "I never could."

Her eyes widened. "You're kidding me, right?" she exclaimed. "You never saw them?"

"No, I never did."

She couldn't believe it.

"You still wanted to meet me? I'm not sure if I could have done that."

Andrew's response was honest.

"I thought about that. The guys at work gave me a hard time about what you might look like, but I figured if you weren't my type or I wasn't attracted at all we could still spend the day together and let it end there." He sighed. "Okay, if you really want to know," he said teasingly, "had you ended up being four hundred pounds with lots of facial hair and only two teeth, the kids and I were going to meet back at the car for a quick getaway!"

Alyson laughed, shaking her head. She was impressed with him even more. Once the humor of his words faded, their eyes locked. She looked away first.

"Are you hungry?" Andrew asked her. "Would you like to go get some breakfast?"

She was hungry. "That sounds great." His eyes were so blue, she could get lost in them.

Andrew reached for the carry-on bag she had on her shoulder and placed it on his own.

"Thanks," she told him, smiling. They left the gate area and got on the slow-moving escalator toward the parking garage.

Alyson suddenly felt a small, warm hand in hers. She looked down, startled to see little fingers touching her red polished nails.

"I like your nails," five-year-old Eric said. "Did you get to watch a movie on the airplane? What did you have to eat? I just got my school pictures back, and they're in my dad's car. Do you want to see them?"

Alyson thought he was so cute. "No, there wasn't a movie on the airplane, and they fed us peanuts, something to drink, and a sandwich. And I would love to see your pictures, Eric." She looked down at his upturned face and smiled. Looking up again, she noticed a startled expression cross Andrew's face as he watched his son interacting with her.

They reached the end of the escalator and went through the automatic exit doors. It took a few minutes to locate where he had parked the car. Kate ended up being the first to spot the midnight blue Daytona. Andrew put Alyson's suitcase and carry-on in the trunk and opened the front door for her. She got in, thanked him, and put on her seat belt. The kids climbed in the back.

Before they left the garage, Eric proudly thrust his school pictures under Alyson's nose. She opened the large white envelope with the cellophane window and pulled them out.

"Oh, Eric, you look so handsome!" she exclaimed. "I really like your shirt."

Eric beamed from ear to ear. "Do you want one?"

"Definitely, I would love one," she told him with a big smile. He made her miss her own boys.

Kate watched the two of them and rolled her eyes as if she couldn't believe how annoying her brother was being. She yawned and looked out the window.

Traffic was light on a Saturday. Andrew turned into the parking lot of a Village Inn restaurant southeast of downtown and turned off the car.

"Alyson," Kate said, seeming much more awake, "we are really close to my school." She pointed past the restaurant. "It's on that street over there."

"It is?" Alyson moved her head and looked. "What do you like best about school, Kate?"

Eric piped up, "I like recess."

"She wasn't asking you, Eric." Kate sighed and shook her head. Then she smiled and answered Alyson.

"I love school, but I'm not sure what I like best. My teacher is really nice and so are my friends. Sometimes my dad comes to my class and teaches. A few weeks ago he told us about early Roman architecture—we've been studying about ancient Rome."

She sounded more grown up to Alyson than just nine.

Kate looked at her dad and smiled. "Right, Dad?"

Alyson's eyebrows rose. "Really?" she was impressed. She watched Kate look at Andrew. It was easy to tell they were very close. "Sounds like you have a smart dad," she told her.

"Yep, he's always teaching me lots of stuff. We're best friends," she said matter-of-factly.

"You're lucky to have such a good best friend, Kate."

Eric piped up, "Can we go get some breakfast—I'm starving?"

"Sure, let's go, guys," Andrew said. "I could use some breakfast myself." He got out and walked around to open Alyson's door. By the time he pulled the handle, Kate and Eric had already jumped out, heading eagerly to the entrance of the restaurant.

Inside they were seated within minutes. Then they were handed menus and four glasses of ice water were brought to the table. The conversation dwindled while everyone looked at the menus trying to decide what to get. The pictures made everything look good.

A waitress with blond hair clipped back in a ponytail and a friendly smile came to the table a few minutes later. She took everyone's orders and said their food would be out promptly. Kate and Eric started coloring the pictures on the kids' menus while they waited.

When the food arrived, Kate softly said a blessing and they started to eat. She and Eric were energetic and talkative throughout the meal, but well-mannered.

Alyson enjoyed watching Andrew interact with them, his love apparent. In half an hour everyone had finished eating. Andrew paid the check up front at the cash register and when he came back, Alyson thanked him for breakfast.

"You're welcome. Did you enjoy it?" Andrew asked.

"It was really good. I love French toast made from cinnamon-raisin bread. Thanks, it hit the spot."

"My omelet was good, too. Kate, Eric, are you ready to go?" They nodded and stood up. On the way to the car, Eric held Alyson's hand again.

"Thank you, Dad," they told him.

Before they left the parking lot, Alyson said, "I brought you each a little gift from Alaska. Whenever my parents went on trips, I always loved it when they brought me something."

Eric's eyes lit up at the mention of a gift. Kate's did, too, but she tried to be more subtle. Kate was closest, so Alyson handed hers to her first. It was a little, clear globe with a small Eskimo girl inside wearing a white parka. When shaken, it looked like snow was falling on her. Alyson gave Eric a book with bright pictures about a young sea otter that became lost.

"Thank you, Alyson," they both said.

"You're both very welcome. Andrew, I have something for you, too."

A look of surprise flashed across his face. She handed him a jar of homemade blueberry jam. It was a vibrant, deep blue. He turned the jar around on all sides.

"Ryker, Cade, and I picked the berries late August on Flat Top Mountain near Anchorage. My mom and I made the jam together. Do you like blueberries?" Alyson wanted to know.

"I love any kind of berries—I wasn't expecting anything for me, though. Thank you. I can hardly wait to try it." He turned the jar around again, looking at the jam before setting it on the seat.

"You're welcome. I hope you enjoy it."

"Don't worry; I definitely will." He started the car and headed downtown, past Temple Square. When Alyson saw the spires of the Salt Lake Temple rise up in front of her, she caught her breath. It was always such a beautiful sight. They continued east through The Avenues to a monument called Ensign Peak. Andrew talked about the history of the area.

The view of the city from their final vantage point was wonderful. Andrew showed Alyson the office building where he worked as they drove to drop off Kate and Eric in Rose Park. Their mom was at a play practice at a stake center there.

Alyson got out of the car with Andrew and his kids, but wasn't planning on going inside. "Kate and Eric," she said. "I enjoyed meeting you today. Thanks for sharing your dad with me. Can I give each of you a hug good-bye?"

They both nodded and thanked her again for the gifts.

"I'll be right back, Alyson" Andrew said. "Or did you want to come with us?"

She wasn't interested in meeting his ex-wife at the moment. She shook her head. "No, that's okay. I'll wait for you here."

"Okay, see you in a second," he said and smiled.

She watched them walk along the sidewalk to the front door of the church. Kate and Eric turned back to wave before going inside. She got back in the passenger side of the car, leaving her door open, and glanced around the front lawn and surrounding landscape. There wasn't any snow on the ground which seemed strange to her for November.

It wasn't very long until Andrew came bounding back to the car at a slow jog and got in next to her. He gave her a big smile, full of energy. "The kids are all taken care of. What would you like to do now?" he asked her.

Alyson smiled, excited to have him sitting next to her again. "I do need to pick up a few things I can't get in Anchorage. Could we head back downtown? Sorry, we were just there, huh?"

"That's not a problem, we aren't very far, and I would be glad to take you there."

She gave him an appreciative smile. "Thanks. That would be great."

Andrew parked on the street close to where they were going. He got out and went around the car to open Alyson's door. Once she got out, he locked the car and put enough change in the parking meter for an hour and a half.

It was a block from where they parked to the entrance of the building formerly known as Hotel Utah, originally built in 1911. When they entered the front lobby, Alyson's eyes were drawn upwards in the spacious multi-level foyer, with tall marble pillars in jade green. Classical music was being played on a black grand piano near the center and small groups of people talked or sat listening in the large open area.

Alyson needed to go to a specialty store on the lower level. They took the stairs instead of the elevator. Andrew showed her where the clothing section was at the back of the store.

"They should carry everything you need," he said.

"Great, thanks," she replied before starting to look around. She was looking for a specific kind of dress and the store carried several. She found a few that she liked in her size and was directed to a dressing room so she could try them on.

"If you need any different sizes, you let me know, and I'll be glad to help you, okay?" one of the sales clerks told her.

"Okay. Thank you." Alyson smiled and opened the door of the dressing room, hanging the dresses inside. She was about to shut the door when Andrew interjected.

"Alyson, you are going to come out and show me each dress after you have it on, right?"

"Uh . . . I hadn't planned on doing that, but I guess I could," she replied uncertainly.

"Of course you should, and then I can give you a guy's opinion on each one." He got comfortable on a chair outside the dressing room by the full-length mirrors.

Alyson was embarrassed to be the center of an unplanned fashion show, an activity she hadn't expected would be part of the day. She was glad Andrew's sense of humor kept the situation light and his comments about each dress ended up being helpful.

She wasn't sure about the size of one dress in particular. It fit a little loose, but she liked it more than the others and was concerned a smaller size would make it too tight. She decided to at least try one on to compare.

The clerk found her the other size and handed it over the dressing room door. She put the dress on and looked in the mirror. It fit perfectly. She came out of the dressing room for the last time to show it to Andrew.

"Oh, yeah, that fits you much better—you have a really small waist." His compliment made her blush.

"Thank you," she told him. After she had changed and made her purchase, they left downtown, heading north through Rose Park, past an industrial area, some open fields with grazing cows and horses, and several small towns that were close together.

Andrew left I-15 at the first of the two Kaysville exits, still driving north until he turned west into a well-kept neighborhood of large, stylish homes and neatly landscaped yards. He slowed the car to enter a private driveway, parked, and shut off the car.

"Whose house is this?" Alyson questioned. They hadn't talked about visiting anyone.

"My parents," he answered matter-of-factly.

"Oh." She immediately felt apprehensive. She had barely met Andrew and now she was meeting his parents. It was a bit overwhelming. "Why are we here?"

"Don't worry, we'll only stay for a few minutes. You don't mind, do you?"

Actually she did mind, but didn't tell him. She breathed in deeply to relax. "I guess that's okay, let's go."

Andrew knocked once before he opened the front door with his key.

He motioned to Alyson to go inside first, and he followed and shut the door. She looked around the interior of the beautifully decorated and immaculate home, thinking it belonged on pages of a *Better Homes and Garden* magazine. Every detail became etched in her mind.

On the left of the marbled entryway was a formal living room with a floral sofa facing two wing chairs and thick mauve carpeting bordered in cream. A lighted cherrywood curio graced one wall with collectible figurines and crystal inside. Long lace-paneled curtains at the window and several vases of roses accented the décor.

Past the room on the right was a long hallway next to a set of stairs going down. Toward the back of the house was a family room in burgundy, green, and cream with touches of navy. One side of the family room was open to a dining room with hard wood floors and a connecting kitchen on the opposite side with a tiled island in the center.

Grant, Andrew's dad was watching a football game in the family room. He was in a wheelchair. Alyson knew from Andrew's emails that Grant had been diagnosed many years earlier with Lou Gehrig's disease, also known as ALS. Andrew introduced him. Alyson could see the resemblance between them right away. She liked his dad immediately. His open friendliness put her at ease. She could see where Andrew got his sense of humor. The three of them talked for a few minutes.

Elyse, Andrew's mom, had been working on a grocery list in the kitchen. She stood up from the table when they came in. She was several inches taller than Alyson, with stylish, short blonde hair and blue eyes like her son. She greeted Alyson warmly, remembering their earlier conversation on the phone. She couldn't talk very long as she was leaving to go to the store.

After Elyse left, Alyson and Andrew went out to the backyard and garden. The perimeter was bordered with rose bushes, trees, and a variety of plants. On the south side was a wood-latticed pergola with a sign above saying "Grandma's Garden." Mountains loomed in the background.

"The view of the mountains is amazing. They look close enough to touch. With the sun coming through the scattered clouds and a light dusting of snow—it's gorgeous," Alyson said looking eastward.

Andrew's gaze followed hers. "Those are the Wasatch Mountains. That one," he pointed to the closest peak, "is Francis Peak. We went on family hikes there, growing up. I've taken my children a few times. You have lots of mountains in Alaska, don't you?"

"We do. I love the mountains. There are four mountain ranges around the city of Anchorage—Chugach, Kenai, Talkeetnas, and the Alaska Range. But where my house is there are no mountains as close as these."

"Do you like to hike?" Andrew asked, pulling out one of the wrought iron patio chairs from the matching table for her to sit on.

"Thanks," she said.

Andrew moved a chair out for himself and sat down.

Alyson got back to answering his question. "I do like to hike as long as the incline is gradual and the mosquitoes aren't too thick. I love weaving in and out of the forest or hiking along a river." She pushed her bangs out of her eyes.

"I like to hike, too, but didn't for a long time after I returned home from serving my mission in Chile. I was so sick of walking everywhere." His eyes became reflective.

"You served your mission in Chile? What was that like?" Alyson wanted to know.

"It was a great place to be and I learned a lot about the people, the culture, and the language. A few months before I came home, I lived in an apartment in Pichilemu with a shower outside—and no hot water whatsoever."

Alyson's eyebrows rose, "Outside, like where outside?"

"It was off to the side of the building, and there was a narrow shower door that hit a little below my knees and about mid-chest. At the time, the water that came out from the spigot was brown and the winds from the Andes mountains blew through the little town all winter long making it even chillier. It wasn't a good time—but you deal with it. In other areas we didn't have much food to eat and that wasn't easy either. I used to dream about food at night. Yet those are the kind of experiences that make you stronger and appreciative of what you have." He nodded his head up and down slowly. "It was good."

Being with Andrew felt right; it was comfortable. Alyson had a hard time realizing she was sitting there, far away from home with such a good-looking man she hadn't even known existed a month before.

The weather grew cooler despite the sun, and Alyson shivered.

"Are you cold?" Andrew asked her. He didn't have a coat on and he was probably getting cold.

"I am a little," she admitted.

"Do you want to go back inside?" he wanted to know.

"Sure, thanks." She stood up, pushing the chair she had used closer to the table. Andrew got the door, and they went inside the house.

"Will you come downstairs with me for a minute? I want to show you some pictures."

"Okay, sure," Alyson said. She followed him down the thickly carpeted stairs, resting her hand on the light oak banister for balance. They turned the corner past two bedrooms, and she saw several framed pictures of different sizes running the length of one wall in the hallway.

Andrew pointed to one close to the beginning of the arrangement. "These are my maternal grandparents. They went through much worse during World War II compared to the challenges I had on my mission. They were separated for over a decade but remained completely faithful to each other."

Andrew told her a couple of interesting stories about them and commented on a few of the other pictures hanging on the wall before they went back upstairs. On the way up, he pointed to another arrangement of pictures on the wall above the stair well—all wedding pictures. He was the oldest of seven—five boys and two girls. The pictures were hung in order of their ages. Andrew's picture was not on the wall, nor his youngest sister. She was single. There was also a picture of his parents on their wedding day.

He was telling Alyson everyone's names when Grant came from the family room and joined their conversation. "Someday, mine will be back up there in the first spot where it belongs," Andrew said.

Grant spoke up teasingly, turning to her. "Would you like to apply for the job, Alyson?"

She was tempted by the light-hearted, yet unexpected comment, to race to the seclusion of Andrew's car. Her feelings about the day so far were overwhelming enough without the prospect of a proposal, but she managed to answer calmly, with a smile.

"Hmm, I don't know. I'll just have to think about that," she said.

Everyone laughed.

Grant laughed heartily. "I see," he said. "Good answer."

The front door opened and Elyse came in carrying several grocery bags. She took them into the kitchen and put them on the tiled-counter top island in the middle of the room.

"Mom, is there anything else in the car that needs to be brought in?" Andrew asked her.

"No, that was all, thank you." She began to put things away in the cupboards and the large refrigerator. "Andrew, have you offered this young lady some lunch? I'm sure she's hungry. I would be glad to make you both something."

Her concerned comment made Alyson smile.

"Thanks, Mom, but I'm going to take her out for lunch after we leave. Do you have any suggestions about where to go around here that is good?" he asked.

She stopped what she was doing and faced her son. "Well . . . there are quite a few restaurants at the Layton exit, which isn't far. Most of them are good, so take her there and let her choose, but go soon because I'm sure she must be hungry."

"No rush, I'm fine—thank you, though," Alyson reassured her. In a few minutes they headed toward the front door.

"Thank you both," Alyson said on the way out. "I enjoyed meeting you. You have a beautiful home."

"It was nice meeting you too, Alyson," Grant said.

Elyse agreed and added, "You are welcome to come visit us anytime."

"Okay." Alyson laughed. "Thank you, again." She walked out the front door Andrew had opened and as they left, he called to his parents, "Thanks, I'll see you later."

The freeway exit he wanted was five minutes away. From there they could see several restaurants grouped together. Alyson noticed a Marie Calendar's, a choice not available in Alaska. She had heard the home-style food was good, especially the pie, which was her favorite dessert.

"What looks good to you, Alyson? I want you to pick, whichever one you would like," Andrew told her, exiting the freeway and turning east. He took the next left.

"Marie Calendar's sounds good to me. Let's go there. I get to pay for lunch, since you treated me at breakfast."

"No, I've got it covered," Andrew said firmly.

"I would really like to," she tried again.

"No, I'm taking you out, like I planned," he insisted.

"Okay," she said, reluctantly giving in. "That's really nice of you. Thanks." She hadn't planned for him to pay for her meals all day long.

"It's my pleasure." Andrew smiled flashing his white teeth. "Here we are." He parked and jumped out of the car to open her door.

"Thanks," she told him as she got out, double checking that she had her purse. Her lips were feeling dry and she needed some Chapstick. She found some in her purse, used it, and put it back. She put the purse strap over her shoulder.

They walked inside the restaurant and a delicious aroma of freshly baked apple pie assaulted their senses; Alyson's hungry stomach rumbled in response. A glass counter in front of the dining room displayed several kinds of pie.

Two other groups were ahead of them waiting to be seated and, once they were, a young hostess led them to their table. It wasn't a booth, but it was cozy.

Andrew pulled one of the chairs out from the table so Alyson could sit down.

"I need to switch sides," she told him. "I'm left-handed and will bump you if I sit in that one." That hadn't come up at breakfast because they had sat across from each other.

"Oh, okay." Andrew pulled the other chair out and after she was situated comfortably, he sat next to her. A bus boy brought them ice water and two menus.

"Is anyone else in your family left-handed?" Andrew wanted to know.

"My dad is. We were always switching chairs when our family went out to dinner. You do know that people who are left-handed are more creative, right?" Her eyes twinkled.

"Absolutely," he said. "And those of us who are right-handed are always right." He grinned.

"Is that so?" A smile appeared on her face, matching his.

"Yes," he continued, "and because we are always right I think you need to order the special—artichoke chicken with mushrooms in a creamy sauce over pasta." His face was serious but his eyes weren't.

"That does sound tempting but I think I'll order something else. Maybe the cook wouldn't mind if I ordered part of this," she pointed on the menu, "and a little of this," she pointed to something else, "and create my own lunch."

Andrew laughed, and she joined in. Once it died down, she picked the menu back up to study it seriously, hoping to decide what she did want before the waitress returned. Something on the lighter side like a sandwich or a salad sounded good. She had to save room for a piece of pie.

There were a lot of choices.

While she looked, she could feel Andrew's eyes on her, his gaze constant. Finally she looked up. "What?" she asked him.

He didn't answer, and his blue eyes didn't waver from her face.

She took another drink of water, trying to create a distraction. It didn't work.

"You are embarrassing me," she blurted out, feeling more uncomfortable by the minute.

"Why?" He sounded surprised. "You should take it as a compliment. I'm memorizing your features so I can remember what you look like after you are gone." He was serious.

Alyson looked at him, not knowing what to say. Suddenly an intense feeling began building inside her.

The waitress arrived to take their orders. Andrew placed his first. Alyson needed the extra few seconds to decide. She told the waitress she wanted a turkey club sandwich on whole wheat bread and a piece of sour cream lemon pie.

The waitress made a few marks on her note pad and picked up the menus. "It should only be a few minutes. Would you like some more water?"

"That would be great, thanks," Alyson replied. The waitress returned with a pitcher of water, refilled both glasses and left it on the table. As the minutes ticked by, Alyson's appetite lessened considerably as the strong feeling continued to overwhelm her. It was constant and her body started shaking like it would if she was cold, even though she wasn't.

Andrew didn't notice anything unusual and while they waited for the food to come, he told her a funny story about his children. She listened as closely as she could, despite the strange thing happening to her.

"One night after work, I picked Kate and Eric up from the babysitter's house and stopped at the grocery store on the way home. I got what I needed, paid for it, and we returned to the car. The kids climbed in the backseat and put their seat belts on while I put the bags of groceries in the car. A couple of the bags went on the floor below their feet because the trunk was full. We left. Halfway home I started hearing chewing noises coming from the backseat. It was weird because I couldn't figure out what they would have found to eat. I hadn't bought anything that didn't need to be prepared first.

"I asked Kate what they were eating, but it was Eric that piped up first. He told me they were eating 'fishsicles.' I had no idea what he was talking about. I pulled over to the side of the road the next chance I had and turned to look in the backseat. I discovered they had opened a box of frozen fish sticks, and that was what they'd been eating."

Alyson wrinkled her nose, "Yuck. Did they end up getting sick?" she asked

"No, thank goodness, but from then on we had a new name for fish sticks!" Just then the food arrived at their table. The waitress also set down extra napkins and a bottle of ketchup.

"Can I get you anything else?" she asked, her eyes moving back and forth between them.

"We're good, thank you," Andrew told her.

She nodded and left to take care of the other customers in her section.

Andrew leaned close to Alyson and whispered a blessing over the food before they started to eat. The bread on her sandwich had been toasted perfectly and the ingredients were fresh. It came with a generous side of French fries and she offered some to Andrew.

"Sure, I'll take a few, thanks." He put some on his plate. "You need to try some of what I ordered."

She took a bite and wiped the corner of her mouth with her napkin. Her lunch was fine but after tasting his, she began to think maybe she should have ordered it after all. She tried to eat her sandwich but each bite stuck in her throat, so she drained another glass of water. The overwhelming feeling pushed everything else to the background. She couldn't recall any time in her life she had felt something so powerfully. She felt drawn to Andrew, like they were connected in some way. She was glad her pie went down a little easier than the sandwich did, but she gave half of it to Andrew.

There was no time to linger since once they were finished eating she needed to get to the airport. She thanked Andrew again for lunch on the way back to the car. The parking lot was less crowded with the lunch rush over. He turned west toward the freeway entrance, and then south to return to Salt Lake.

During the drive, part of her wished time would stop. She wasn't ready for their time together to end, thinking about how far apart they would be when she left. She wondered if or when she would see Andrew again. That was a depressing thought.

In less than thirty minutes they reached the exit and turned west, driving another ten minutes before arriving at the airport. Andrew got in the appropriate lane for short-term parking, entered the garage and looked for a parking place. He found one on the third level close to the elevator, pulled in, and shut off the engine.

"Well, here we are," he said.

Alyson nodded, not trusting her voice to speak.

"Are you ready to go?" he asked

She was able to respond now that she had gotten rid of the lump in her throat. "I guess so. I don't have another choice, right?" she said, only half joking.

He chuckled, opened his door, and got out, walking around the back of the car to open her door. She double-checked to make sure she had everything, picking up her purse and carry-on bag. By then Andrew had her suitcase out of the back. He lifted it easily and insisted on taking her carry-on bag, too.

"Thank you," Alyson said, appreciating his help.

The automatic double doors to the terminal were around the corner. On the way inside, at the check-in counter and through security to the gate, Andrew kept the flow of conversation going practically by himself. She was lost in her thoughts.

The gate she was leaving from was a third of the way down the concourse on the right side. Once they reached it, they sat down to wait. It wasn't long before she spotted her friend, Caren, with her daughter in her arms and her son in tow. Alyson waved. She was glad to see them. Caren looked tired but her smile was warm.

"Hi, Caren," Alyson said, leaning forward to give her a quick hug. "This is Andrew," she said and gestured toward him. "Andrew, this is my friend, Caren."

"Hi, Andrew, I'm glad to meet you," Caren said, extending her hand. "How has the day gone, you guys?" she asked.

They looked at each other, smiled, and then smiled back at her. Andrew answered first.

"It's been great. I think Alyson enjoyed it." He glanced at her. "She hasn't talked very much since we finished lunch."

Caren looked at Alyson, trying to read her face.

"It's simply because I have so much to think about," she told them. They waited for her to say more but she didn't. She was very conscious of

Andrew's nearness and struggled with her feelings. It was hard for her to breathe. He kept looking at her, but she didn't make eye contact, her gaze wandering while she tried to relax. She did manage a smile.

After a few minutes of Alyson's silence, Andrew gave up on figuring her out and turned to Caren. They talked until the flight number was announced over the intercom.

Caren stood up and started getting her things together. "It was nice to meet you, Andrew," she said and turned to Alyson. "I'll see you in few minutes." She went ahead to board the airplane and get her children settled before the majority of the waiting passengers got on.

Andrew and Alyson stood close together near the check-in counter for one last minute of privacy.

"Do you have a phone number of where you'll be staying in Kansas? I want to give you a call tomorrow," he told her.

"Sure, hang on a second." She hadn't expected that question and was glad he asked. She found the piece of paper she had written it on in her purse and handed it to him. He copied it onto something else and put it in the pocket of his jeans before handing her paper back. His eyes stayed on her face, waiting until she looked directly into his. He opened his arms to give her a hug, but she stood there hesitating until he asked, "Is it okay?"

She didn't respond verbally, just moved closer.

His arms went around her in a firm embrace, causing the feeling she had since lunch to grow stronger, as if her whole body was on fire. It scared her. Andrew didn't let her go right away and bent his head down closer to her ear.

"Did you have a good day?" he whispered.

She nodded. Any reply got stuck in her throat. What was wrong with her? She sensed his questioning uncertainty, but was lost in her own. She raised her eyes to look at him and tried to smile. Just then the voice on the overhead speaker called her flight number. The last few minutes were gone. It was time to say good-bye, and Andrew's unblinking stare was searching her face.

"Good-bye, Andrew," she said. "I'm really glad I got to meet you. I had a wonderful day. And thanks again for breakfast—and lunch."

"No problem, it was my pleasure. I'll call you. Have a good flight," he said as she moved away and began her walk through the gate to the entrance of the plane. She could feel his eyes on her back, but she didn't turn around. She was just trying to breathe.

Chapter Twenty

"Wait on the Lord: be of good courage, and He shall strengthen thine heart."[21]

The flight went quickly. Caren and Alyson talked briefly about how the day had gone, but Alyson struggled to stay focused on the conversation. Thankfully, Caren's children kept her distracted, so Alyson didn't seem rude. She closed her eyes for awhile but didn't sleep. The flight was over in no time.

Caren's mom, Sandra, met them at the gate in Kansas City after they landed. They followed the signs to baggage claim, which wasn't very far from the gates. The airport was small. Their luggage was some of the first on the conveyor belt, and it didn't take long too gather it up. On the way to the car, Caren and her mom were talking, catching up, and Alyson was glad to have her thoughts to herself. The night air outside the terminal was cool, not cold, and felt wonderful to her.

The drive to Caren's parent's home took half an hour. Alyson used the opportunity to doze off; she hadn't recovered from the previous night's red-eye flight. She woke up sleepily when the motion of the car stopped, glanced around, and saw they were parked underneath a carport next to the front door of a home. It was built of brick and the outside porch light was on, illuminating the area.

The car was unloaded quickly with so many hands helping. Inside, Caren's mom showed them where to put their things. Alyson was sleeping on an air mattress on the floor of the office, and Caren and her children were in an adjoining spare bedroom. It was late and everyone was tired. They said good night.

When the bathroom was free, Alyson brushed her teeth, washed off her make-up, and removed her contacts, yawning repeatedly during the process. She returned to her temporary bedroom and attempted to read her scriptures, nodding off after a few verses. She gave up. She switched off the lamp on the desk across from the bed and climbed under the covers, falling asleep within seconds of her head hitting the pillow.

A few hours later she woke up. The intense feeling that had started at lunch with Andrew was still with her and the more awake she became, the stronger it grew. She was so tired and could feel tears starting to form in her eyes. She slid out of bed and dropped to her knees to pray. She wanted to understand what was happening.

She didn't receive a discernible answer instantly; however, she stayed on her knees to listen. Gradually her concerns receded, replaced by a calming, peaceful feeling. It wasn't long before she was able to fall back asleep, no longer worried.

The next day, Sunday, her thoughts repeatedly took her back to Utah, and Andrew.

She went to church in the morning with Caren and her parents. The small, college branch was different from the family congregations she was used to, but the reverent atmosphere was the same. The meetings ended at noon.

After eating a light lunch and putting Caren's children down for a nap, she and Caren cleaned up the kitchen. It didn't take long to put away sandwich ingredients and the rest of the apple and orange slices in the refrigerator. They sat back down at the dining room table to discuss and organize their sightseeing plans for the upcoming week.

"Alyson, you seem miles away and you're pretty quiet. Are you doing all right?" Caren asked her, focusing on Alyson's face.

Alyson thought about how to explain what she had been feeling. "I'm just tired; I didn't get much sleep. Something happened yesterday with Andrew—I'm still trying to make sense of it."

"What do you mean? What happened?" Caren asked, concerned.

"I felt so . . . close to him. It was the most amazing day. The sooner it came time to leave and catch my flight, the more I didn't want to go. I kept wondering when I would see him again." She hesitated. "When we were having lunch together I got a very strong feeling inside. It made me feel—like he and I had deep connection—a connection that would normally come after a relationship developed over many years. Caren, honestly, the feeling hasn't left. I've never experienced anything like this. You know what I went through with Jared; I can barely imagine the thought of having a serious relationship with someone else, but I'm finding myself wanting to be with Andrew already. Isn't that silly?"

Caren looked at her intently taking in her serious face and carefully spoken words.

"Wow, that is really something! I only talked to him for such a short time before we left Salt Lake, but he came across as a very nice guy—and good looking." She smiled. "Alyson, you've got to call him and tell him what is happening. Just talk to him. You never know what God has planned for you, but you need to find out if Andrew could be a part of it."

"I gave him your parents' phone number before I left and he said he would call me, but he hasn't. I don't want to seem . . . I don't know, over-anxious or anything," she told Caren.

"Alyson, you have to call him! Go do it right now so you can tell him what's been happening with you. Besides, who knows, maybe he is feeling the same thing."

"Well, if he is, then why hasn't he called me?" Alyson asked nervously.

"Just go call him!" Caren's voice grew louder in exasperation.

"All right, all right, fine. I will." Alyson got up from the table and walked back to her room to get his phone number. She waited before dialing hoping to get her heart rate slowed down. Andrew had mentioned he spent most Sunday afternoons at his parents' so she called there first. The connection went through, rang once, twice, three times, stopping on the fourth.

"Hello," Elyse answered.

"Hi. Is Andrew there?" Alyson asked.

"Yes, he is, just a minute, please."

"Thank you," Alyson told her. She heard her footsteps gradually get fainter, other background sounds, and then a shuffling as the receiver was picked up again.

"This is Andrew."

On cue, her heart rate sped up again. "Hi, Andrew; this is Alyson."

There was a long silence.

"Alyson? Hey, I've been trying to get a hold of you," he exclaimed. "The number you gave me didn't work. I tried it at least three times, hoping eventually someone would answer that knew you, but I think all I did was make whoever's number it was annoyed. By the third time I called, they were pretty adamant that they had never heard of an Alyson or anyone from Alaska. I decided that you gave me the wrong number on purpose."

Alyson looked again at the paper she was still holding, thinking.

"Tell me what the number was," she asked him.

He repeated it back. It was the same number she had written down. Confused, she glanced at the telephone she was using to check the number it showed. The answer became obvious.

"Oh no, I reversed the last two numbers. I'm so sorry, Andrew. I had it written down wrong to begin with."

He laughed. "I thought for sure you were trying to get rid of me, and I figured I would have to put our date in the category of a learning experience. I was kicking myself for bringing my kids, too, something I don't do on a first date—by the way, they really thought you were nice."

I don't believe it! To think that he was worried that I didn't like him after all I've been going through in the last twenty-four hours. I haven't been able to think about anything else.

"Andrew, did you really think I didn't like you? That is so far from the truth!" Alyson tried to explain.

"Well, I thought things were going pretty good between us. By the time we got to the airport and sat down at the gate you would hardly look at me. When I gave you a hug good-bye, you were so quiet. I was no longer sure."

Her voice was softer when she spoke again. "That is because I was feeling so much, I didn't want the time we had to end. I barely got any sleep last night, and I felt so drawn to you. I'm not sure what to make of all of this." She more or less told him the same thing she had told Caren.

"Alyson," Andrew began, the tone of his voice matching hers, "I felt something, too—something special that I haven't felt with anyone else I've dated since my divorce." His voice had gotten softer. "My divorce was very hard and something I didn't want. We were married for twelve years, and she decided it wasn't for her, never telling me once that she was unhappy. We went through a bitter custody battle and she basically tried to push me out of our children's lives. That has left permanent, emotional scars. She also tried to mess with my head by saying no one else would ever want me. That was certainly a challenge I accepted." Andrew laughed.

Alyson heard his laughter but could feel the underlying pain that with it. Those words made her sad and a little angry. To her, Andrew was such an amazing person.

"I never had any problems getting all the dates I wanted and even a few marriage proposals. I guess I had to prove something to myself, and I did. But with each woman I've dated or began to get serious with, something always ended up not being right." He stopped talking. Someone in the background asked him a question.

"Alyson, can I call you back later tonight after I get home? I need to go."

"Sure, Andrew, that's not a problem. I feel much better about things." Her voice was lighter.

"That's great. Me, too. I'll talk to you later tonight," he said.

Caren was anxious to hear how the conversation had gone.

Alyson filled her in. Caren encouraged her to go with this new relationship and see what would come of it. Later that night, Andrew called, as he said he would. Alyson had been reading and quickly set the book aside as soon as she heard the telephone ring. It was late in Kansas and she hurried to pick it up so it wouldn't wake anyone.

Not much past the "hellos," Andrew asked Alyson an important question.

"If we did decide to pursue a relationship and things got serious, I couldn't move to Alaska. My children are here and I share custody with my ex-wife—I'm sure you don't want to leave Alaska. Don't you think it would be hard to have things work between us?"

She was honest. "Andrew, if it came to that point and I knew we were supposed to be together, I could leave Alaska." Where she lived was a small concern compared to being happy with someone she loved.

He was startled. "Really? I didn't think you would even consider leaving your family and friends."

"I wouldn't like leaving them, but I believe a wife supports her husband and you need to be in Utah because of Kate and Eric. I would never expect you to live where you couldn't see them all the time." Her voice was subdued but definite.

"Wow. I guess . . . we don't have to worry about that then," he answered, still acting as if he found that somewhat unbelievable.

"Yesterday was really wonderful and I don't know when we will get to see each other again—Alaska is so far away. I'm going to be in Kansas for over a week. Is there any way you could come here next weekend? We could spend more time together before I go home. Maybe you could drive—I'm not sure how far it is from Salt Lake."

Did I just say that?

Alyson wasn't sure where that idea had come from or why it entered her mind and came instantly out of her mouth.

A long silence followed. She started worrying.

Andrew spoke. "I don't know how far it is to Kansas from here. I've never thought of driving—it might work."

His hesitation was audible.

She wondered if he thought seeing each other again wasn't a good idea. She mentally kicked herself for bringing it up. She needed to be a little more rational and not so impulsive.

Why would I want to get involved with someone else this soon, anyway? Good grief, we met on the Internet.

As suddenly as her fears had come, Andrew dispelled them with his next words.

"I would love to come see you and spend more time together. Both of us felt things we need to define. You're right, Lawrence, Kansas, is a bit closer than Anchorage, Alaska. Let me do some checking on distance as well as flights and get back to you once I have more information. I'll give you a call tomorrow."

She immediately felt relief.

On Monday when Andrew called, he told her it would be quite a drive to Lawrence from Salt Lake City and he could only manage getting Monday off from work with such late notice. If he spent most of the time driving there wouldn't be much point in coming. He was checking on available flights. They agreed if it was supposed to work out, it would.

Tuesday, Alyson, Caren, her children, and Sandra spent a full day sightseeing. There were many nearby historical points of interest from the early days of their church's history. It was close to ten that night when they checked in at a motel with two connecting rooms. Caren got her children ready for bed right away and put her son in the room with her mom. She and Alyson shared the other one.

Sleep sounded great to Alyson too, but she remembered that Andrew wanted her to call him. While she waited for the bathroom, she did call. The phone barely began to ring before it stopped.

"Hello?" he answered.

She shivered a little when she heard his voice. "Andrew, hi, it's me. We just found a motel, so I'm giving you a call. How are things going?"

"Alyson—hi." His laughter warmed her and she could feel his smile. "Everything is great here, thanks for calling. Have you girls been having fun?"

"We have. It's been a wonderful day."

"I'm glad. I have some good news." His voice sounded excited.

"You do? What's up?" She hoped it was what she wanted to hear.

"Do you think I could get a ride from the Kansas City airport late this Friday night to where you are staying?"

"Really?" She grinned. "You're coming here?" Excited anticipation washed over her like a burst of sunshine escaping a passing cloud. "Did you get a good deal on a ticket?" she asked him.

Andrew sounded happy. "It was a strange the way it all worked out— honestly, it shouldn't have. There's a travel company online that lets you name your own price for a ticket. What you do is type in the specifications of your trip as well as what you are willing to pay and then it is reviewed. In a relatively short amount of time the company accepts your offer or declines. It's set up so that you can enter only one request per flight—company policy.

"That is what I did. I typed in the amount I wanted to pay and the travel dates and waited. My request came back denied. I'm not sure why, but I decided to do it again. Maybe because I really wanted to see you." That made Alyson smile.

"When I checked back later it had gone through. I couldn't believe it!" The volume of his voice dropped. "Maybe we're supposed to see each other this weekend."

She got goose bumps. "I'm so glad you're coming. I prayed that everything would work out the way it was supposed to and left it in God's hands. I guess we got our answer." A warm feeling spread through her.

They didn't speak for a minute or two, lost in their thoughts, trying to understand what was happening. Alyson wrote down the flight information Andrew gave her, and he said he would call to reconfirm on Friday before leaving Salt Lake, in case something changed.

Caren was standing impatiently nearby, waiting for Alyson to finish talking so she could find out why she was acting so excited. She finished talking to Andrew, and then told Caren he was coming to Kansas. Her words tumbled out in a rush.

Caren wanted the details. Alyson explained what had happened. Caren's surprise almost matched hers.

"Caren, I'm so embarrassed. I forgot to ask you and your mom if it was okay for Andrew to stay over the weekend with your parents."

"Don't worry about it. Of course it's fine. I'll talk to my mom. I promise she won't care—it'll be great!" She walked over to Alyson and gave her a hug.

Chapter Twenty-one

"There is no fear in love; but perfect love casteth out fear."[22]

A few more days of sightseeing helped the week pass quickly for Alyson until Friday finally arrived. Time dragged. She had a hard time keeping her eyes off her watch. It was close to ten when they left for the airport. Once they arrived and parked, Alyson's excitement was almost uncontainable.

The terminal wasn't crowded. Alyson found the gate and waited for the plane to land while trying to calm her rapidly beating heart. The plane arrived on schedule and ten minutes later, the passengers began to disembark. Their faces looked tired as they searched for welcoming greeters or signs directing them to the baggage claim.

Several people got off before she saw Andrew. As soon as he saw her, his face broke into a huge grin. She had butterflies in her stomach as he approached, thinking about the fact that he had come a long way just to be with her.

"Hi, Alyson! Whew! I finally made it! It's been unbelievable." He gave her a hug. "Two hours before I had to leave, I was given a project at work I had to finish. Then I couldn't find my keys. I left my coat in the car back in long term parking. I had two layovers—the first one was late due to bad weather and I almost missed the second. It has been a long day, but I'm here." He looked at her tiredly and caught his breath. "Are you glad?"

"Yes, I'm really glad! Today has gone so slow for me. Thanks for coming, Andrew; it's great to see you!" She remembered what it had been like since she saw him in Salt Lake—how hard it was to sleep the first night, their conversations on the phone, and the emails that had started over a month ago. She knew him better on the phone or through letters than in person. That explained the awkwardness she was feeling right now.

"Sorry about your coat," Alyson said. "I'll bet Caren's dad will have something you can use."

Caren chose that moment to walk over and join the conversation. "Hi, Andrew. How are you?" she asked, laughing. "I didn't realize when I first scheduled my trip with Alyson that I would be sharing her with you. But really, I'm glad you could come." She turned and introduced him to her mom, Sandra.

Andrew hadn't checked any luggage, so they left the terminal without stopping at the baggage claim. They got situated in the van and headed back on the dark highway toward Lawrence.

Once they arrived at the house, Caren's mom showed Andrew where he would sleep downstairs. He set his luggage next to the couch and she handed him an armful of clean-smelling bedding and a pillow.

"I really appreciate you letting me stay here for a few days," he said, as they walked back upstairs.

"It's no problem. We're glad to have you," she replied. "I hope you will be comfortable on the couch."

"I will. It'll be fine." He smiled gratefully.

Everyone went to bed except for Andrew and Alyson. They sat down side by side on the living room sofa to talk. During the next hour, Alyson fought to keep her eyes open. Finally, they told each other good night and went to their rooms.

Early the next morning, Alyson got ready for the day before following the fragrant smells coming from the kitchen. She wanted to see if she could help with breakfast. She made orange juice, finishing when Andrew came in the front door. She was surprised to see him. She had thought he was still asleep.

He was dressed in black nylon pants, Nike running shoes, and a white T-shirt. He caught her admiring gaze as he turned toward the kitchen, where she was standing.

She blushed, happy to see him.

"Good morning, beautiful!" his confident voice boomed.

"Good morning." She gave him a smile. "I was sure I would need to wake you up for breakfast, but it looks like you already went running this morning. I'm impressed!" she teased.

"Yes, I was up a while ago and needed some fresh air." He ran his fingers through his hair to smooth it out. "How did you sleep?" he wanted to know.

"Okay, I was out almost immediately after my head hit the pillow but couldn't sleep as long as I would have liked." She paused before adding, "You know how that goes. I'm still not used to sleeping alone."

He nodded his head, completely understanding that change caused by divorce.

"So what's going on today?" he asked her.

"I'm not sure, except breakfast will be ready in about fifteen minutes."

"Then if the bathroom is free, I'll get cleaned up right away and join you."

"That sounds good. See you in a few minutes," she added.

In almost exactly fifteen minutes, a piping hot breakfast of fluffy scrambled eggs seasoned with snipped chives, a generous stack of buttermilk pancakes, and a platter of crisp bacon rested on the dining table. Once everyone was situated comfortably around the table, the food was blessed and plates eagerly filled.

The conversation over most of the meal focused on Andrew. Caren and her parents asked him several questions about himself.

After everyone finished eating, Andrew and Alyson offered to do the dishes. Caren's parents had things to do during the morning, including preparing for the next day at church.

The plan everyone agreed on was to take the kids to see their grandpa's horses and afterward go out to lunch. Caren wanted to go to one of her favorite fast-food restaurants, which was not available in Alaska.

Andrew and Alyson finished loading the dishwasher. She started it while Andrew wiped down the table and the white speckled counter tops. He rinsed out the sink when he was done. The kitchen was sparkling clean.

The two of them walked over to a nearby church recreation building. It was deserted that morning. There was a large multi-purpose room in

188

the center of the building that was used for Sunday meetings and was separated with a divider. At the back of the room was a recreational area with puzzles, books, games, a ping-pong table, and a piano on wheels.

Andrew and Alyson took turns playing the piano. They played a few rounds of ping-pong, and then sat down to talk—the main activity of the entire weekend. They spent hours and hours talking over the next few days to learn all they could about each other.

Later that day they saw some of Lawrence, checked out the horses and stables, and stopped for lunch at an old-fashioned drive-in. They feasted on juicy burgers, thick, salty fries, and shakes that were every bit as good as Caren had promised.

Andrew and Alyson laughed and joked—sitting beside each other in the van as they ate. Their eyes lingered on each other's face; Alyson could tell he knew like she did that something was happening between them. Their previous spouses had broken their hearts and trust, something neither of them were willing to give easily again. Yet they couldn't discount the fact that they had met, despite living such a great distance apart. Something was drawing them together.

That night they went for a walk around campus.

Stars and an occasional streetlight illuminated the sky. It was chilly and grew colder by the minute, but for the time being, they didn't care. They ended up sitting on a bench under a white-slatted pergola they found in a grassy clearing. It wasn't long before Alyson started shivering. They were mostly quiet, gazing at the stars in the dark sky and the area around where they sat.

"Here, I can help you get warm," Andrew said, putting his arm around her, drawing her closer to his side and the warmth of his own body. She didn't protest. They could see their breath in the cold air create tiny clouds of moisture that dissipated into the night. Their eyes locked. Andrew leaned his face nearer to Alyson's, waiting.

Her heart started to beat faster, the cold suddenly not as noticeable as it had been only minutes before. Andrew didn't move closer, continuing to look in her eyes, the exact shade of his own. He smiled, keeping his gaze intently on her face. The waiting was driving her nuts, and she moved toward him until their lips met. The kiss was gentle. They broke apart to search each other's eyes, again, now wide in the moonlight. Andrew initiated the next kiss, which lasted longer than the first.

Alyson's first thought when their lips met was that Andrew's lips felt different from Jared's. She hadn't kissed another man for more than fourteen years, and it felt strange. It took her a little while to remember that it was okay. She wasn't married anymore. The cold finally drove them indoors, their cheeks flushed from the brisk outside air, as well as from kissing.

Something amazingly unexpected was occurring in Alyson's heart, even though her apprehensive mind was fighting to keep her grounded. Before she knew it, the weekend was over, and Monday arrived with its imminent departures.

Andrew's flight left about an hour before Alyson and Caren's did. Alyson walked with him to his gate. He double-checked his seat assignment and bags, satisfied everything was in order, and then they moved out of the main path to a less busy area. Andrew drew her close for a long hug, gently touching her face and lifting her chin upwards so her eyes focused on his.

Lowering his voice to a caressing whisper, he said, "Oh, Alyson, I have had the most wonderful time with you. It has been better than I could have imagined." The tone of his voice became wistful, "And now we'll be far apart again." Something flashed over his face for an instant, and he looked as if he was struggling to keep his emotions under control. The intensity of what Andrew said next scared her.

"I want to take you home with me right now so we can be together always."

Those words shook her abruptly into reality. The little time they had known each other flashed like a neon sign in a dark store window. Her response came out in a rush as old fears took a firm hold on new emotions and she tried to sound practical in an effort to cover her own similar feelings.

"Neither of us is ready for that, Andrew. Remember you've been divorced longer than I have, with more time to adjust. I've loved being with you. You're a great guy and we'll certainly have to figure out a way to see each other again soon." She glanced at her watch, using practicality to cover up what was going on inside of her. She was fragile and needed to take the relationship one step at a time. "You better go catch your flight."

His eyes softened with understanding. "Yes, you're probably right. You just have an overpowering effect on me. I'm going to miss you." Laughingly, he twisted a few strands of her hair. "It must be your bewitching eyes and gorgeous smile!"

The tenseness between them was gone. Departing passengers on Andrew's flight were called again to board. They gave each other one last hug and a kiss good-bye.

"I'll email you as soon as I get in," Andrew told her.

"Sounds great. Thanks again for coming. I'll talk to you soon," Alyson said. She watched as he walked through the gate until she could no longer see him. She turned away to catch her own flight, feeling a enormous emotional letdown because he was gone and wondering what would happen next between the two of them.

Chapter Twenty-two

"Rise above the storm and you will find the sunshine."[23]

Alyson was home, but she was different. A new sparkle brightened her eyes and her steps were lighter. The challenges she left were no longer as heavy. Her boys hadn't stopped being a handful, and loneliness still visited her often, but each passing day brought more hope as her relationship with Andrew developed. They emailed each other almost every day and she drew bursts of energy and optimism from his letters. The links in the protective chains they both had around their hearts were beginning to loosen and fall away.

The rest of November passed quickly. Alyson and her boys celebrated Thanksgiving at her parents' home with extended family. Despite the difficult year she'd had, she knew her life held many blessings. Her family was a big blessing.

Each week at church she received support and encouragement from the members and dear friends she had made there. Every day that passed, she felt a little more victorious as it became easier to move farther away from the pain. When she first considered ending her marriage, she was filled with fears and self-doubt. She had turned a corner.

One evening in December, after the children were in bed, Alyson sat in front of the computer checking her email, anxious to see if Andrew had written. She clicked her mouse on her inbox. Andrew was coming to Anchorage. He missed her and wanted to meet her boys and extended family. He would arrive after Christmas and stay over New Year's. She could hardly wait.

On the morning of Christmas Eve, Alex woke up sick. Alyson stayed home all day, finishing last-minute projects and presents, and preparing food for the next day's dinner at her parents'. Jared was in town for Christmas, and she had invited him to come for a Christmas Eve dinner that night, hoping it would feel more normal for the boys.

They had dinner, then a program, which included reading the story of the Savior's birth in Luke, singing carols, and reading Christmas stories. Afterward, they ate homemade cookies and treats, and drank eggnog and spiced cider. The traditions they celebrated were the same as every year before, but the magic of Christmas Eve that night felt broken. Jared left early. After the boys had put out the stockings and were in bed, Alyson went to her room and cried.

On Christmas morning, they opened their gifts, which didn't take long. The children were cheerful and excited, even Alex, who didn't really know what all the fuss was about, had fun and seemed to be feeling better. Alyson made sure to keep her lonely thoughts to herself so she wouldn't spoil things for them.

"Ryker, I'm going to go start breakfast. Can you and Cade please pick up the scattered paper and ribbons and put them in a garbage bag?"

"Sure, Mom." He followed her into the kitchen to get a bag from the box underneath the sink.

She mixed up the batter for waffles and plugged in the waffle iron to preheat. When the indicator light went off, she sprayed the inside surface with a nonstick coating, then added the appropriate amount of batter for one waffle. She put some frozen turkey sausage links in a pan on the stove to brown and sliced bananas into strawberry yogurt.

She glanced in the living room and was about to ask one of the boys to set the table until she saw how nicely they were all playing together. She decided to set it herself. She made two more waffles and then called the boys for breakfast. She looked around the table at each of them, glad they were together, yet the lonely feeling inside of her persisted. There was a gaping void in her life that they couldn't fill.

Ryker and Cade helped with the dishes, and Cade took the garbage outside. When he opened the front door to carry it out, he yelled excitedly,

"Mom, come here quick! Look what someone left for us!" His eyes were glowing in thrilled amazement.

Alyson walked over to the open door, feeling the freezing cold air hit her bare feet. She looked down on the porch to see what Cade was talking about. There sat several brightly wrapped packages. Together they bent down to bring them in and set them in the middle of the living room floor. The boys all started talking at once. Even Alex seemed excited.

She handed out the gifts one by one. Ryker and Cade both got portable CD players and Jayden and Alex got musical books and a toy. She got a bread machine—someone must have known how badly she wanted one.

Cade's eyes began to tear up a little and he said, "Mom, who do you think would do this for us?"

Alyson's voice was touched with awe, "I'm not sure Cade, but it was so nice. Maybe someday we can do it for someone else." Her spirits had lifted immensely and, despite her earlier feelings of loneliness, she was reminded that there were people who cared about her family.

At noon they left for her parents' home. Christmas music played all the way, and Alex fell asleep. Her parents' yard was blanketed in fluffy, white snow, deeper than what sparsely covered Anchorage. Down the long driveway, they passed the house and the reflection of twinkling, colored lights on the Christmas tree shone through the glass of the front window. Her dad's face appeared next to it and he waved.

She stopped the car in front of the garage and shifted to park, but before she could finish turning the key in the ignition, the older boys jumped out and raced to the front door. Jayden climbed out more slowly, after being overly helpful in undoing Alex's seat belt. Alex headed immediately toward the edge of the backseat, to make his escape. Alyson had to grab him quickly before he could tumble over the edge.

"Thanks for trying to help, Jayden. Next time you need to let Mommy unbuckle Alex, okay?"

She couldn't quite catch his reply. Her mom had appeared at the door and, suddenly, in a burst of speed, Jayden ran to his grandma's open arms. Alyson followed with Alex's hand in hers, his small feet eager but not very successful at walking on the icy driveway without her help.

"Merry Christmas, Alyson," her mom greeted her as she came inside the house.

"Thanks. Merry Christmas to you," she responded before giving her a hug. Her dad came around the corner and he got one, too.

"How were the roads?" he asked.

"They weren't too bad, but I'm sure they'll be icy by tonight. I'm glad I won't be driving on them again until tomorrow," she said.

"I see," he said. "Well, come in and sit down. We're still waiting for Michael and Vicky. When they get here, we'll open presents."

Alyson looked at the tree in the corner of the room. Underneath the lowest branch were quite a few wrapped gifts. She saw the ones they had brought off to one side where Ryker put them.

"That sounds great, Dad."

Her older brother, Reid, had been sitting across the room, reading a story with his two-and-a-half year-old daughter. His girlfriend, Heather, hadn't come. He stood up, gave her a hug, and wished her a "Merry Christmas."

Elizabeth turned to her grandsons. Ryker and Cade were next to each other on the couch and Jayden sat in front of her on the floor making "vroom-vroom" noises with a toy truck. Alex was on his mom's lap.

"So guys, what did Santa bring you this morning?" their grandma asked.

Cade piped up. "I got some clothes, new Legos, and a book. Something happened after breakfast that was even more exciting."

"Oh? What was that?" her eyebrows lifted slightly over her hazel eyes.

This time Ryker answered. "Cade was taking the garbage outside to put it in the big garbage can, and he almost tripped over some presents on the porch . . ."

Cade interrupted, "I didn't almost trip, Ryker. I stopped as soon as I saw them."

Ryker grinned. "Whatever."

Jayden jumped in next. "Grandma, somebody left us presents while we were sleeping. I got a new book that talks and a little train. It doesn't talk so I have to say "choo-choo" when it goes around the track."

"Wow, that's exciting, Jayden. You'll have to show it to me the next time I come to your house. Did your mom get a present?" she asked.

Cade answered. "Oh yeah, she got an automatic bread maker. Ryker and I both got CD players and a game. Jayden got a book. So did Alex. The train is for both of them."

"That is really neat, you guys, that someone would do that for your family." She looked her daughter's direction and smiled. Alyson met her mother's eyes over Alex's head of loose curls.

Michael, his wife Vicky, and their daughter, one month younger than Reid's, had arrived. Six excited grandchildren were chattering at once. Grandpa passed out the gifts. Once the grandchildren were busy with something new, Elizabeth, Vicky, and Alyson went to the kitchen to finish the final preparations for dinner.

Dinner that night was ham with all the trimmings, rolls, salads, and a variety of homemade cookies and fudge for dessert. The rest of the evening, they played games and talked. When Alyson went to bed that night in one of the guest rooms, she was grateful. In spite of the obvious absence of Jared, it had been a special day.

Andrew flew into Anchorage on the twenty-ninth. She was more than ready to see him. Olivia, her neighbor, offered her family room couch for him to sleep on.

Alyson cleaned the house and did the shopping—planning to make meals around what Andrew said were some of his favorite dishes. The laundry was caught up, the kids ready, and she had baked a batch of chocolate-chip pecan cookies.

His flight was supposed to be in at seven. She was busy all day with her preparations and the time still went by slowly. She was going by herself to pick him up at the airport. She wanted some time alone with him before he met the boys.

The last several days, the temperature had been below zero. That night was no different, and the sky was dark and clear. Alyson started the car, letting it run for five minutes until the engine warmed up enough for her to drive. Traffic was light on the way, with rush hour long past. She parked in the parking garage after finding a spot near the entrance, not wanting to have to walk very far in the dimly lit, chilly interior.

Inside the terminal, she checked the nearest monitor for all arrivals. She found the right gate number and passed through security. Andrew's flight was running behind schedule, but there was a bookstore across from the gates she could browse while she waited. She was flipping through her second magazine when his flight number was announced over the intercom. She walked to the gate to wait.

A steady stream of people entered the terminal for several minutes before tapering off. Alyson scanned each face looking for Andrew's, disappointed each time it was someone else. For several minutes, no one came through the door at all until a group of three people exited with the flight crew behind them.

Alyson started to worry even more after the gate door was closed until she noticed a few people hadn't found their parties either. They were inquiring at the desk. She got in line behind them. Her heart sank when she overheard the airline employee explain the flight had been overbooked. She assumed that was what happened to Andrew. She would have to come back later sometime that evening, depending on when he arrived.

When she got to the front of the line, she explained to the agent that the passenger she was waiting for hadn't gotten off either. They were both checking the passenger list for Andrew's name when out of the corner of her eye she saw a movement by the gate door. Glancing over, she saw Andrew walking toward her. He was there after all, acting as if there had been no delay.

"Hi, Alyson, I'm here. Did you save me a hug?" he asked once he stood next to her.

She looked at him strangely, wondering where he had been for the last several minutes. "Andrew, you are here. What happened?" Her words came out in a rush. "I've been waiting and waiting, thinking for sure you had missed the flight. You're the last one off. The agent said the plane was empty and anyone else would be on a later flight. I figured you hadn't made it."

He laughed. "Well, I guess they were wrong, huh? Because here I am. Aren't you glad to see me?"

"Of course, I was only concerned when I couldn't find you. Is everything okay?" she wanted to know.

"Yes, everything's great. Sorry about that. I waited until the aisles were clear then walked to the bathroom at the back of the plane. I wanted to brush my teeth and wash my face before I saw you He let out a deep sigh. "It has been such a tiring day. I guess I took longer than I realized. Come here." He pulled her close into a hug. "Were you really worried I hadn't made it?"

Alyson stepped back to look at his face, her lips mimicking a pout only part in jest. "Yes. I could barely contain my excitement and anticipation, and when you didn't get off the flight my emotions, like a popped balloon, deflated instantly. She took a deep breath.

Andrew took her hand in his and smiled. It's okay. Let's go."

Chapter Twenty-three

"The Lord will give grace and glory: no good thing will he withhold from them that walk uprightly."[24]

Andrew asked questions about Anchorage as they drove through the now icy streets toward Alyson's home. She pointed to different landmarks and places she thought would interest him on the way. When they pulled up in front of her house, she turned off the ignition and started reaching for the door handle on her side of the car.

Andrew touched her arm. "Would you wait a minute before getting out?" he asked.

She moved her hand and turned to face him. He put his arms around her for another hug.

"It's really great to see you, Alyson! I have so looked forward to coming." His warm breath was near her ear and sent delicious shivers down her neck. "Are your boys okay with it?" He seemed nervous.

"Don't worry," she reassured him. They're excited to meet you. It'll be fine, I promise. Let's get out of this car, though, before it gets any colder."

Ryker and Cade were at the kitchen table playing Skip-Bo. Jayden and Alex were on the floor of the living room with toy trucks and blocks scattered around them. All four looked up eagerly when their mom and

Andrew came in.

Alex immediately toddled over wearing a smile and lifted his arms to be picked up. Jayden was right behind him to hug Alyson's leg before he peered shyly up at Andrew with big brown eyes, thickly fringed with dark lashes.

Alyson introduced Andrew to each of her children. They said hello and the room fell silent. Then suddenly everyone began to talk at once. The boys and Andrew got better acquainted until it was time to get the sleepy youngest two off to bed. They had family prayer. When they finished, she invited Andrew to come upstairs to Jayden and Alex's bedroom while she got them ready for bed.

"Everything looks so clean and organized," Andrew commented on the way.

She changed Alex's diaper and put him in a soft pajama sleeper. Jayden got his pajamas on most of the way before he needed help. She supervised them brushing their teeth. She tucked the boys in, kissing each of their cheeks, switched off the lamp, and plugged in the night light. Andrew stood back and watched.

Jayden spoke up in a hopeful voice as they were about to leave the room. "Andrew? Will you be here tomorrow?"

Andrew walked to the side of his bed and crouched down to Jayden's eye level. "I sure will. You think of something fun you want to do, okay?" He patted him on the head.

Jayden got a huge grin on his face. "Okay. Good night, Mommy. Good night, Andrew."

They shut the door softly and returned downstairs.

The next morning Andrew was over early to help Alyson make breakfast. She was making French toast. She beat the eggs, milk, cinnamon, and a dash of vanilla and took several slices of whole wheat bread from a bag in the cupboard. Andrew took over from there. She appreciated his help with something she usually did by herself. She made orange juice, and then set the table, including an unbreakable bowl for Alex on his high chair tray. She called the boys to come eat.

Once everyone was seated at the table, Ryker said the blessing and the platter of warm egg-dipped bread was passed around. Alyson cut a piece for Alex into little chunks and put it in front of him. After everyone else had theirs, she put two pieces on her plate. The second bite was in her mouth when Cade jumped.

Jayden, who was sitting next to him, had knocked over his glass of orange juice. It had splattered on Cade's pants and made a puddle on his plate and the table. Jayden's lower lip protruded, and his eyes began to fill with tears.

Alyson waited for the angry words to erupt as they usually did when a similar mishap happened. Before the boys or she could speak, Andrew said, "Hey Jayden, it's okay. It happens with my kids all the time. Eric, who is five, usually spills on his sister and she runs to get a towel to clean it up."

Jayden lifted his wet eyes to Andrew's face. "Really?" he asked.

"Yes, that's right. Other times, I'm the one that spills on her and she runs to get a towel to clean it up."

He grinned and Jayden giggled. The tension in the room was broken.

Andrew went on, "But since you don't have a sister to run and get a towel, maybe your mom could throw me one?"

"I think I could do that," Alyson said smiling. She grabbed a roll of paper towels off the counter and tossed them to Andrew. He caught them mid-air.

She gave Cade some direction on getting the juice off his pants and told him and Ryker as soon as they finished eating to go upstairs make their beds, and brush their teeth. She sent Jayden to the bathroom to wash his face and hands.

Alex was banging his bowl upside down on the highchair tray. Alyson only noticed a few pieces of bread on the floor underneath the chair. She assumed he had eaten the rest. She lifted him out, his sticky hands facing away. Several pieces of bread fell off his pants.

"So that is where you were hiding it, stinker," Alyson said to him, hugging him close. She carried him over to the sink to wash his hands, squirting some hand soap on one of his palms. She tried to rub his hands together under the warm running water. He kept shaking them, spraying water on the counters and backsplash behind the sink. She towel-dried them as well as she could, along with her shirt, and put him down. He went off to find a toy.

Andrew had stacked the dishes and silverware on the table while Alyson had been occupied. She carried them over to the sink for a quick rinse before putting them in the dishwasher. She walked back to the table to pick up the syrup and butter, as well as a few stray knives. She had barely set them down on the kitchen counter when Andrew's arms went around her waist, and he gently guided her backwards. He sat down on a chair he had pulled away from the table with her captive on his lap.

She laughed in surprise, catching the light smell of his cologne.

He put his head off to one side of her face, close to her ear. "That was a delicious breakfast, Alyson. Thank you, and by the way, you look pretty to me, even without your makeup on."

She had been embarrassed earlier that morning when he came over before she had her contacts in or even any lip gloss on. She turned her head to the side, closer to his. "Well, thank you. I appreciated your help with the cooking. Is this something I should get used to or are you the kind of guy who expects a barefoot wife to wait on you hand and foot?" she teased.

"Oh absolutely . . . and it looks like you're a fast learner. That is important." His voice was lower when he continued, "It would be a welcome change for me and my children to have someone around who cooked and took care of the house. My ex-wife was gone a lot. Her priorities were different from yours. I would love to have a wife who wanted to be with me and our family more than anywhere else."

Alyson scooted off his lap and turned around to give him a hug. "Gee, Andrew, how is it we keep agreeing on so many things?"

Instead of replying, he leaned forward and kissed her.

When Jayden and Alex went down for naps that afternoon, Alyson left Ryker in charge. He and Cade were playing a game on the computer and hardly even noticed they were leaving. She and Andrew decided to see a movie—*You've Got Mail*. They laughed a lot. Afterward they stopped at a computer store to look for accessories for Alyson's computer.

They were teasing each other when Andrew pulled into the parking lot of the store. Once the car stopped, Alyson was ready to quickly head for the warm building. She glanced at Andrew. He didn't seem anxious to get out.

The laughter in his face had faded, and he was looking at her with tenderness, or something deeper. The change wasn't just on his face, either—it was in the air. For a few seconds she wondered if something was wrong. Those worries evaporated as soon as he spoke.

"Alyson, I want you to know . . . I've fallen in love with you. I've never felt like this before."

Her heart instantly soared; her mind wondered how that could be. His first marriage had lasted twelve years—surely there had been love.

"What about your first wife?" she questioned. Part of her still distrusted words of affection.

"I did love her," Andrew told her, "but I was never in love with her. It's so different with you. I've told you that I've dated a lot of women since my divorce, yet this feeling I have for you is something completely new. I resigned myself to believing that I would never experience this kind of love in my life." His voice became husky with emotion. "But now you, my beautiful girl, have changed all that. It feels so different and so amazing—I really think we could make this work."

Alyson took a deep breath, ready to be honest in return. "Andrew, I have been feeling some of the same things. I just haven't had the nerve to tell you. There have been times I've wanted to, but something always held me back. Maybe because I've initiated things in our relationship that normally I wouldn't. With this, I guess, I wanted to hear you say it first. I'm so glad you feel it, too. You've made me very happy. I love you."

Andrew leaned across the seat and kissed her, holding her close as he moved his hands gently through her hair. She felt safe in his arms, as though he truly valued who she was—a new experience. It was exhilarating! She wanted to dance and shout to the world that she was in love!

By the time they got home, Alyson didn't think her children could do anything wrong the rest of the day to upset her. And there was something about Andrew's presence that was soothing and comforting, too. Even if things were stressful, he made her feel it would be okay.

The next day was New Year's Eve, and they spent it with the children. The morning was slow and relaxing, no schedule to worry about or place they needed to be. They played Legos, read stories, and watched a Disney movie until everyone was hungry.

Alyson went to the kitchen to make lunch and Andrew followed her, offering to help. She put a pot of water on the stove. Once it was boiling, she added noodles for macaroni and cheese. The boys would like it. She and Andrew chose leftovers from the night before. He dished them up and reheated them in the microwave.

She added milk and the powdered cheese mix to the drained noodles until it was the right consistency and called the boys to the table.

"Thanks, Mom, I love macaroni and cheese—you're the best!" Ryker told her after he saw what they were having.

"Can we have applesauce with it?" Cade piped up.

"Sure, that would be fine. Will you get it out of the pantry and bring it to me with some spoons?" she asked him.

"All right!" he said, as he scrambled out of his chair and went into the kitchen.

"Can we have it with cinnamon?" Jayden asked.

Cade got the cinnamon out of the cupboard and brought it, too.

Several minutes later, Andrew pointed to the big picture window in the dining room. "Look outside."

The older boys were sitting with their backs facing the window. They turned around in their chairs to see what was happening. Everyone else could already see the window but hadn't been paying attention to anything outside.

Giant snowflakes were coming down steadily, making the sky and the ground white.

"This looks like perfect weather for a snowball fight," Andrew said. "Anyone want to take me on?"

"Sure, I'm in," Ryker said.

"Me too," Cade added.

The boys got into their snow gear—boots, snow pants, coat, gloves, and hats. Andrew had a warm jacket but nothing else. Alyson got him some extra gloves out of the closet.

"What about your feet?" she asked him. He was wearing Nikes.

"I'll be just fine," he assured her.

Jayden wanted to play outside while the others messed around. She got him ready, too. She cleaned up the kitchen as they headed out to the backyard.

Ryker and Cade had little time to prepare any reserve ammunition because Andrew started throwing snowballs right away. For the next half hour, they chased each other around the house and yard, laughing and calling out teasing comments. The snow kept coming down hard. Soon they were all soaked.

Jayden stayed off to one side in the corner of the backyard playing, occasionally looking up to watch them when they came closer or were loud. Alex and Alyson watched the action out the window. Andrew won, but Ryker and Cade didn't make it easy. They came inside with red faces.

There was even frost on their eyelashes and on the hair sticking out from under their hats. Andrew hadn't worn one so his hair was very wet.

The outerwear they had so recently put on came off in a pile at the front door. Small chunks of snow clinging to the fabric fell on the floor and started to melt into puddles. Alex thought those were fascinating to play in and headed toward them as soon as he realized they were there.

Alyson redirected him to his toys in the family room while the mess was cleaned up. She took the wet coats and snow pants and put them on hangers. She hung them upstairs on the shower curtain rod above the tub in the bathroom to drip dry and turned the gloves and boots upside down. She placed them near a heating vent.

Back downstairs, she went into the kitchen to make hot chocolate with lots of marshmallows. She set out cookies for dunking. Andrew came to the table with the others, and they dug in. It wasn't long before they were feeling much warmer.

Jayden and Alex went down for their afternoon naps, and Ryker and Cade cleaned up the kitchen. She and Andrew were taking them to the theatre at the mall to see the latest Star Trek movie. They were so excited, they were willing to do practically anything she asked.

The doorbell rang. Jared's mother, Marilyn Clarke, had arrived to babysit.

"Hi, Grandma," Cade said, as he let her inside. Ryker took her coat and hung it in the closet. Alyson introduced her to Andrew, and then filled her in on their plans.

"We'll probably be gone two or three hours. Jayden and Alex should sleep for half of that. Thanks so much for watching them,"

"No hurry, just have fun. I'll see you when you get back. Drive carefully." Marilyn closed the door behind them.

The boys loved the movie and rehashed their favorite parts with each other as they left the theatre. Andrew wanted to shop for souvenirs for Kate and Eric, so they went to a different part of the mall.

That night the whole family went over to Rick and Caren's to play games, talk, and eat snacks while welcoming the New Year. Olivia, her husband, Brad, and their children came, too. After midnight struck, they said their good-byes and left for home. Alex was sound asleep in his car seat when they arrived.

Andrew lifted him easily into his arms and took him upstairs to his crib. Alyson guided Jayden, his drowsy eyes barely staying open. She put him right to bed, too, pulling his thick plaid comforter close around him before giving him a kiss on the top of his head. Ryker and Cade followed as soon as they finished brushing their teeth.

"I'm too tired to stay up late tonight, Andrew." She yawned before she could finish the sentence. They had gone back downstairs and were sitting on the couch for a minute, enjoying the quiet. Every night since he had come they had talked for quite awhile after the kids were in bed, but Alyson had no energy left tonight.

Andrew gave her a warm hug, holding her for a few minutes. "You do look beat. Definitely go crash right away—I love you." He gently lifted her chin to bring her lips closer. He gave her one long, lingering kiss. "Sleep well, Alyson."

"You, too," she yawned again. "I'll see you in the morning—I mean later today."

She walked with him to the door. He hugged her one more time briefly and left for Olivia and Brad's to get some sleep. Alyson locked the front door, sliding the dead bolt firmly into place before heading upstairs. In her room she eagerly laid down under the warm covers of her bed, certain she would fall instantly asleep. It didn't happen. Her thoughts reviewed the last year.

She remembered when it started, having no idea the changes in her life it would bring. It was hard to comprehend all that had happened. She was glad that last New Year's Day she hadn't seen the future or knew what was coming down the road. At the same time, now that she was beginning a brand new year, she could see the personal growth that had occurred. Her faith in God was stronger than ever because she had chosen to face the trials that came. What if she had turned away from Him and wallowed in anger and self-pity? Who knew where she might be tonight. She would never want to relive the past year but knew the inner strength and peace that forgiveness was helping her find would not have come any other way.

On Friday they slept in and didn't have breakfast until it was practically lunchtime. Alyson let the boys stay in their pajamas longer than usual watching cartoons. That afternoon, during nap time, she did some laundry and caught up on things around the house while Andrew took the two older boys out.

Ryker and Cade did their best to show him around but on the way home, they ended up lost. Andrew eventually called her to get directions. When the three of them finally made it home, dinner was ready for the boys. An hour later, she and Andrew left to meet friends for a seafood dinner out.

"I like Anchorage a lot more than I expected," Andrew told her on the way to the restaurant. She glanced at him while he was driving.

"Why is that?" she asked, curious.

"I wasn't expecting it to be so big. I thought it would have more of a small town feel and everything would be really expensive. I didn't think it would have a Wal-Mart!"

Alyson laughed. "Of course, we're cultured enough to have Wal-Mart. We even have more than one."

Andrew blushed. "You know what I mean. It's more normal than I expected—and the scenery is great. I'd love to go fishing sometime."

"Maybe you'll have to come back when the salmon start running and go fishing with Reid."

"That would be great. So who are we meeting for dinner tonight?"

"Caren, Olivia, and their husbands—the same two couples we hung out with on New Year's Eve."

"Oh good. They seemed like nice people. I liked them." He looked down the road. "Which one do I take?"

"Turn left on C Street. We're getting close now." Alyson glanced up at the road. "The restaurant parking lot is the next right, Andrew."

He turned into it and drove to the other side of the restaurant before he found a parking place. When they went in, they were the first of the three couples to arrive. The others came within five minutes.

Alyson gave Caren and Olivia both a hug and said hello to their husbands. Andrew started talking with the guys, and she turned her attention back to her girlfriends.

Olivia whispered in her ear. "You look so happy. How are things going?"

Alyson's huge smile gave her enough of an answer before she spoke softly. "It's going so well. The boys seem to love him. He's helped me a lot with things around the house like cooking and dishes, and he is appreciative of whatever I do. He is so positive. I love that."

Olivia and Caren's smiles were both big. "I'm so glad," Olivia said, giving her arm a tender squeeze.

The hostess arrived and seated them for dinner.

Saturday was a chilly, overcast day. In the morning Andrew and Alyson took the youngest two boys for a drive south of Anchorage on the Seward Highway along Turnagain Arm. Ryker and Cade wanted to hang out with friends instead.

The scenic road hugged the coast, bordered by high rocks and sparse trees with an occasional waterfall, or currently frozen splashes of cascading ice down the rugged face. They passed Beluga Point and Bird Creek, not able to see much because of the gray weather. Andrew took pictures anyway.

They exited the Seward Highway onto the Alyeska Highway toward Girdwood, passing the turnoff for Crow Creek Mine on the way. Originally it was a mining camp started in 1888 and a part of Alaska's historic gold rush. Nestled beneath the Alyeska ski resort in Girdwood were several shops.

"Do you mind if we stop and go inside a few of the shops?" Andrew asked Alyson.

"That's fine with me. You go ahead while I get the boys out."

Andrew leaned over and gave Alyson a quick kiss. "See you in a minute." He left the car.

Jayden and Alex were only too eager to be released from their constraining seat belts. Alyson walked with them outside for a little while to get rid of some of their wiggles. When they went into the gift shop, Andrew was looking at some jade and carved ivory. Alyson held on to Alex's hand, which he didn't like. She gave Jayden a few instructions.

"Jayden, while we are in this store, we only look with our eyes, not our hands, okay? Some of the things are fragile and we don't want them to break. Can you be very careful for Mommy?"

Jayden agreed. He lasted about five minutes, then couldn't resist touching the furry coat of a tiny stuffed seal. Alyson was glad it wasn't breakable; it was next to some crystal figurines that were.

Alex kept whining and trying to get Alyson to let go of his hand.

"Jayden, did I tell you not to touch anything?" He nodded. "Don't do it again."

She reached down and picked up Alex who wasn't excited about being held and started kicking his feet. She found something in her purse to distract him and he settled down. She looked back to Jayden. The pointer finger on his right hand was extended and touching a penguin made from the crystal.

"Come here, Jayden." He pulled his hand back quickly. Luckily the penguin didn't fall. It was close to a crystal walrus. He walked sheepishly toward her. Alex chose that moment to throw the compact she had given him to hold onto the floor. He giggled as it fell.

The manager of the store brought it over to her. "Is this yours?" he asked her, smiling insincerely.

"Uh—yes, thank you." He walked away and Alyson glanced at Andrew who was oblivious to her plight. He was poring intently over the glass counter displaying gold nugget jewelry inside. She was stressed out and took both boys outside, hoping Andrew wouldn't be much longer. Jayden protested loudly on the way. She tried to ignore the looks coming from a few of the customers; however, she couldn't ignore the happy look on the store manager's face when they left.

She sighed and glanced at her watch. Andrew had been inside the store close to a half an hour. She unlocked the car, helping Jayden climb in, and put Alex in his car seat. He started to cry.

"I'm sorry, Alex." She dug in the diaper bag for the goldfish crackers and gave some to him and Jayden. Silence ensued for a few minutes. She went back to the front seat and sat down, putting her seat belt on. The goldfish began to look pretty good to her, too. It was past lunchtime. She was trying to not get irritated with Andrew.

When he came to the car a few minutes later, she was extremely relieved. Before he started the engine, he turned to her. "Are you doing okay?" he asked, watching her face closely.

She sighed but smiled. "I'm doing fine. Did you get some nice things?" He showed her an ulu—a traditional rounded blade knife used by the Eskimos for hunting, fishing, skinning, and fileting—a carving of a whale and one of a sea otter in soapstone, and a very nice pen with a gold nugget on the clip.

"Thanks for being so patient. I'm sure it wasn't very fun for you or the boys, but I found something for my parents I know they'll love."

Alyson's irritation dissolved, glad she hadn't complained. They stopped for hamburgers on the return trip to Anchorage. When they came out of the restaurant, it was snowing. On the way home, it gradually came down faster and heavier. Driving became hazardous as the winding roads turned slick from the frozen moisture. The steady thumping of the windshield wiper blades, along with the motion of the car, put Jayden and Alex to sleep. Despite the inclement weather outside, it was cozy inside with the car surrounded by the falling snow.

That night her parents were coming over for dinner to meet Andrew. They had originally planned to get together earlier during his visit at their home but Nate and Elizabeth had been fighting a flu virus—finally they were feeling better. Since the dinner had been moved to her home, Alyson invited her two brothers and their families to come.

She had decided to keep the meal simple and had put hamburger and spices in the Crock-Pot that morning for sloppy joes. She asked her mom and sisters-in-law to each bring a salad. She had made brownies the night before.

Her parents were the first to arrive. She was in the kitchen talking with Andrew when the doorbell rang. He went with her to answer it.

"Hi, Mom and Dad. Come on in." She took the salad from her mom's hands so she could take off her coat and boots. Alyson set it on the kitchen counter and went back to the entryway, offering to take her parents' coats. Before she took the coats upstairs, she introduced her parents to Andrew.

"Andrew, this is my dad, Nate, and my mom, Elizabeth—Dad, Mom, this is Andrew."

Andrew shook both of their hands and the three of them started talking.

"Come in and sit down, you guys, I'm going to put these away and I'll be right back."

She went upstairs and put the coats on her bed, and then stuck her head in Ryker and Cade's room to tell them their grandparents had arrived. They went downstairs with her and greeted them with hugs.

Jayden had already found them and was sitting next to his grandma on the couch. Alex was nearby. The doorbell rang again. This time Cade opened it and both Reid and Michael with their families arrived at the same time. It was crazy for a few minutes as everyone came in, took off their winter gear and found a spot to sit. Alyson did introductions again. When she went back upstairs, her arms were full of coats.

She went to the kitchen to finish the last minute preparations for dinner. Vicky came in.

"What can I do to help you?" she asked, looking around the room.

"Everything needs to be set out on the table and we need a pitcher of water." Alyson pointed to half of a sliced lemon on the cutting board. "You can add that when you fill up the pitcher—thank you."

Alyson put out paper plates, napkins, cups, and silverware, and undid the twist ties on two packages of hamburger buns. She set those next to the Crock-Pot and uncovered the salads.

Vicky had added ice to the water from the freezer and was filling the last cup with the lemon water. Alyson surveyed everything.

"Can you think of anything I forgot?" she asked her sister-in-law.

Vicky checked out the table. "We need salad dressing for the tossed green salad. Other than that everything looks good. Oh, and the bag of potato chips."

"Those are on the counter by the toaster. If you want to grab them, I'll get the salad dressing out of the refrigerator. She took out a bottle of raspberry vinaigrette and ranch dressing and put them on the table next to the salad.

"Okay, I think that's it. Let's tell everyone dinner is ready and have a blessing so we can eat."

Vicky went to the family room to tell the children, and Alyson told the adults talking in the living room. Once they were all assembled, she asked Andrew if he would offer the prayer. When he finished and said "Amen," the children rushed for the food.

"Kids . . ." Alyson said loudly to get their attention. Immediately the room quieted down. "If you're under twelve, you need to eat in the kitchen. Moms, could you help serve your children, please?" She turned to help Jayden who was filling his plate with potato chips.

"Jayden, you can't just eat chips, you silly goose. I want you to have at least one kind of salad. Which one do you want?" He pointed to the fruit kind and she put some of the chips back. She made him half of a sloppy joe, got him a fork, a napkin, and a small glass of water, and then found him a seat.

Her mom had Alex in his highchair and was giving him some small pieces of a sloppy joe and some fruit. She had put water in a sippy cup with a lid. "Thanks, Mom," Alyson said. "I'll take over, and you go fix a plate for yourself."

"I don't mind," she said.

"I know, but it's okay. Go sit with Dad and Andrew and relax." Alyson handed her an empty plate off the table, and then checked on Ryker and Cade. They had everything they needed. Andrew walked over to her and put his arms around her shoulders.

"Are you ready to eat, Alyson? I waited for you."

"You didn't have to do that." She smiled up at him, feeling tired, but happy at the same time.

"I know, but I wanted, to. Shall we make some plates for us?" Before she answered, he handed her an empty plate and got one for himself.

"Ladies first . . ." he gestured toward the table. Alyson chuckled.

"Why thank you, kind sir," she said, trying to imitate a southern accent.

Andrew gave her a light kiss. They filled their plates and joined the other adults.

The evening went well. It was apparent Alyson's dad liked Andrew right away. She could tell her mom did, too, but she was more reserved about showing it. After dinner, they played a few games of Pit and UNO and had dessert. It was early when the gathering broke up. Alyson's parents had a long drive ahead of them and the road conditions were even icier from the continuing snow.

Alyson hugged them both good-bye, and they shook Andrew's hand again, telling him they had enjoyed meeting him and wished him a safe return flight. When the last guest had gone and the younger boys were in bed, Andrew helped Alyson finish cleaning up the kitchen and quickly straighten the rest of the house. They sat on the couch to talk. It was their last night together before he left.

When Sunday morning arrived, they were tired from staying up late the night before, but it had been worth it and they made it to church on time. Alyson introduced Andrew to her friends, enjoying the expressions on their faces and the smiles.

She made lasagna for dinner, one of Andrew's favorites. She didn't mind cleaning up and washing the dishes afterward. He was playing with the boys. He helped Cade build a small battery-operated robot, part of his science project for school. When it was finished, they took turns playing with it.

When the house quieted for the night, she and Andrew had a few hours left before she needed to drive him to the airport. He was catching a red-eye flight out of the city. The time flew by. During part of it, Alyson fell asleep on the couch. Andrew woke her up when it was time to leave. When she realized she had been sleeping, she felt terrible.

"I am so sorry, Andrew. I can't believe I wasted the last of our time together sleeping." She yawned and rubbed her eyes, trying to become more awake.

"Don't worry, Alyson." Andrew's words were reassuring. "I watched you while you slept and thought about the wonderful time I've had with you and your family. It's been amazing. I'm going to miss you even more now, you know." He lightly touched her face with his hands and she turned to kiss his fingers.

"I'm going to miss you, too," she said softly. She sat completely up and gave him a hug. "Time to go." They grabbed their coats and left for the airport.

Alyson didn't park this time. She dropped him off at the curb in front of the airline check-in counters. Andrew jumped out and got his luggage from the back of the car, shutting the door with a firm push. She stood shivering outside the driver's side of the car. He wrapped her in a big hug, and they clung together for a moment before he needed to go. Then he was gone.

When Alyson made it home and went inside the house, she noticed immediately how empty it was without Andrew. She checked on the boys and then went to bed. She was still cold. She wrapped the covers like a cocoon around herself and fell asleep to dream of Andrew.

Chapter Twenty-four

"You can't have a better tomorrow if you are thinking about yesterday all the time."[25]

Date: Monday, 4 January 1999, 9:32 AM MST
Subject: Back Home

Dear Alyson,

I'm back. Hope you slept well. You've made it impossible to forget you. The whole trip seemed like a dream. Thanks to all of you. Look forward to hearing from you soon.

Love,

Andrew

Date: Monday, 4 January 1999 8:36 PM AKST
Subject: Cherished

Dear Andrew,

Hi! Thanks for your message. I'm glad you made it home safely. Things have been busy and I'm sure they will continue to be that way until I get caught up again.

213

While going through the routine today, I kept remembering moments spent with you here. They were such wonderful days, but way too short!

I wish I had kept one of your shirts or something to bring you close again. I really love the smell of your cologne. I keep closing my eyes to feel your arms around me. You have such a good heart and make me feel cherished. What woman in her right mind could ask for more? I will call you tomorrow. Sleep well!

Alyson

Date: Tuesday, 5 January 1999, 7:28 AM MST
Subject: Shirt off My Back . . .

Dear Alyson,

Does it matter which shirt? Maybe one that keeps you warm at night when you go to bed? Something of yours would be similarly great to keep you close to me.

You're beautiful to me. I love your hair, your eyes, your dimples, your lips and, above all your smile, and that is just the beginning. Soon, when it is right, we will be inseparable.

I think February would be a great time for you to come and visit. I want you to spend some more time with my children and we need to be together so we can decide where to go from here.

Let me know what dates would be good so I can start checking on ticket prices.

Love,

Andrew

Date: Tuesday, 5 January 1999, 10:33 PM AKST
Subject: FW: This is what's happening . . .

Hi Andrew,

Thought you might like to read this from my mom. I have thanked God so many times that he gave her to me for my mother. She really cares a lot. She will have a hard time having me gone from Alaska, but more importantly, she wants me to be happy.

—Original Message—

From: Elizabeth
To: Alyson

Date: Tuesday, 5 January 1999, 8:50 AM AKST
Subject: Re: This is what's happening . . .

Alyson,

I am pleased that things went well. I prayed that they would and that this visit could have a deciding influence on the future. I only want you to have the happiness you deserve. As for any reservations or hesitation I might have, I think you know why—I only want you to be happy. I just want both you and Andrew to take your time because it is not only you two, but six children who need a happy, stable home.

I was distracted last Saturday with all that was going on and the grandchildren clamoring for my attention. I would have liked to talk more with Andrew, but didn't get the chance. He seemed like a nice guy. I just don't want you to end up with another "smooth talker."

Love,

Mom

Date: Wednesday, 6 January 1999, 6:09 AM AKST
Subject: Some extra cash

Good Morning!

Hope you got some sleep. It was great to talk to you twice yesterday. I can still hardly believe all this is real, except I feel so much. Thank you for your strength and your love.

Did I tell you one of my tole paint projects finally sold? I was beginning to wonder, but someone bought the whole set for close to $90. Wish I could sell a few more. They are time-consuming, but it was exciting to know someone would pay for something I made.

I will write later since we probably won't get much time to talk on the phone today.

Lots of love from me to you!

Alyson

Date: Wednesday, 6 January 1999, 12:53 PM MST
Subject: Great Sale!

Alyson Dear . . .

That's great about your artwork! Seems like the scriptures talk about the worth of an industrious woman. I think we can make this work.

I knew at the time I shouldn't have teased your mom about you looking as good as she does when you reached her age. It was assuredly an honest thing but one that I should not have passed on to her. Putting together a package to send—

Love,

Andrew

Date: Wednesday, 6 January 1999, 3:30 PM AKST
Subject: Re: Great Sale!

Dear Andrew,

Hi! You must have misread my mom. I forwarded her email to reassure you. Trust me she liked the compliment!

Everything went well with Alex's doctor's appointment. The doc isn't worried about his frenulum at this point as he is eating well and if later (around age 3) he develops a lisp we can go from there.

I'm running into some possible obstacles, leaving the first part of February, with arranging childcare but I still have some other options to explore. Probably would work better if I split the kids up. We will see. I just want to be with you.

Have to run, I will talk to you soon.

Love ya,

Alyson

Date: Wednesday, 6 January 1999, 6:20 PM MST
Subject: Love is in the air

Sounds like a good thing. I haven't gotten tickets yet. I would like to have you here; just let me know when you can come. The earlier I start, the better the deal, and the sooner I can make it happen.

I was just talking about the "smooth talker" thing your mom mentioned. While I will compliment, I am careful that the comment is valid. I just knew that I coming off as a little insincere when I made the comment directly to her. Good to know things went well with Alex.

I love you very much,

Andrew

Date: Wednesday, 6 January 1999, 5:44 PM AKST
Subject: Re: Love is in the air

Hi,

I miss you so much! I did some more discussing and I think things will work out fine with the kids. Michael and Vicky will probably stay here and house-sit and Ryker will stay in town for school. So why don't you plan on getting tickets for the fifth of February (Friday) until Sunday the fourteenth.

This is my second draft, by the way. Somehow I lost the first one. I've been trying to remember where you got that "smooth talker" comment, then realized it was at the bottom of the letter from my mom, I hadn't scrolled down far enough before forwarding it all. She was referring to how Jared had been. She wasn't implying anything that you had said. I know she was flattered by your compliment. Don't feel bad—I know you were sincere.

Alyson

Date: Wednesday, 6 January 1999, 9:03 PM MST
Subject: Re: Re: Love is in the air

Babe,

I'll get to working on the new dates for your trip.

I'm not hurt, I only know that I, along with my parents and siblings, want to establish and maintain great relationships with potential in-laws. The fact is, I really like your parents and hope to love them both for their own attributes and as an extension of you.

I won't bring this up again. I will love them and see if they can reciprocate. I just want everything to be great. Let me know how I can help them. My former in-laws refused invitations to join my family, other than for the reception, even before the wedding. I'm sure this facilitated her leaving later on. I really want things to be different between our families and us.

I love you with all of my heart,

Andrew

Date: Thursday, 7 January 1999, 4:32 PM AKST
Subject: Reassure me

Dearest Andrew,

After we talked this morning, I have been thinking a lot and I still have some concerns I need to share with you. Since we have been talking about a time frame to make things permanent between us, I do think about everything that is involved. Being the woman that I am, it's part of my inherent gender characteristics that cause me to be emotional as well as to talk through things five different ways. I hope you'll understand that I do need reassurance.

It isn't the detail stuff I'm worried about that leaving Alaska would involve, although it will be a pain at times. It is that I would be leaving my family, my friends, my home. Please just hear me out again. Like we talked about on the phone, I feel totally safe here. It is what I know best and I have a support group that is big; I know I can call on so many people and they would come in a second to help me, unconditionally with love and care. I haven't had close female friends for a long time because of the way Jared was. I wouldn't let them get close. Now I have three dear friends who I can turn to without hesitation, who accept me for who I am, who make me laugh, and who understand me.

They have been a major help in pulling me through last year.

Then, of course, there are my parents. They mean everything to me and have always been there for me, and my brothers and their families, along with other friends at church here. Alaska is a part of me and my life. That is something I will be leaving behind.

Now Andrew, there is you. I know for sure how I feel about you; I know for certain I love you very much. You have so much to offer that is important to me. You seem to genuinely love me and want us to be together. I feel your goodness inside and out.

I know you are and would be a wonderful father, something I have to have for my kids. You bring me so much joy; I just love to be with you.

I guess it all comes down to this—like I told you, I would go anywhere with you. Circumstances being what they are, Salt Lake has to, and would, be our home at this point in time. I do not question that. But I have to really, really know, because of everything and everyone I would be leaving to be with you, that it will be worth it. I have to know for sure that you are my best friend and that you will be there for me as I adjust. I can tell you I am going to have days in the future when I will feel homesick and lonely as well as moments that I will feel overwhelmed from the changes. I'm realizing the reality of it more because we have been talking about marriage.

I have grown independent and fairly self-sufficient, which partly comes from feeling secure and comfortable here, something that I won't feel at first after moving to a totally new area. My role as temporary head of my home will also change. I do know that is right, and I'm certain with you it will be a partnership. I will get to know your family and love them; I have no doubt. I will make new friends over time, but at first you will be *it*! I just need to know that you will be patient as I learn to fit in there.

I, in turn, will try to be what you need by being a good wife and mother, taking care of our home and supporting you as husband, father, and provider. Please don't think in any way I am trying to discount the changes for you, Kate, and Eric. Again, all I am asking for in explaining this is reassurance. I want you to be able to understand all I'm feeling, and how together we can make this work.

Know how much you have already added to my life, and how much happiness I have felt because of you.

I love you Andrew!

Alyson

Date: Thursday, 7 January 1999, 9:17 PM MST
Subject: One Together

To My Love,

While I heard you today, it seems I wasn't listening. In retrospect, while I could easily sense all was not well, I was trying to fit you into what might be, unemotionally, an ideal plan. I understand this is an important part of who you are; one of the reasons that women are so amazing is that their capacity to love emotionally is unbounded.

I wish that I could be with you tonight. If you could feel my strong embrace, let me hold you gently in my arms, and look into my eyes, you would see and know what I would be for you.

I love you, Alyson. I have been granted substantial opportunity to learn and understand many things, but this is still new. Know that I have never loved another woman like I love you

You are constantly in my thoughts. Believe that I would never do anything intentionally to hurt you.

Let me know with whom you choose to associate. Extended family here could be a great help, but our family of eight would come first—always. Other friends here could become a great support. We can decide with whom to mingle together, and there will also be new friendships that we discover and develop on our own

Let me know what you prefer. I am prepared to take as strong a role as you desire to protect and integrate our family into society here.

I hope with all of my heart that we can be together soon,

Andrew

Date: Friday, 8 January 1999, 6:22 AM MST
Subject: Good Morning

To My Dearest Friend,

I love you, cherish you, and can hardly wait to be together again. Hope to hear from you soon.

Andrew

Date: Friday, 8 January 1999, 7:09 PM AKST
Subject: Dearest Friend

Hi!

So I'm your dearest friend? I *do* want to be that to you and to have you be mine. I am leaving shortly to go out for dinner with my mom, but I wanted to send a quick message. I love you and think of you constantly.

I had a fun time with Caren, Olivia, and my mom sewing dresses and things for the wedding. I was a bit surprised in talking with mom that she is encouraging me to stay longer than two weeks in Salt Lake next month, since that directly affects her as my main babysitter for the boys. I hope that sounds okay to you. I don't want to wear out my welcome, especially with your parents. They are already being so gracious to let me stay with them. However, I would love more time with you. Think about what would be best regarding time with your kids. Being with them is important to me, too.

We have much to discuss for the future, and I would like you to show me more of Salt Lake, so I can get a better feel for things. I do want to meet some of your friends, just don't overwhelm me with everyone!

Please tell Eric I am thinking about him since you said he was sick; I hope he feels better soon. I know he is in good hands.

I received an interesting letter from Jared. He said he has been putting in applications for a part-time job for when he isn't flying. Maybe something good will happen in that direction. I do feel he wants to make things right on the financial end. He mentioned more than once that he knows it is part of his repentance process to meet his obligations to the boys and me.

I was thinking today, it was just last week we were together, so how come it seems like a long time ago? Maybe because you took part of me with you and I feel it missing?

Love You!

Alyson

Date: Friday, 8 January 1999, 10:08 PM MST
Subject: Your Trip

Alyson,

I would love to have you come for as long as possible and don't worry, my parents will be happy to be accommodating. I agree with your mom that we need to have more time to work things out and I will have you around the children as much as possible while they're with me. Then when they're back with my ex-wife we can have some time to ourselves.

That would really help if Jared meets his responsibilities as we will be caring for a large family together and will have to spend wisely. I'm not worried though. I'm sure we can do it.

Hope you had a nice dinner with your mom. Got some videos for the kids tonight and we're staying in so Eric can rest. They both have mentioned they're looking forward to your visit.

Love,

Andrew

Date: Friday, 8 January 1999, 10:47 PM AKST
Subject: Re: Your Trip

Dear Andrew,

Hi! I did have a nice dinner. We had Mexican cuisine, Chile Verde with tortillas and seasoned rice—and it was good. Our whole conversation centered on one person in particular—actually, he could be someone you know!

So is everything okay with you?

By the way, I heard through the grapevine you caused quite a stir at church last week. Want to know more? The general comment from many of the women was "Wow, he's good-looking!" Then taking it further someone said, "Tell Alyson, 'I told her so!' " This came from someone who told me I would find someone neat but that I should look outside Alaska. Pretty interesting, huh?

Tell the children I am also excited to see them both and to spend time all together.

Love,

Alyson

Date: Sunday, 10 January 1999, 9:57 AM AKST
Subject: Trying to understand each other

Dear Andrew,

How are you today? It was good to talk to you last night, but it sure can be frustrating sometimes when we talk on the phone, since we aren't face to face. We can't see each other's expressions or pick up on non-verbal cues, and it can be easier to misunderstand one another. I hope I'm not too confusing, being the emotional person that I am, since I often feel confused myself. I know you're trying hard to understand me. I do give you credit.

I appreciate you so much and the effort you make in trying to communicate clearly. I think we are progressing there. It's just this man/woman thing added to being far apart. I hope you know I never intentionally want to hurt you or make you feel bad with anything I say—or don't say well.

Also, our past relationships play a big part in how we perceive things because of how we've been hurt. But like I said last night—when I don't try to explain "us" logically and how these feelings I have could be there, how we feel a bond, and so forth, then I feel peace inside without any doubts.

I always want to make you happy; you deserve nothing less than that. I know, in turn, treating you well will bring me happiness. Thanks for being patient. Again it is a continued learning process.

Enjoy your day. You are always close in my thoughts and my heart.

Tell Kate I would love to go to the gymnastics meet with her when I am there.

Love,

Alyson

Date: Sunday, 10 January 1999, 11:31 PM MST
Subject: Re: Trying to understand each other

Dear Alyson,

It really would be helpful to be physically close to one another whenever we have misunderstandings; hugs can definitely help.

Sounds great to have you attend a gymnastics meet. Sleep well, and imagine that I am close, whispering reassurances to you.

Love,

Andrew

Date: Monday, 11 January 1999, 7:43 AM AKST
Subject: Making a difference

Hey Handsome,

Thanks for the pictures! How old were Kate and Eric in them? Were the flowers they were holding ones you planted? They were nice.

I really enjoyed talking to you earlier in the day. I would be all for creating a new, stable, and strong family from two that have had such difficulties. It will be a challenge, but I feel that together you and I can make a difference in our children's lives.

Thanks for your advice on fixing the tub. I picked up some caulking. I guess I will work on that tonight.

And thanks also for the advice on dealing with Jayden's pent-up anger and frustration over Jared's absence. I also purchased a blow-up toy punching bag for Jayden today, and I talked to him about what it was for. He seemed to like the idea. I appreciate your input. We can do so much more if we help each other and share ideas, as long as it is done without criticism. I feel that is how it was today.

I'm looking forward to being with you soon, and permanently later. You are adding much to my life and I hope I am doing the same for you.

XOXO and much love,

Alyson

Date: Monday, 11 January 1999, 9:26 PM MST
Subject: Why I love you

Dearest,

I think that the pictures I just had developed from the camera I brought to Alaska were about four years old. Not bad still.

I don't tell you enough what you mean to me. My words can seem shallow compared to other ways of expression, but some of that will have to wait until we're married. You bring happiness and stability to my world. You bring beauty and excitement. You bring experience and a sense of relief. You would be, for the children and me, a real mom and a real wife—something we need in our lives. You give me the will to fight on.

The ideas that we try are ours together; I ultimately want them presented as such. I must be one with my wife. I am well aware that nothing else will work. Successes from either of us are ours for we will be one.

No one truly successful can be such without the support of one who loves him. I want you by my side. Together we can take whatever credit there will be. It is imperative that there never be jealousy between us and that there be no "between us." After all is said and done, I LOVE YOU!

Andrew

Date: Tuesday, 12 January 1999, 11:27 PM AKST
Subject: Why I love you, too

Hey Babe,

The more time we spend talking on the phone, the more I miss you and feel lonely. It just makes me want to be together since when we talk I feel closer, although I know you think talking is not enough.

I made you something tonight, but you'll have to wait and get it in person.

Jayden was telling me again that he wants a new daddy and he asked me who it would be. I said, how about Andrew? He said, "Yes, he is my good friend!" Maybe you can write him, and he would enjoy writing you, I'm sure. That might help with all he's going through. Talk to you soon!

Alyson

Date: Wednesday, 13 January 1999, 11:07 AM AKST
Subject: Letter for you . . .

Dear Andrew,

We have a letter for you. We will put it into our computer and send it to you. I got your card. It made me feel happy. I liked the music and the picture. I got a punching bag from that store that has toys. It is a punching guy. His name is Steve Austin.

Andrew likes Mommy.

I like to paint and color. My favorite color is red. I got candy for Halloween and Christmas. It is really good to eat. I like candy and pizza and peanut butter and jelly sandwiches. I like these things. What do you like?

Good-bye,

Jayden (age 3)

The children began to occasionally email one another. Alyson also emailed Kate and Eric and Andrew did the same with the boys. The changes were affecting all of them. As she and Andrew continued with their courtship, they made sure the children were involved and everyone was in agreement about moving forward.

Date: Friday, 15 January 1999, 1:53 PM AKST
Subject: Re: Court

Hi handsome and wonderful guy,

Thank you for that beautiful card! It was very romantic. You are learning!

So many thoughts went through my head while we were talking about how things went with court and your ex-wife. Of course it will be better when it is all on paper and signed, but it seems like blessings keep arriving. You continue to make me happier than I ever imagined I could be. Our future is so full of promise and endless possibilities. Some challenges, yes, but I feel in my heart—and I'm trying to trust it—such joy and so much gratitude to God. When we do what is right regardless of how hard it is, He certainly keeps his end of the deal. I will only be happier when we can be together as husband and wife. Does that mean I have only had a taste of what's to come? Wow!

I think of what a good friend said to me just yesterday when the two of us were talking. She told me I am different—that I seem really alive instead of just going through the motions. Then I guess being "really alive" feels awesome. I would never go back!

Hope you feel as I do and can understand. I guess it's like you've told me several times that you have never felt this way before. Neither have I.

I love you so much.

Alyson

Chapter Twenty-five

"True love cannot be found where it truly does not exist, nor can it be hidden where it truly does."[26]

Andrew sent Alyson another email as soon as he completed booking her reservations to fly to Salt Lake City. They would have about two and a half weeks together. They both knew and agreed that their relationship was reaching the point where it was time to end more separations. It was frustrating to be so far apart when they wanted to be together all the time.

Andrew met Alyson at the airport with a big hug and hardly let go of her hand for a second. She collected her luggage from the baggage claim and a few minutes later they left.

They took the on-ramp to the freeway, heading north. When they passed through the newer area of Rose Park, Andrew pointed out houses for sale, telling her they would need something similar in size for their future family.

He showed her his former home, and she noticed the nicely land-scaped yard he had carefully tended and several fruit trees. He took her out to dinner and later drove north to his parents' to drop her off. Grant and Elyse were warm and gracious, just like the first time she met them. She felt very comfortable staying in their home.

On Monday night after work, Andrew picked up Kate on his way out of Salt Lake to meet Alyson. The three of them went out for pizza at a small Italian restaurant. During dinner they talked and helped Kate with her homework. Afterward they went swimming at a local indoor pool. Kate seemed glad to share Andrew with Alyson for the evening. She hinted to her dad to hurry and propose with her there.

Andrew didn't seem amused by her input and tried discreetly to tell her so. Alyson found the whole situation endearing but was relieved when the topic switched to other things.

During the following week, while Andrew was at work, Alyson checked the classified ads each day for possible houses, calling on some to get more information. Several of his family members invited her to lunch on different days, and she spent a lot of time with his parents.

On Thursday night, Andrew had both children with him and they were going to stay for the entire weekend. They played Scrabble, rented a video, and talked. The next day Kate had school, so she left with her dad while Eric stayed at his grandparents' with Alyson. He helped her make two kinds of cookies that afternoon. Alyson cooked lasagna that night for dinner and made a coconut cream pie for dessert. That pie ended up endearing her to Grant.

Saturday, the thirteenth, they took the children shopping, out to lunch, and then to look at several homes on the market. Alyson had a lot of time on her hands during the day while she was visiting and wanted to make a dress for Kate, so their last stop was the fabric store to buy what they needed.

That night, Alyson helped Kate and Eric make valentines for their dad. She enjoyed their company, their cheerfulness, and the open love they shared with Andrew. The respect they had for him was easy to see.

At 8:30 PM, the kids were settled and Andrew and Alyson hugged them good night. They left together for dinner at a fancy restaurant where Andrew had made reservations. She sat close to him on the drive over, glad to be alone, but thinking about how nice the day had been with his children.

The restaurant was in Bountiful. When Andrew parked the car, he put his arm around her and gave her a light kiss on the cheek.

"You look beautiful tonight," he said softly in her ear.

That made Alyson smile. "You look very dashing yourself," she responded, giving him a kiss.

The restaurant's interior was classy, decorated in black and white with crisp, linen tablecloths, luscious, full green plants and several appropriately placed artificial trees to lend privacy. There were modern-style prints on the walls, low lighting and classical jazz playing in the background. Most of the tables were busy with customers despite the late hour.

They enjoyed a seafood dinner and, although they barely had any room left when they were finished eating, they decided to share a dessert.

"Oh, that was wonderful, Andrew. Thank you so much." Alyson leaned back in the soft leather-cushioned chair after finishing the last bite of pie.

"You're welcome. I'm so glad you enjoyed it. I wanted you to have a really great time since tomorrow will be our first Valentine's Day together. What would you like to do now?" he asked.

"I don't know. Anything you want is fine with me. I'm just enjoying your company." She glanced at her watch and noticed it was 10:30 PM They had started dinner late.

"Great! Would you go for a drive with me?"

"Sure, that sounds good," she answered.

Andrew paid the bill and they left. The inside of the car was drafty when they climbed in, and Alyson zipped her navy blue jacket higher, burrowing her hands deep into its large pockets.

"My Alaskan gal isn't cold, is she?" Andrew teased. "This should be spring weather in comparison to what you're used to."

She laughed. "It probably is colder back home, but I definitely feel the nip in the air with that breeze blowing outside."

"Oh, darn. I guess you'll have to scoot a little closer to me and we'll see if I can help you out," he added.

It didn't take long for the four-cylinder engine to emit enough heat through the vents to warm her up as they drove through Farmington and Centerville.

"How are you doing?" Andrew asked her. He had noticed her droopy eyelids and frequent yawns.

"Tired. I'm not a late night person like you," she told him.

Andrew glanced at the clock on the dash of the car. It said 11:32. "Would you mind if we turned around? If we get off at the fifth south exit in Bountiful and head east up the hill, there's a great view of the valley."

At that moment, she would have preferred to go back to his parents' and call it a day, however part of her was interested in seeing the view. "That's fine," she told him, hoping she could sleep in tomorrow.

The stars were out in all their sparkling glory and the panoramic vista of the Salt Lake Valley and surrounding area was amazing from the grounds of the Bountiful temple, high on the hill. The vast city lights shimmered and sparkled against the dark winter sky and they could see as far west as the Great Salt Lake, as well as the surrounding towns beneath the looming Wasatch mountains.

She sat in Andrew's car and the glowing beauty of the magnificent white temple mesmerized her. The lighted grounds reflected off its granite surface and the contrasting night sky gave it a hint of blue.

"Would you get out and walk with me for a little while?" Andrew's voice interrupted her wandering thoughts.

Glancing back at the small clock on the dash, she saw it now said 12:02 AM

"It's really gotten late. Are you sure you want to get out of the car?" she asked him. "That breeze has turned into a sizable wind, and I think I'm finally warm all over."

He seemed a bit frustrated by her response, and then pursued it anyway. "Come on. Let's go for a few minutes," he said.

"Okay," she replied with a little sigh. "If it's really important to you, I will."

"It really is," Andrew said.

Alyson had to push the car door with more force than usual against the wind so it would open far enough for her to get out. Her long hair instantly whipped around her face and blew into her eyes. She pulled her coat tighter around her and felt the chill pierce quickly through her slacks to the skin on her legs instantly causing goose bumps all over.

Andrew took her hand in his and they moved side by side, their steps on the paved walkway creating very little sound against the boisterous wind. They walked beside the tall, black wrought-iron fence that bordered the temple grounds. Its widely spaced bars offered no protection from the biting weather.

Within moments Alyson started to shiver. They continued until they were close to the main entrance of the temple. Andrew let go of her hand and moved to her right side, closest to the gate. He knelt down. Looking up at her, he reached to take both of her hands in his.

She finally figured out what was happening, and her heart began to pound, feeling several emotions at once. She had wondered when and how this moment would come. Looking deeply into his blue eyes, not missing the seriousness and look of humility reflected in his face, she waited, holding her breath.

"Alyson," he said intently focused on her. "I would be honored to have you for my wife. Will you marry me?"

She was overcome with happiness and excitement. The love she felt for him shone from her eyes. She pulled him to his feet and wrapped her arms tightly around him. "Yes, Andrew. Oh, yes, I would be honored to marry you!" she exclaimed.

They hugged like that for several minutes. She was lost in her thoughts of what brought them to this point and anxious to move forward together. When they finally broke apart to walk back to the car, Alyson no longer felt the cold.

"I was wondering when you were going to propose," Alyson told him. "I was even beginning to worry that I would go home not knowing where things stood between us."

Andrew glanced at her.

"I'm sorry. I'm sure you were trying to figure it out, especially since we have been looking at houses and talking details of you moving here. I just wanted to make this special and do it right. You're the first girl I ever really proposed to. I thought Valentine's Day would be romantic, the perfect time you could look back and remember. I also wanted it to be in front of this temple.

"Now you know why I kept checking the time in my car while we were sitting. I wanted to make sure it was officially the fourteenth before I asked you." Andrew laughed. "You had me worried for a minute when you didn't seem anxious to get out of the car and take a walk with me. I was thinking I might have to carry you out."

"Sorry. I didn't know." Alyson smiled sheepishly. "Thank you, Andrew for making tonight so wonderful. I will always treasure the memory. I love you!"

Leaning forward, she gave him a lingering kiss.

Alyson woke up the next morning feeling deliciously happy, remembering she was officially engaged. When she opened the door of her room a few minutes later, she almost stepped into the middle of a large vase overflowing with twelve gorgeous, long-stemmed, pink and red roses. In the center of the vase floated a helium-filled heart-shaped balloon with the words "I Love You" on it. A white, sealed envelope with her name written in Andrew's handwriting across the front leaned against the arrangement.

She opened the card, savoring the sweet words he had written, feeling as if she was going to burst from so much joy. Andrew came down the stairs in search of her. He saw she had found his gift. His smile was enormous.

"Happy Valentine's Day, sweetheart," he said, pulling her in for a hug.

Kate and Eric were close behind him, eager to give her a hug too, and admire the flowers.

"Were you surprised?" they asked her.

"I was," she said, laughing. "I almost tripped over them, in fact."

"Oops, that would have made a big mess on Grandma's carpet. I'm glad you didn't," Eric replied.

"Me, too. Hey, is anybody else around here hungry?" she said.

Everyone nodded. They went upstairs for breakfast.

Later that evening, Andrew's extended family gathered at his parents' home for dessert. Alyson was overwhelmed by so many people, but impressed by the close ties they shared. Andrew had typed up the news of his and Alyson's engagement in an email format to announce it, since that was how their relationship began. When there was a lull in the conversation, he asked for everyone's attention. Once the room became quiet, he handed the paper to his dad and asked him to read it.

When Grant finished, the room erupted in cheers and excited voices. Andrew and Alyson were surrounded by pats on the back, hugs, and congratulations. They announced the date was set for early April. Once things calmed down, they slipped away to Grant's home office to call her family in Alaska. They both talked to her parents and each of her sons, whose excitement was as exuberant as what they had experienced in Utah.

The rest of her trip flew by.

She completed Kate's dress and worked out details for the wedding with Elyse and with Andrew's sisters, who generously offered to help. She and Andrew had their engagement pictures taken and shopped for rings. After visiting several jewelry stores, they found the ring they both liked.

Before she left they put earnest money down on a piece of property for the new home they were going to have built. They looked at several house plans, knowing lots of space would be needed for their soon-to-be family of eight. Tentatively, they decided on one.

Chapter Twenty-six

"I count no more my wasted tears;
they left no echo of their fall;
I mourn no more my lonesome years;
this blessed hour atones for all.
I fear not all that Time or Fate
May bring to burden heart or brow,—
Strong in the love that came so late,
Our souls shall keep it always now!"[27]

Andrew and Alyson had a lot to do to prepare for the wedding and the move.

Andrew worked on the plans for their home, checking out other models. One afternoon he called and said he found a rambler-style, two-story house on the south side of the city. It had six bedrooms and three bathrooms, with a large family room downstairs and many unique touches. He sent Alyson the new floor plans and a video. She agreed with Andrew that it would be a perfect choice for their family. They would finalize the plans with the builder a couple of days before the wedding, although the house would not be finished until August, Andrew found an apartment for them to rent until it was completed.

His parents gave them two round-trip airline tickets for a honeymoon in Orlando, Florida, and volunteered to host the wedding luncheon at the historic Lion House in downtown Salt Lake City. Andrew scheduled the photographer, had the announcements printed, and made reservations for Alyson and the boys to fly to Utah.

Alyson prepared to move, going through household items, clothing, and furniture. She and Andrew had several discussions by phone detailing what they each had so they wouldn't pay to move duplicate items. The mover was scheduled to come a few days before she left Alaska. Their belongings were supposed to arrive in Utah three weeks later.

She made her white satin wedding dress with Caren and Olivia's help. The pattern included a sleeveless, fitted bodice, tailored floor-length skirt with a slit in the back and a waist-length jacket, also made of satin overlaid with lace. It was a simple, but elegant, design with buttons in the back. She wanted it to be a completely different style from the dress she wore when she married Jared.

The boys were staying in Alaska until after the wedding and after she and Andrew returned from their honeymoon. Her mom would be in Salt Lake for the wedding, and her dad would bring the boys to Salt Lake the day before the reception.

Alyson's sister-in-law, Vicky, drove her to the airport on her last morning in Alaska. On the way, they talked about the changes in her life over the past eighteen months. It was emotional for Alyson to think of all she was leaving behind; however, her happiness in a future that included Andrew reminded her that what she was doing was right. She was sure many new experiences were ahead of her. Not all of them would be easy, but she was certain that God brought her and Andrew together and that the new direction she had chosen was the one He meant for her to take.

When she left Alaska, the plants and trees in Anchorage were just beginning to revive after the long winter. In Salt Lake City, there were signs of spring everywhere—budding tulips, daffodils, crocuses, gladiolus, irises, and pansies. Blossoming fruit trees displayed an array of cheery shades, including vibrant green. The season of rebirth and promise matched the feelings in her heart.

Her separation from Andrew was finally over.

The next morning, Alyson and Andrew spent several hours at the builder's design center with a consultant, poring over samples for the interior and exterior of their new home. When they finished they went out for lunch.

Elizabeth flew in on Thursday, the day before the wedding. Andrew and Alyson picked her up from the airport. She was staying with his parents, too. By then, most of the preparations for the wedding were finished, other than some touch-up ironing on Alyson's dress and Andrew's last-minute packing. After dinner, he kissed Alyson good-bye.

"I'm not sure if I'll be back here before you go to bed. Remember how much I love you. Try to get some rest, and I'll see you in the morning." Andrew hugged her tightly.

"I'll miss you. Don't forget you need some rest yourself tonight," Alyson said to him on his way out the door.

"Don't worry, I'll get some. Sweet dreams. I'll see you in the morning."

Alyson slept soundly for the first half of the night, but not so well during the second half. She periodically checked the bedside clock to see if it was time to get up. Eventually, she gave up on sleep—a common occurrence in her relationship with Andrew. She got up quietly, not wanting to disturb her mom sleeping in the same room.

She showered in the adjacent bathroom, washing her hair twice with sunflower-scented shampoo before finishing with a moisturizing conditioner. She dried off with a towel and wrapped herself in a thick, white, terry-cloth robe Elyse had left in the closet for her use.

She went upstairs to finish getting ready in the half bath off the kitchen, so the downstairs bathroom with the shower would be free. She put on her make-up, finished blow-drying her hair and curled it with a curling iron.

Elyse came in the kitchen as Alyson left the bathroom, holding her cosmetic bag and curling iron to take back downstairs.

"Good morning, Alyson. Are you feeling nervous about today?" she asked cheerfully. "You look beautiful."

"Thank you. I think what I'm feeling inside comes more from excitement than nerves. It's hard to believe this day has finally arrived," she said.

"I know what you mean. It's all so wonderful, I can hardly believe it. Dear, be sure and get yourself some breakfast—whatever you can find that looks good, okay? I need to finish helping Grant get ready and then get dressed myself. Is Andrew up?"

"I'm not sure if he's up now. When I came upstairs to finish getting ready, I think he must have still been asleep because it was quiet," she explained.

"Well, you better go check in case he isn't up yet. It snowed last night. You'll need extra time driving, the roads are probably going to be icy. Don't you need to be at the temple about an hour and a half early?"

"Yes, something like that," she answered.

Elizabeth came into the kitchen and joined them.

"Good morning, Mom." Alyson walked over and gave her mother a quick hug. "Looks like you're all ready to go. As soon as I put this stuff away and get dressed, I'll be ready, too. Do you know if Andrew is awake?"

"I think he just got in the shower," she replied. "Have you eaten anything?"

"Not yet, I'm going to grab a piece of fruit or something. I'm not very hungry right now, and there will plenty of yummy things to eat later at the Lion House."

Alyson peeled a banana, eating it while standing next to the tiled counter top, too jumpy to sit and relax at the table. Elizabeth made a piece of toast and got some yogurt out of the refrigerator. Once Alyson had eaten her fruit, she excused herself to finish getting ready.

Downstairs, she replaced the borrowed robe on its original hanger inside the large closet of the guest room. She had shopped for a dress to wear for the wedding luncheon, wanting something new for the occasion. She had finally found one she liked in sage green—her favorite color.

She put the dress on with light-colored, matching pumps. A touch of perfume on her wrists and in the hollow of her neck, along with a narrow, silver choker sparkling with tiny crystals in a subtle zigzag pattern completed her ensemble. Before she left the room, she glanced around once more to see if she had everything she needed. When she was certain, she opened the bedroom door to go out.

Andrew stood in the hallway waiting for her, looking very handsome in his black tuxedo. Their eyes met, lighting up at the sight of each other.

He spoke first. "Good morning, Alyson. You look incredible! Are you ready to go?"

"Thank you," she smiled. "I am. Mom was upstairs finishing breakfast when I last saw her. Let me see if she's done, then we can leave."

Andrew took the dress bag she had been holding and slung it over his arm. He picked up a small blue suitcase he had set down by his feet when he gave Alyson a hug.

"I'm going to get the car started and let it warm up for a few minutes, then you and your mom come out as soon as you're done. I'll put these things in there while I'm at it."

"Thanks, honey, I love you. See you in a second." She blew him a kiss.

Snow was lightly falling on the drive south on I-15. The overcast sky was a pale gray but no inclement weather could dampen their high spirits. Andrew's car had trouble keeping traction up the steep, icy hill above 500 South as the gradual incline wove through a neighborhood of beautiful and elegant homes.

They drove due east for a short distance before turning north onto Bountiful Boulevard and through the gates of the immaculate temple grounds. The freshly fallen snow thinly covered bright, blooming tulips, daffodils, and pansies bordering the front walkway in artistically arranged displays. The dusting of white created a unique presentation for the new spring plants. Alyson wanted to believe the fresh snow was an Alaskan touch just for her.

She and Andrew checked in at the front door. Passing gorgeous arrangements of silk flowers, beautiful paintings, and elegant furniture, they reached the dressing room entrances, Alyson went to the left, Andrew to the right. Elizabeth and Alyson's destination was the bride's room where Alyson would change into her wedding dress.

The room was lovely with gilded mirrors gracing the walls in front of dressing tables and more vases of huge, exquisite flowers on nearby low tables—the petals were velvety soft in shades of white, ivory, and pale yellow, and their muted-green leaves gave a delicate contrast.

Alyson smoothed her hair, retouched her lipstick, and made a few last minor adjustments to her dress. She hugged her mom. For a moment her mind took her back to her wedding day with Jared. She had also stood in a bride's room that day with her mom, checking her dress and feeling excited and nervous—savoring an experience she had never planned on having twice.

A unexpected stab of pain seared her heart and suddenly she felt like crying. She knew she had to stop instantly; she couldn't go there. She had to look forward, not back. She pictured Andrew's face, reminding herself of the happiness he brought into her life. Her childhood dream couldn't be destroyed by Jared, unless she allowed it. She could still have that dream; in fact, it was waiting for her. Alyson gave her mother a huge smile. "Thanks, Mom, for all your help. I'll see you soon."

"You're welcome, sweetheart. I want you to be happy. I pray this day brings all you have ever hoped for. I love you." Elizabeth hugged her again.

Alyson found Andrew. He took her hand in his outstretched one and pulled her close to his side. He complimented her on her dress.

"You made it, right?" he asked.

She nodded.

"It's not quite what I expected, but it looks amazing. I like it a lot." He kissed her cheek.

"Thanks." She smiled at him. "I'm glad."

The thirty-foot high room they entered was flooded with light, the walls bathed in delicate colors from tall, stained-glass windows. A huge, crystal chandelier brilliantly shimmered, its brightness reflecting off the mirrors covering the walls on opposite sides of the room.

Andrew and Alyson couldn't stop smiling. Their heads were bent closely together, hardly believing they would soon be husband and wife. They talked softly, wrapped in the peaceful beauty surrounding them, savoring the moments together in the beautiful room.

When the end of Alyson's first marriage tore her life and heart to pieces, she didn't believe a day like this would ever happen again, afraid she would never find real love. She looked at Andrew's face, studying it intently, as if to freeze this moment in time.

"Andrew, there's something I want to tell you while we're here." She stopped talking until she was certain her voice wouldn't break.

"I felt so much pain and heartache when my marriage with Jared ended, like what you went through with your first wife. There were crushed dreams and broken promises, and at times I hurt so badly I thought I couldn't live through it. The emotional damage was so wrenching at times, surviving to face another day felt impossible. In my darkest hours, the only thing that carried me through after pleading on my knees in prayer was the promise that God has said He will never give us more than we can bear." She looked past Andrew, remembering.

"There's a scripture I love. I can't remember the reference but it's about a lost man being converted through God's love. It says something to the effect that his soul was filled with such great joy and light, it was equal in comparison to the depth of his pain.

"Andrew, I want you to know that this is what I have experienced with you. The overwhelming happiness, the brightness and hope you've brought to my life, making me feel more loved and accepted than I ever felt with Jared . . . it truly has made all that I suffered because of him worth it to feel this way with you. Thank you—I can only imagine what greater joy is to come as we start a new beginning today as husband and wife. I love you, Andrew."

Moisture gathered in the corners of his eyes as he looked at her, trying to absorb what she had just told him. "Do you really feel that way?" he asked, keeping his gaze steady on hers.

"I really do. I can't recall another time in my life when I've been so happy," she said, her voice soft and sincere.

"Thank you, Alyson. You have no idea what that means to me. You have brought so much to my life also. I've been looking a long time to find someone like you. When my ex-wife betrayed me in the manner she did, my whole world imploded. It was nearly impossible for a period of several weeks to stop my body from physically shaking. I had for the first time in my life trusted another person completely, and the depth of her betrayal was overwhelming. Her intention was clearly that I lose my mind—maybe worse—but God gave me the power to avoid that.

"When we're married, I will pledge all that I am, committing to you forever, holding nothing back. I will not let prior events or people dictate our future. You are an overwhelmingly important part of my life. I cry your tears and feel the warmth of your smile on my lips. I'm already much further into the 'bonding as one' process than I ever was with my former wife throughout our marriage. It is imperative to me to represent the warmth within your life and never the cold wind. Today, I'm giving you my whole heart and unconditional love." He put his arms around her and held her close.

A short time later, surrounded by family and friends, Andrew and Alyson solemnly, yet with long-awaited anticipation and excitement, spoke their vows. They promised one another, before God, to forsake all others and become one. Andrew leaned across the altar and kissed Alyson for the first time as his wife. Alyson felt her heart would burst from the overwhelming warmth of his love.

From that moment on, they agreed that their marriage was like night and day compared to what they had experienced in their past relationships. Things were not perfect and it was not easy trying to create one new, stable family from two traumatized ones; in fact, it often seemed impossible. But something was hugely different. Andrew respected her, cherished her, and showed her every day how much he cared about her. His love was real. She saw it in his eyes, heard it in his voice and felt it in his touch. She didn't have to fight an unseen wall to be as close to him as she wanted—a wall that with Jared had always felt insurmountable—because with Andrew there never was one.

Conclusion

"Peace I leave with you, my peace I give unto you: not as the world giveth, give I unto you. Let not your heart be troubled, neither let it be afraid."[28]

In the middle of the night, almost a year and a half later, the shrill ringing of the telephone woke Andrew and Alyson in their dark bedroom. Andrew picked it up and Alyson felt his body tense, her heart rate responding immediately by escalating. He handed the phone over to her, and she placed the receiver to her ear, afraid to hear the voice on the other end.

It was her former father-in-law, not at all who she had expected. He got directly to the point. Once his words registered, she could not believe they were true, hoping she was caught in the middle of a bad dream and would wake up any minute.

Jared had been killed that morning while attempting to land an airplane at the Nuiqsuit Airport, 135 miles east of Barrow, Alaska. He was the pilot in command. The landing gear did not properly deploy and the turbo prop-driven Piper 1040 scraped the ground before climbing again, struggling to gain altitude.

He had pulled up, attempting a go-around, hoping that the gear would properly engage so they might land safely. In the process, the wheels suddenly dropped and the plane abruptly banked sharply to the left before nose-diving into the tundra.

A fire broke out on impact and three of the ten passengers, those closest to the front of the airplane, had died with Jared.

Alyson's mind was numb with shock.

"No," she told Jared's dad. "No, he can't be gone." Her voice broke.

"I know, Alyson, I can't believe it, either," he said. "It doesn't seem real, but it is."

"How will I ever tell the boys?" she asked him, her mind fighting the implications. She remembered well the unreal sadness she had experienced when she was seven and her own father had died in an airplane crash. Her heart ached for her sons even more because she knew clearly the grief they would experience.

"I don't know—I'm sorry," his voice broke, "I'll call you later once there are more details about the arrangements and the funeral."

"Thank you for calling me," she paused, "I'm sorry, too." She hung up the phone and told Andrew what had happened. He held her as her body began to shake with sobs. The years she spent as Jared's wife, the birth of their children, the memories and the heartache of their divorce blocked everything else. She couldn't believe it was true, how could he be gone?

Once her mind had a firmer grasp, she felt confused, not knowing how to deal with the news in relation to Andrew. She was uncertain how her display of grief would make him feel. He brought so much good to her life, and she loved him dearly, but a small part of her still loved Jared—not in a romantic sense; those feelings had died a long time before. She loved him as a person, a friend, as someone who had played a big part in her life.

He had called their home three days earlier. When she answered the phone, her first thought was to tell him his insurance payment for the boys' medical coverage was late. But something stopped her and she listened. Though she didn't know it then, that would be the last time she ever talked to him. She was glad beyond words it had been a positive conversation between them.

He had sounded tired on the phone. When she asked him how flying was going, his voice perked right up and he sounded pleased. He told her about a herd of caribou he saw from the air on a recent flight, running across the tundra, and how beautiful the sunsets were so far north.

They only talked for a few minutes. Jared was short on time and wanted to talk to each of the boys. Before she put down the receiver to go and get them, he told her the medical payment was in the mail and she should get it soon. He said he was sorry it was late.

She thanked him—so glad she hadn't brought it up. She could not believe now that he was truly gone. It was unreal.

She felt a heavy weight settle on her shoulders, realizing how much greater her responsibility for their boys had become. She was deeply thankful they had Andrew. She hardly slept the rest of the night; instead, she spent it worrying and crying.

The next day after school, she and Andrew gathered the boys together to break the sad news. It was hard to watch their emotional reaction. It reminded her of when they learned she and Jared were getting a divorce. Their world was being rocked hard again.

Ryker reacted with anger. Cade was more stunned. Jayden tried to comprehend what it meant while Alex was too little to understand much at all. They cried together for awhile, and then the older boys said they wanted to be alone. They went to their bedrooms. Andrew held her as she cried again.

A few days later, they flew to Anchorage for the funeral and to say good-bye. It was nice to spend some time with extended family and friends and feel their support. Alyson was glad when it was time to return to Utah. That was her home now and where her family needed to be.

She worried about the timing of Jared's death, knowing the issues he was dealing with in his life. She struggled with feelings of concern and sadness, wondering what was going to happen to him. She prayed about it many times until she got to the point where she had to give the heartache to God and let it go.

Jared was in His hands.

Four months later, Alyson discovered she was pregnant and it was time to experience joy.

The following October, she delivered a healthy, beautiful baby girl. Madison had lots of dark hair and startlingly blue eyes, the exact shade of her parents'.

From the Author

Ten years have passed since my marriage was torn apart. Since then the pornography industry in all its deceptive forms has continued to grow at an alarming rate. My former husband didn't get the help he needed to save himself, our marriage, or our family. It doesn't have to be too late for someone you love.

No one anywhere can tell me pornography is not a big deal or not a horribly destructive force, far-reaching in its influence. No one can tell me it doesn't destroy lives—it has forever marked mine.

Sharing this personal story was difficult and painful at times, but if it can save even one other person's life, marriage, or family from the pain, heartache, and destructive effects pornography addiction causes, then sharing it will have been worth it.

I know my former husband would agree.

—Diony S. George

Resources

Below are several signs that may indicate a problem with pornography:

- Loss of interest in sexual relations or insatiable sexual appetite
- Introduction of unusual sexual practices in the relationship
- Diminished emotional, physical, social, spiritual, and intellectual intimacy
- Neglect of responsibilities
- Increased isolation (such as late-night hours on the computer) and withdrawal from family
- Unexplained absences
- Preference for masturbation over sexual relationships with spouse
- Unexplained financial transactions
- Sexual relations that are rigid, rushed, without passion, and detached

Although further information should be gathered, if these signs are present in a relationship, it is possible there is a problem.[18]

The following resources are available to help deal with the problem of pornography.

You can file a complaint with Federal Communications Commission at: www.fcc.gov

For Internet exposure to hard core pornography you can report to www.obscenitycrimes.org and it will be forwarded to the U.S. Department of Justice in Washington.

To report child pornography or other sexual exploitation of children: www.cybertipline.com

For the protection of children and families: www.nationalcoalition.org

Preserving Family Values in a Media-Driven Society: http://familysafe.com

Promoting a Decent Society Through Law:
www.moralityinmedia.org

Keeping Children Safe Online: www.getnetwise.org

Keys to Recovery: www.no-porn.com

Relationship Rescue for Wives and Girlfriends of Internet
Pornography Addicts: www.pornaddicthubby.com

Girls against Porn: www.girlsagainstporn.com

Notes

1. http://www.familysafemedia.com/pornography_statistics.html.

2. Louise May Alcott, http://womenshistory.about.com/cs/quotes/a/qu_lm_alcott.htm.

3. Thomas Moore, http://www.brainyquote.com/quotes/authors/t/thomas_moore.html.

4. Brad Wilcox, quoted in *Confronting Pornography: A Guide to Prevention and Recovery for Individuals, Loved Ones, and Leaders*, edited by Chamberlain, et al (Salt Lake City: Deseret Book, 2005), 78.

5. A.A. Milne, http://www.goodreads.com/author/quotes/81466.A_A_Milne.

6. M. Russell Ballard, "Let Our Voices Be Heard," *Ensign*, Nov 2003, 16.

7. Edward Teller, http://thinkexist.com/quotes/edward_teller/.

8. Rabindranath Tagore, http://thinkexist.com/quotes/rabindranath_tagore/2.html.

9. Jewish Proverb, http://thinkexist.com/quotes/jewish_proverb/.

10. Mother Teresa, http://www.brainyquote.com/quotes/authors/m/mother_teresa.html.

11. Gordon B. Hinckley, http://www.goodreads.com/author/quotes/313356.Gordon_B_Hinckley.

12. Carl Bard, http://www.worldofquotes.com/Carl_Bard/1/index.html.

13. Kenji Miyazawa, http://www.brainyquote.com/quotes/authors/k/kenji_miyazawa.html.

14. John L. Harmer, *A War We Must Win* (Salt Lake City: Bookcraft, 1999).

15. Lili Anderson, LCSW and Christian B. Anderson, LCSW, quoted in *Confronting Pornography: A Guide to Prevention and Recovery for Individuals, Loved Ones, and Leaders*, Edited by Chamberlain et al (Salt Lake City: Deseret Book, 2005), 183.

16. Marsha Means, *Living with Your Husband's Secret Wars* (Grand Rapids: Fleming H. Revell, 1999), 163.

17. Ephesians 4:31–32

18. James 4:10
19. Proverbs 3:5–6
20. Richard M. Nixon, http://quotationsbook.com/quote/13794/.
21. Psalms 27:13
22. 1 John 4:18
23. Mario Fernandez, http://quotations.about.com/cs/inspirationquotes/a/Teacher12.htm.
24. Psalm 84:11
25. Charles F. Kettering, http://en.thinkexist.com/quotes/charles_f._kettering/.
26. Anonymous, http://www.famousquotesandauthors.com/topics/true_love_quotes.html.
27. Elizabeth Akers Allen, "At Last," http://www.love-poems-love-quotes.com/love-poems/at-last.html.
28. John 14:27

Book Club Questions

1. What is the book's message?

2. How did the fact that this book was based on a true story affect your reactions to it?

3. Do you think Alyson was right to give Jared a second chance at their marriage? Why or why not?

4. What emotions did you feel toward Jared? Anger? Sadness? Empathy?

5. Do you think Jared sincerely tried to change?

6. Do you think Alyson's character showed strength or weakness throughout the book? Or both? In what ways?

7. How did you feel about Alyson's relationship with Andrew?

8. Did the details in the story help you feel you were right there, experiencing the same things the characters were?

9. Was the book helpful in teaching you what signs to look for in someone who may be struggling with a pornography addiction?

10. Did you feel the book presented a message of hope to others facing similar issues?

About the Author

Diony is a wife and full-time mother of seven. Her life-long passion for books and desire to help others heal from the pain of pornography's influence on marriage and families, prompted her to write *Torn Apart*, which is based on her own experiences. Originally from Alaska, she enjoys traveling, cooking, appliqué quilting, and spending time with her family. She currently lives in Salt Lake City, Utah, with her husband, Daryl, and four of their children who are still at home.

To order additional copies of her book, schedule a speaking engagement, or to become involved in promoting decency visit her personal website at, www.tornapartbyporn.com. She can also be contacted by email at dionygeorge@gmail.com